The Governess

Lynette Rees

Dedication

For Alan, who was a kind and faithful friend.

© Lynette Rees 2020
Contact Lynette:
http://www.lynetterees.com
Blogs:
https://lynetterees.wordpress.com/
http://www.nettiesramblings.blogspot.com
Email: craftyscribe@yahoo.com
Facebook author page for latest updates:
http://www.facebook.com/authorlynetterees/

Chapter One

December, 1885

'It certainly won't seem like Christmas this year,' Emily sighed as she dropped the newspaper she'd been reading onto the table in front of her sister. She turned away to heft a box that was resting in the corner of the room and placed it on the table before her.

Clara picked up the newspaper, leafing through it until she arrived at the page where advertisements were placed either seeking work or offering it. It might be their only option now there were five in the family with no breadwinner to support them. At least she and Emily were now grown up, but Meg and Edmund were aged ten and eight years old respectively. Mama brought in a little income with her dressmaking skills, but the family's finances were fast filtering out.

Emily began sorting through the wooden box of decorations that she'd brought down from the loft in preparation for putting up the much smaller Christmas tree that had been gifted to them this year.

'Some of this is pure tat!' she moaned.

Clara smiled wistfully. 'I suppose they are rather old, but Mama says each piece we hang on the tree is a treasure as it holds a memory of a Christmas past.'

'But it would be nice if we could buy something new to cheer us up. You know, we don't deserve to be living like this,' Emily continued to complain. 'If Papa hadn't passed away, we wouldn't be forced to move out of here.' She tutted under her breath.

That much was obvious. Clara laid down the newspaper in a pensive moment. It was true enough what Emily said. Their father had been Reverend Albert Masters, vicar at St. Bartholomew's Church in the village of Foxbridge. A highly respected member of the community he'd been too – a pillar of it, held in high esteem by one and all.

'To be fair, though, the church hasn't forced us out of here straight after Papa's death. It has been a good six months now and maybe they'll allow us a little more grace.'

Emily quirked an anxious brow. 'I very much doubt it!' she scoffed as she folded her arms. 'The sands of time are running out and the new vicar is due here soon. We've only been fortunate up until now because there have been a couple of lay preachers who've landed here and been put up by the benevolence of various members of the congregation. When the new vicar arrives we'll have to vacate for sure as this will be his home then and no longer ours.' She tossed back her flame-coloured hair as if in defiance.

Clara nodded. 'I know, Em. I suppose I've been putting off the inevitable but now I think as the eldest here the only thing to do is for me to look for a suitable job,' she said as she chewed on her bottom lip.

Emily blinked. 'A job? But what on earth could you do, Clara?'

Clara sniffed loudly. 'I'm not useless you know. I could teach, for one thing. I have plenty of experience of teaching at Sunday school. I've been doing that for years.'

'Yes, I know you have and that's to be highly commended of course, but you'd have to train.'

'Not for what I could do. I've been studying the adverts in the newspaper.' She opened up the page and flattened it out with her hand. 'There are several adverts where people are seeking someone to tutor their children.'

'You mean as a governess?' Emily's eyes widened.

'Yes, and why not?'

'But what would you teach them?'

'Well let me read a couple of the adverts to you and you tell me if you think I'm capable?'

Emily nodded. 'Very well.'

'Right, first there's this one: *"Governess sought. The lady in question would need to be from a respectable background and competent at teaching reading, writing and arithmetic to two young boys aged five years old."*'

'Hmm, that one sounds straightforward enough, go on.'

'Then another says: *"Young lady required to teach two girls and one boy, ages thirteen, twelve and eight years old respectively. The successful applicant would need to be competent at teaching English, mathematics and in use of the globes. Also, an interest in dancing, singing and piano playing would be a distinct advantage. Required to live in on premises. Own living quarters offered. Three meals a day provided. Salary moderate."*'

Emily nodded. 'Yes, you could do all of that. What does "use of the globes" mean, though?'

'Geography of course! Teaching the children about other countries in the world besides this one.'

Emily nodded knowingly. 'Ah, I've no doubt you could teach that sort of thing as you're so clever, but to live in somewhere else other than with your family? Won't that be rather lonely for you, Clara?'

Clara shrugged. 'I suppose it might, but it would lessen the load here with one less mouth to feed and I can send my wages home as I shan't need much if I have my bed and board. So, what do you think, Em? Is it worth a try?'

'Is what worth a try?' Mama chose that moment to enter the kitchen. Her cheeks were flushed from the chill wind whipping up outside. She carefully laid her wicker basket on the table. Untying the ribbons of her bonnet beneath her chin, she removed it along with her cloak and hung them both on pegs on the back of the door.

'Clara was just explaining how she might apply to become a governess,' Emily said.

Mama raised her eyebrows in surprise. 'I don't think there's a need for that as yet. I've got plenty of work to keep me going. I've just been asked to make a wedding gown for Mrs Pettigrew's daughter!'

Clara smiled. As far as she was concerned, Mrs Pettigrew was a villager who had delusions of grandeur, always thinking she was a cut above other folk because her husband was the village baker who was doing quite well for himself indeed. He'd even opened a second shop in the nearby village of Crownley. Ever since then, Mrs Pettigrew seemed to consider herself above mere mortals and could be quite tiresome with her efforts to show off. No doubt her Lillibeth would demand the gown be made with the finest of fabrics, embroidered – of course! – with small seed pearls sewn into its bodice. She could well imagine it now. Hours of work for Mama for a pittance in return and all for a spoilt young madam, although Clara fully appreciated that Mama liked to maintain an air of optimism.

'But think, Mama, when we move from here, we'll have to pay rent somewhere else. This will be our final Christmas at The Vicarage,' she said.

Their mother nodded sadly before letting out a long sigh. 'You're right of course, Clara, but I never wanted it to come to this.' She sniffed back a tear.

'I know you didn't,' said Clara, rising out of her chair to hug her mother. 'None of us did, but truth be told we need to buckle up our belts. Look, you take a seat and I'll unpack the shopping. Then I'll put the kettle on to boil and we'll discuss this.'

Mama smiled and did as she was told. She was looking so weary lately and Clara guessed Papa's death had taken its toll. They had been such a close couple. A couple to be admired.

'What are you doing with that box?' Mama asked as she turned towards Emily.

'Sorting through the Christmas decorations, Mama.'

'Oh, I don't think it would be right for us to put up a tree or decorations this year,' Mama said, shaking her head and causing Emily to frown.

'I don't know why though,' replied Clara as she took a hunk of muslin wrapped cheese from the basket and placed it in the cool pantry. Returning to the table, she carried on. 'We could use the small Christmas tree that Jake has left for us.'

Jake was Emily's friend. He was more than a little sweet on her sister, although Clara wasn't so sure her sister returned the same sentiment towards him.

'Please, Mama,' Emily pleaded. 'Just a little tree in the corner of the parlour. You know how much Papa loved Christmas.'

It was true, Christmas was Papa's favourite time of the year and he'd loved preparing his Christmas day sermon. No one was to set foot in the parlour when he was planning for that! He went above and beyond to narrate the Nativity story to his flock in a new way each Christmas. It would be a sad Christmas this year with Papa no longer here.

***

Mama reluctantly gave in, allowing them to adorn the parlour with the Christmas tree and decorations, along with paper lanterns, chains, stars, and snowflakes the girls had made themselves from cut up pieces of coloured paper. Later, Clara slipped away to apply for both governess jobs. Sitting at her father's oak wood desk, she penned:

The Old Vicarage
Rodden Row
Foxbridge
December 15th, 1885

To whom it may concern,

I should like to apply for the post of a governess. I am twenty-one years old and currently still residing at the family home. I have seven years' experience of teaching young children in the Sunday school at St. Bartholomew's Church where my late father was vicar. I am literate, numerate, and able to play the pianoforte to an acceptable level. I am also conversant in French and have a sound knowledge of global geography. I am an excellent communicator and get along well with young children.

Should I be successful as an applicant then you will find me truthful, loyal and trustworthy. I can obtain references supporting this

*at your request and shall be able to live in on the premises with you
and your family.*

I look forward to hearing from you in due course.
Yours faithfully,
Miss Clara Masters

She wrote two identical letters to apply for both jobs she had seen in
the newspaper, sealed them in envelopes and made her way to the
village post office.

***

As Clara entered the post office, she heard Mrs Pettigrew boasting
about her daughter's upcoming wedding to a crowd of women who
were waiting in the queue. The postmaster, Mr Fothergill, shook his
head to hear such chatter. It was obvious he wanted to hurry them
along as he had things to be getting on with.

'Oh, your Lillibeth will make a beautiful bride,' a lady wearing a
big fur-trimmed hat fawned, obviously trying to find favour with Mrs
Pettigrew. The woman always had a group of hangers-on around her,
clinging on to her every word. Maybe this lady was expecting an invite
to the wedding, which would surely be a lavish affair. Imagine the
wedding cake her father would bake for the occasion for a start. No
expense would be spared.

'Yes, she's following me with her bone structure,' Mrs Pettigrew
beamed. She hadn't noticed Clara slipping in through the door and
waiting patiently in the queue behind her. 'My mother was the same:
high cheekbones and alabaster skin. We're all extremely fortunate to
be blessed with good looks on that side of the family.'

Pity you can't say that about your other daughter Esme, Clara
thought to herself, stifling a giggle. The girl was one of the plainest
young women she'd ever seen. She was very tall and well built, more
like a man than a woman. Her face was long – reminding Clara of a
horse –but her eyes were small and beady like a bird. Esme was a few
years older than Lillibeth and, as yet, Mrs Pettigrew had had no luck
finding her a husband.

Mr Fothergill cleared his throat as if to remind the group where they
were, but Mrs Pettigrew jabbered on and on. Finally, Mr Fothergill,
holding his patience no longer, slammed his hand down on the wooden
counter.

'If you do not wish to be served, ladies, then I suggest you leave my
shop and allow other customers to come forward to the counter.'

Mrs Pettigrew lifted her chin and stared at the man. This wasn't just a post office; it was also a general store that sold a little of everything from sacks of potatoes to ladies and gents gloves. Mrs Pettigrew had been a good customer up until now. As if realising his error, the man's face grew red. He had dared to come into conflict with the most influential woman in the village and in front of her cronies to boot!

Thinking on her feet as to how the situation might be resolved, Clara looked at the postmaster.

'Maybe if you could just serve me quickly, Mr Fothergill. I need to send two letters quite urgently and don't wish to miss today's post. That's if you don't mind, of course, Mrs Pettigrew?'

Mrs Pettigrew's features relaxed and she smiled at Clara. She had no wish to upset her as her mother was making her precious daughter's wedding gown. 'Yes, go ahead, dear,' she said good-naturedly, though Clara noticed how she glared at Mr Fothergill. If looks could kill he would have keeled over that very second from the penetration of the woman's hard stare. But if he lost her custom, he would lose that of her acquaintances too. He wasn't a foolish fellow either so Clara knew that he realised it.

As the group of women parted like the Red Sea to allow her through to the counter, she smiled at him. He was quite elderly and she would hate to see him lose his livelihood due to the likes of Mrs Pettigrew.

As she approached and the women continued to natter, she whispered to him, 'I would try to make some sort of amends if I were you. Maybe apologise to Mrs Pettigrew in front of her friends?' she suggested.

Mr Fothergill nodded gratefully. 'Yes, I think you're right. I'm just so tired. I've been standing here since early this morning and now with Christmas upon us, I'm busier than ever.'

Clara smiled sympathetically. She well understood as the poor man had to attend to both the post office counter and the shop floor. His wife, Matilda, used to help out but she had been in poor health of late.

Clara placed the two envelopes on the counter. 'Do you think both of these might arrive by morning?' she asked hopefully. The newspaper where she'd spotted the adverts was already a couple of days old, so she figured some applications would have been received by now. It would be nice if she were able to attend an interview for the position before Christmas. With ten days to go until the big day itself, it would soon be upon them.

He strained to read the addresses. 'Ah, Crownley and Stapleton. Neither are too far away, so I don't see why not.'

He took the relevant coinage from her outstretched hand and affixed a postage stamp on each envelope, placing them in a wooden box beside him. As she passed the ladies, she looked at Mrs Pettigrew.

'Mr Fothergill is under a lot of pressure with his wife being ill of late. I'm sure he didn't mean to be so irritable. I know what a kind and forgiving person you are, Mrs Pettigrew.' Clara made sure to say this loud enough for the woman's friends to hear, fully aware there was no way Mrs Pettigrew could reprimand the man now. Mrs Pettigrew just nodded and smiled at her as she left.

Once outside Clara let out a long breath. Life in Foxbridge was never without its ups and downs, that was for certain.

Chapter Two

When Clara returned to The Vicarage, the place was in an uproar. Meg and Edmund were squabbling over a wooden toy train right in the middle of the kitchen floor while Emily was preparing supper and muttering under her breath. Mama was in her workroom finishing off an order for Farmer Downing and his wife in time for Christmas. She had sewn a smart brocade waistcoat and cravat for him and a new dress for his wife as they were invited to the local farmer's ball at the village hall. It would have seemed like a typical evening had it not been for the Christmas tree in the corner of the parlour and the paper decorations adorning the place. Just one person was missing: dear Papa. This time last year he would have been fussing around in the background, gently explaining to Meg and Edmund why they needed to stop squabbling and why Emily should stop her moaning about little things when she had a lot to be grateful for. Then he would softly chastise Mama for working too hard. After supper, he'd settle down in his favourite chair by the fireside, dozing away as Mama would smile and pick up her knitting, click-clacking in time to his rhythmic snores as she sat opposite him like a pair of bookends. It tore away at Clara's heart to know he was no longer here, nor ever would be again. Everyone missed him so and needed him even more.

'Will you pair please stop squabbling,' she said as she laid down her baskets. She had purchased a few Christmas presents for them all.

'It's not my fault!' declared Meg crossly with her hands folded beneath her chest as her lips formed a pout. 'Edmund won't share with me. I wanted the train to go under the legs of the table so we could pretend it's a tunnel, but he wants to keep it all to himself!'

Edmund's shiny eyes looked up at Clara from where he was playing on the rug. He was close to tears. How could she possibly resolve this? The children were grieving too and maybe their frustration at not having their father around was spilling over into their games with one another.

'I'll tell you what,' said Clara with a big smile. 'How about we compromise a little?'

'Compo-what?' said Edmund, scratching his head.

'It means we find a way of working together, silly!' said Meg as she shook her ringleted head and rolled her eyes.

How did she know that? No doubt it was something Papa had explained to her – that would be just like him to do so. She could well imagine him with a secret smile on his face taking both children on either knee as he sat in his favourite chair, flames crackling in the hearth. He had a way of speaking in a quiet tone that made them listen and concentrate even harder on just what he had to say.

'Yes, that is correct,' Clara said firmly. 'Meg and Edmund, you must find a way of working things out together. Now Edmund, what is so wrong about pretending under the table is a tunnel for the train?'

'Because it's far too big of course!' he said.

She couldn't argue with that. 'All right then, what could we use instead?'

'How about the little table by the fireplace?' Meg suggested. The little low table was one Papa had used to set down his cup of tea or cocoa on and more often than not he was so tired that after taking just one sip he'd nod promptly off to sleep, forcing Mama to gently rouse him so he might finish his drink.

'Hmm, that's a good idea,' Clara said thoughtfully, then she turned to look at her younger brother. 'Shall we use that small table instead then, Edmund?'

'I suppose so,' he said sighing, while the glint in his eyes told that he liked the idea but didn't want to show his sister she had the upper hand.

And so a difficult situation which could have blown out of all proportion was resolved.

That evening, Emily dished up rabbit stew with hunks of fresh bread she had baked earlier. The aroma was divine. For all her moans and groans, Emily was a fine little homemaker and would make someone a good wife someday.

'Did you manage to post your letters earlier?' Mama asked across the dining table.

'Oh yes,' said Clara. 'But there was a right to-do in the post office.'

Mama raised an inquisitive brow. 'How so?'

'Mrs Pettigrew and her cronies were in line when I arrived and she was showing off so much about Lillibeth's upcoming wedding that she held up the queue, causing Mr Fothergill to grow most impatient.'

'I can well imagine,' smiled Mama.

Feeling serious for a moment, Clara said, 'Mama, do you think you might be taking on too much making Lillibeth's wedding dress and trousseau?'

'Heavens no!' Mama answered a little too quickly. 'Mrs Pettigrew will be paying me handsomely for my work and it should keep us going for some time to come. Plus, of course, we all know she will ply me with some of her husband's delicious baked goods!'

'Oh yes, Mama!' shouted Meg. 'Share some with us, won't you?'

Mama laughed. 'Of course I will.' Then she turned to Clara. 'But why do you have misgivings about this, Clara? I've made wedding gowns before.'

Yes, Mama had made several beautiful gowns for young ladies in the past but that was before Papa had died. She hadn't been grieving then and she wasn't getting any younger either. Clara had noticed how she squinted her eyes some nights as she'd sewn by candlelight to finish a gown for a bride. On one or two occasions, Mama had even stayed up all night to do so. One morning Clara had arisen from her bed in the early dawn and caught her mother then setting down her work.

Clara said nothing about any of that though, instead she said, 'I just worry about you sometimes, that's all.'

Mama smiled. 'There's nothing for you to worry about, rest assured.' But even as she said the words, she rubbed her weary brow. It was clear that what she was saying was belying how she really felt – thoroughly exhausted. And to Clara, there was no disguising that fact as they were two of a kind, both compassionate sorts who put others above themselves.

***

The following morning, Clara was up bright and early to go shopping for her mother. This time she fancied a change and decided to walk into the village of Crownley, a short walk through Foxbridge to the bridge itself, then over the river which divided both places. On the way there, she felt the chill breeze from the north wind and wrapped her muffler tighter around her neck. Thank goodness she'd remembered her woollen mittens. As she walked the road she heard a heavy clip-clopping sound coming up behind her, signalling an approaching horse. She began to walk faster to get onto the little path where there was no room for a horse nor rider, but the faster she walked the louder she heard the horse's hooves behind. She turned abruptly to see who it might be who seemed to be tormenting her.

Her face froze when she saw that it was Josiah Whitman sat upon his horse as if he owned the very same road. Josiah was the son of Alfred Whitman, the local publican. A bad 'un in every way. Everyone had thought so except for her own dear father who refused to chastise the man, instead preferring to say, 'We must hate the sin but love the sinner…' Aye and a sinner he was and all. Known for his dirty dealings with all and sundry, he knocked around with a veritable gang of thieves, often fencing off stolen items.

Drawing up beside her, he brought his horse to a standstill and said, 'Well if it ain't Miss Clara. How d'ya fancy a ride on this one, m'dear?'

A shiver coursed down her spine, causing her to wrap her shawl around her shoulders as if it would afford her protection in some way.

'No thank you,' she said as she made to be on her way, but he was having none of it. The fear began to take over her. There was something about him and how he looked at her as if he was removing her dress with his eyes. Oh, he'd have liked to have had his wicked way with her. Of all the women in Foxbridge, and there were one or two with questionable morals who loitered around the ale houses, why did it have to be her that he had designs on? She had never been interested in him. Not one iota. Placing her hands on both hips with her basket over the crook of her arm, she raised her chin as her eyes met with his.

'I do not fancy a ride on your horse, not now and not ever. Now please leave me well alone.'

He gave a throaty chuckle. 'Oh my darlin', you don't even realise how beautiful you are, even in temper. In fact, even more so – it demonstrates to me that you have fire in your belly. And if you should come to my bed, then I know you would never want to leave it.'

'Are you talking to me in this manner because my father is dead?' she yelled at him as the tears threatened to spill down her cheeks. Then he was quiet for a moment, and she knew she had got through to him. He'd liked and respected her father.

'Er no. I meant what I said as I've been looking for a good wife for this long while. And your father, well he was a fine gentleman and no mistake. He was one of the only people in this village who saw any good in me.'

'Then out of respect for him, please let me be on my way as I have shopping to get for my mother and the children. They will need to be fed later. Times are hard now my father is no longer with us.'

He nodded solemnly. 'I am sorry to have delayed you, Miss Clara,' he said, and she could tell that he meant it. For the first time, she began to wonder if maybe he wasn't as black as he was painted. She nodded back at him and quickly walked away.

When she arrived at Crownley, the marketplace was busy. There was a visiting fair on the common near the church and lots of new stalls had popped up selling home crafted items for the festive season.

A man was playing a fiddle just outside the church as a young gypsy girl wearing a voluminous green velvet dress tapped a tambourine which had colourful satin ribbons hanging from it. It wasn't a song Clara had ever heard before and she didn't recognise the language they sang in either, but her father once told her that the gypsies spoke the Romany language which originated in India, then spread to the Balkans and eventually Europe. Clara had found that fascinating, along with their wooden horse-drawn caravans which were intricately painted with fanciful designs and etchings. Last year she and Emily had walked through the woods and, on hearing several voices, had hidden behind a tree. The smell of wood smoke had permeated the air and on closer inspection they'd spied a circle of those caravans sited around a campfire. As the sun had set, the gypsies left their caravans and had congregated around the fire as a big iron cauldron of food bubbled away. No doubt it had been their evening meal. For a moment she had wanted to join them but Emily feared them and had frozen, wanting to get out of the woods. For several nights, Clara had returned there all alone to look at the travellers, realising they wouldn't be there forever. And she had been right, as three nights later they had gone. All that had been left behind was a burned patch where the fire had been, cold ashen embers, and a gold-coloured neck chain with a pixie dangling from it. Knowing they were unlikely to return, she had picked up the necklace and placed it in the pocket of her dress. It didn't look worth much. *Probably fool's gold,* she had surmised. A feeling as though someone had been watching her had sent a tingle down her spine, then there had been the crack of a twig which had spooked her enough to have made her run for her life through those woods. It had not been until she had arrived home, gasping for breath, that she had thought that maybe it had been her imagination that had caused her to think that someone had been chasing her. The gypsy folk before her now were a memory of that time and she felt a pang of guilt to know she still had that pixie necklace back home. But still, it was hardly likely they'd have returned for it if it were just fool's gold.

The melody playing now was a haunting one and the gypsy girl banged on her tambourine before shaking it high in the air so the multitude of coloured ribbons seemed to dance in time with the music. She was spinning around as the man played the fiddle on the crook of his arm with the base of it beneath his chin. Oh no, he'd caught her eye and he was looking at her curiously. He had deep-set green eyes, the like she had never seen before, and they seemed to bore a hole into her soul. He was handsome in a rugged sort of way, with dark curly hair and tanned, weather-beaten skin. He filled his clothes very well, as if he worked physically hard and was muscular beneath their confines.

When the pair had finished, a small crowd that had gathered to watch clapped loudly and several threw coins inside the man's cap by his feet. He nodded and smiled at them to show his appreciation as the girl bowed. Clara was about to turn around to peruse one of the market stalls when the man handed his fiddle to the girl and came over to speak to her.

'Now you're not going, are ya?' he asked as a smile lit his face to reveal an even set of white teeth.

'I'm afraid I don't have any money to pay you,' she said, feeling slightly embarrassed. She didn't want to explain that the family were on their uppers and she couldn't possibly afford to part with a penny to a complete stranger.

'It's not paying I'm after.' She noticed a mischievous gleam in his emerald eyes and found herself relaxing in his company, although she had no idea why as she was usually wary of strangers.

'Oh?'

'It's just I feel I know you from somewhere,' he probed.

She shook her head. 'No, but you can't do. I've never seen you before in my life.'

'No, not purposefully, but I've seen you.'

It felt as though her heart had ceased beating. How could that possibly be?

Noting her distress, he chuckled. 'It's nothing bad I can assure you. Last year we were camped at Hartley Woods and you were there with a younger girl. I noticed you looking at us. I never forget a face.'

'You're right,' she said, astonished that he'd even seen her when she hadn't noticed him looking at her.

'Why were you watching so intently? You returned and hid night after night.'

'I don't know,' she hesitated, 'I suppose I was curious.'

He laughed. 'And did you like what you saw?'

She let out a composing breath. 'I suppose I did. I just loved the way you all settled around that campfire and ate and laughed and sang songs during the night.' A thought occurred to her. 'Did you see me in those woods after you'd packed up to go?'

'Aye,' he nodded. 'I did and all and I left a little present for you. I know you picked it up and put it in your skirt pocket. Do you still have it by any chance?'

Slowly, she nodded. Of course, that gold pixie necklace being left in that precise spot was no accident. 'I do. I felt guilty picking it up, but I didn't think anyone was going to come back for it.'

'Sure,' he smiled. For a moment she felt he was making fun of her until he added, 'I noticed you heading for the woods and I waited to leave it there for you. I didn't want anyone else to find it.'

Clara had just opened her mouth to speak when the young girl in the green dress sidled up next to them.

'We have to go now, Patrin,' she said firmly. She smiled shyly at Clara and Clara returned the gesture.

'Aye, I know,' he said reluctantly as the girl walked away with his fiddle beneath her arm. 'Forgive my sister for her impatience.'

'Nice to meet you, Patrin,' Clara said. 'Good luck to you.'

'I know it's you that needs good luck,' he said, gazing into her eyes. 'And I wish it to you too. I hope that pixie brings you good fortune. But please don't make things feel so final, our paths will definitely cross again someday, I feel it in me bones.'

She nodded and, smiling at him, said, 'Thank you for leaving that necklace for me.'

He lifted her gloved hand and placed a kiss upon it. Feeling her face flame, she realised she wouldn't mind crossing paths with Patrin again in the future.

***

By the time she'd purchased the shopping her mind was in a tizzy. Two encounters with two different men within the space of one hour. One man she was beginning to change her mind about; the other was a stranger to her who she didn't realise knew of her existence until this very day. How strange was that?

As she left the open-air market she noticed a commotion going on. Some sort of toff inside a coach was leaning out of it looking incandescent with rage.

'Be off with you, you varmint!' he yelled as he waved a gold-tipped walking cane through the open coach window.

'What's going on?' Clara asked one of the onlookers.

'That nob in that there coach,' explained the gentleman beside her. 'He just got out of it and whacked that old man across his shoulder blades, all because he asked if he could spare any change.'

'Shocking!' said Clara. 'Is the man all right?'

'Well yer can see for yourself, he's still trying to get money out of him. To be honest, the old fella were pestering him a bit and the gent, well, he didn't whack him too hard, just tried to frighten him I expect.'

'But still,' said Clara shaking her head in anger, 'he could have been a little more charitable.'

The man beside her nodded. 'But those rich folks don't give a darn about the likes of you and I. People like the old fella who sleep rough they treat even worse.'

Clara had to admit that the man was spot on. They were both well dressed and well fed. While not in league with the gentleman in the coach, neither were they down and out like the old man. They had a lot to be thankful for. *There but for the grace of God, go I.*

'Someone get him out of here!' the gentleman shouted. 'He's pestering me!'

And with that along came a couple of young men who looked muscular and strong. Having already removed their jackets and rolled up their shirt sleeves, they took the man by both arms, each flanking him either side.

'Come along now, Grampa,' said one in a kindly but firm tone, 'time to get you out of here. I'll buy you a pint at the ale house and a bite to eat.'

The old man nodded and smiled. He gave the gentleman in the coach one last sorrowful look before he was escorted off by the two young men.

'Is the one who offered to buy him a pint his grandson, then?' Clara asked, thinking it would make sense if he was as he had flown to the man's rescue so quickly and calmed the situation, but the man beside her shook his head vigorously.

'I very much doubt it. Don't think he has any kin. 'Tis a turn of phrase calling him "grampa" like that, that's all.'

Clara watched as they marched the old man away across the fields in the direction of The Ferret and The Furlong. Thankfully he now seemed willing to leave at the mention of a pint of ale. Meanwhile, the gentleman in the coach, who was red-faced with indignation, had retaken his seat and was now glaring out of the window. He was a nice-looking, smartly dressed man and Clara guessed that maybe he was in his mid-thirties, but by the way he was staring out of the coach window as if the whole fiasco was the fault of the onlookers who had gathered to watch the debacle, she decided she wouldn't like to encounter him again.

By the time she had walked back home, thankfully without encountering Josiah, she was fair near worn out and it wasn't even midday. She unpacked the baskets and put everything away in the cupboards and larder. Then she called into her mother's workroom to find out how she was doing. Through the open door, she could see her mother adjusting the lace on a blue silk dress that was hanging on a dummy. Mama was concentrating hard and had a pin in her mouth ready to hem up the material. Clara waited for her to remove it and place it on the garment before she spoke; she didn't want her mother to go swallowing any pins. When the sharp metal entered the material, Clara knocked on the door.

'That looks beautiful, Mama,' she said as she entered. Her mother's skill as a seamstress never failed to amaze her and she had the reputation of being the best in the whole of Foxbridge.

Mama smiled. 'I'm glad you like it, dear,' she said proudly.

'How would you like a cup of tea?'

'I'd love one, thank you,' she replied, stretching her fingers.

They sat at the kitchen table sipping their tea in silence for a while, Clara cradling her teacup to warm up her hands. Although she'd worn mittens earlier, it was a bitterly cold day. She glanced across at her mother. Lately she looked so tired. Clara wished she was able to assist her with her dressmaking to give her a rest every now and again, but for some reason that was a skill that didn't come naturally to her. More often than not she'd end up all fingers and thumbs and end up pricking herself with a pin and dripping spots of blood onto a garment, or find herself sewing the wrong seam. She just wasn't meant to be a dressmaker; her skills were in communicating with people and teaching. Although not formally trained as such, she had acquired a good schooling when Papa had sent her to Miss Daley's School for Young Ladies in Crownley. It was probably the best thing he could ever have done for her, even though it had cost a pretty penny. Emily, on the other hand, hadn't wished to go there even though Papa had offered to do the same for her. Instead, she had preferred to leave Foxbridge Village School to stay at home and help with the homemaking, and very good she was at it too. It helped Mama a lot as Emily could carry on with the household chores, allowing Mama to work on garments for customers.

Realising she had been deep in thought, Clara looked across the table to see that Mama had been studying her for a moment. She felt herself blush for being caught off guard.

'A penny for them, Clara?'

'Oh, I don't know if they're worth that much,' she said, sighing louder than she intended to for she didn't wish to worry her mother.

Mama reached across the table to pat her daughter's hand. 'You know we'll manage. You don't have to go out to work.'

'Sorry, Mama. I need to work and not just for the money to help us out. I need to keep active and keep my mind off things. Like you do with your dressmaking, I suppose.'

Mama smiled. 'Yes, although it's hard work it is rewarding. And I don't know what I'd have done without it this past few months, nor you children either.' She dipped her hand into her pocket and retrieved her lace handkerchief to dab at her watery eyes. 'Yes, I do understand.'

Clara nodded. She wondered if those application letters had reached their intended recipients by now. Maybe she had no chance if there was a lot of competition for the posts, but there was one thing she knew for sure: she just had to try.

Chapter Three

It was a few days later when Clara received a reply to one of her application letters, offering her an interview at eleven o'clock in the morning on December the twenty-first at Stapleton Manor. Out of the two adverts, it was the one that concerned her most as the master of the house, Lord Howard Stapleton, had three children, not just two young boys as for the other post.

'You've had a reply?' Emily said, failing to contain her excitement as she clasped her hands together. She seemed more enthusiastic than Clara was. Why did she suddenly have misgivings?

'Yes,' Clara replied shakily as her stomach flipped over.

'Well, why aren't you happy about it? It's what you want, isn't it?' Emily drew closer to her sister.

'It is, yes. I suppose it's like all new things, we fear them until we get used to them. It's not just that though.' Clara took a seat at the kitchen table to read the letter once more as if she'd somehow missed something the first time.

'Then what is it?'

'This is the application to teach three children, not just two young boys as in the other one.'

'That might not be bad though. One of them is a girl, yes?' Emily sat beside her sister and took the letter from her hands. 'Oh, I see, there are two older girls and a younger brother. Look at this fancy notepaper and the fine penmanship. That's real quality. Imagine it though Clara … I'd jump at the chance to bed and board at a fine establishment like Stapleton Manor!'

Clara smiled inwardly to herself. She guessed her sister would think she'd gone up in the world if she acquired a post as a governess somewhere like that.

'Yes, it is such lovely notepaper.' Clara sighed and took the letter from her sister, replacing it in the envelope. Why did the interview have to be so close to Christmas? Why not afterwards? Although she knew that Christmas wouldn't be the same this year anyhow as Papa wouldn't be a part of it. How could she bear to hear the visiting vicar speak of Christmas when her father had done it so well and for so many years to the delight of his parishioners? Maybe then it was a good thing she'd be out of the house for a period of time, even if it meant missing church should she have to work.

'What's the matter?' asked Mama as she entered the kitchen. 'Clara, you've got a face as long as a horse!'

She didn't feel like going through the whole thing again nor worrying her mother, so she said, 'Nothing, Mama. I've just had a reply to my application as governess and I have an interview arranged for the twenty-first of this month.'

Her mother nodded. 'Well at least the interview will be out of the way and then you can enjoy Christmas. I expect they'll want the successful applicant to begin work in the New Year.'

Mama was probably right, what other explanation could there be?

***

Early the morning of the twenty-first of December, Clara was out walking on the mountainside where she stood for a moment to enjoy the view below: the green rolling hills stretching out in the distance, the river flowing between Foxbridge and Crownley and the peppering of mill workers' cottages in the distance. She could even make out the spire of St. Bartholomew's standing loud and proud. Up here, she felt closer both to God and her father.

'Oh, Papa, what are we all to do?' she asked him, her whispered words taken by the breeze and disappearing into the ether.

Sometimes she closed her eyes and waited for a reply carried by the wind. If she just concentrated and switched off from everything, she knew the answer would come, but then from somewhere she heard a loud piercing scream which shook her out of her reverie.

Her eyes flicked open. Someone was in danger by the sound of it. One of the cottages out this way belonged to Jethro and Lottie McWhirter – the latter of whom had to be about eight months or more pregnant by now. The second cottage was derelict and the third belonged to an elderly gentleman. That high pitched, piercing scream had to belong to Lottie McWhirter. Jethro was a wastrel who frittered his wages from the mill on cheap ale and equally cheap women. He was also known to be handy with his fists which were set to fly at the sound of a crossed word or a perceived insult.

She stared hard in the direction of the cottage but could see nothing out of the ordinary. There wasn't even a sign of life there and no smoke from the chimney either, which was strange for such a perishingly cold day. But what if Lottie was going into labour?

Clara hitched her skirts up and made her way down the mountainside, digging the heels of her ankle boots into the grassy verge to stop herself from falling. Thank goodness it hadn't been snowing or icy, but then she surmised she'd hardly have been likely to climb the mountain if it had been either.

'Help me! Help!' she heard the voice cry out, its guttural quality disturbing her greatly.

'I'm coming!' Clara yelled back, trying to establish where the voice was emanating from. There was no one on the doorstep of the cottage, but then she noticed the wooden door of the barn was ajar. As she neared, she saw Lottie on her hands and knees inside.

'It's on its way. The baby is on its way,' she grimaced and then she raised her head and let out an all-encompassing groan which sounded like a wounded animal.

'Don't you fear, Mrs McWhirter,' Clara said in a much calmer voice than she really felt as she approached the woman.

'Where's Jethro?' she asked.

'Where. Do. You. Think?' Lottie forced out each painful word. There were no prizes for guessing where the man was. How could any man leave his wife to squander his wages at the pub when she was so near labour and needed him? Clara could never understand that.

'Right, there's no time for me to run and get Marie Wilton for you,' – Marie was the local midwife, untrained but always good when it came to delivering babies in the village – 'so you'll just have to depend on my help for now and then when everything's over and you and the baby are settled, I'll try to send word to your husband. All right?'

Lottie shook her head vehemently in protest. 'Please, no. He's the last person I want to see.' Then to Clara's horror, she noticed the purple and yellow mottled bruising on Lottie's arms and legs.

'He did all that to you?'

Lottie nodded as tears filled her eyes at the memory of it all. 'Came home drunk last night he did and kicked me down the stairs as his dinner weren't on the table.' She paused to draw a breath. 'Then when he went out this morning, I started to pack a few belongings of mine to get out of here. I don't want no baby brought up in this environment.'

Clara nodded slowly. Poor Lottie having to go through all that. She knelt on the hay beside her and took the woman's hand in her.

'Hopefully you shan't have to go through that ever again, either. As soon as you've given birth and I've cleaned both you and the baby up and he or she has had their first feed, we're getting you out of here.' By hook or by crook Clara was that determined that she wasn't going to rest until both mother and baby were safely out of Jethro's clutches.

'But where will you take us?' Lottie's brown eyes were wide with concern.

'To The Vicarage for now. He won't suspect you of being there as it was only accidental that I was walking your way this morning. Once you've rested for a few days, then I'll get you out of there and to another place of safety.' An idea was forming in Clara's mind of who she could ask for help, but the truth was she didn't know how to find him. Jethro wouldn't think of looking for his wife and child at Patrin's caravan, and when he and his sister moved on with the other gypsies to another town or village, maybe Lottie could settle there and find work.

In amongst all the hullabaloo, Clara had totally forgotten her interview for the post of governess was scheduled for eleven o'clock that morning. It was now twenty-five minutes past nine.

***

Lottie McWhirter lay back with her head resting on a bale of hay as Clara stared at the newborn babe in her own arms. He was a fair size but so far he hadn't cried at all and his body seemed a little limp. Thinking about what her father had done when their sheepdog, Nell, had given birth to pups presented her with an idea. When one pup had seemed almost dead, he had done something to revive him. Clara thought she'd try the same thing. Carefully, she prised open the infant's mouth and inserted the knuckle of her little finger inside to clear away any mucus. She laid the baby on the hay then lifted her skirt to tear at her petticoats for something to swaddle him in. If he was dead, how was she going to explain to Lottie? The woman now lay exhausted, all effort spent as her head lolled to one side. For a moment she was out of it with exhaustion, but soon she would ask.

You can't die, I won't let you! she said inwardly to the baby. She lifted him into her arms and rocked him, but still nothing. Even tapping the newborn's back didn't seem to work. Seeing a trough of clean water in the corner, she took the baby there and began to splash the cold water onto his face. It wasn't long before he let out a loud ear-piercing cry which left Clara almost weeping with relief. Lottie looked up at her and smiled with tears rolling down both cheeks.

'It's a boy,' Clara said. 'A beautiful baby boy! You'd better give him a feed. Now I'm going to pop inside your house and get a fire underway so I can boil some kettles and make you a nice brew and something to eat. Then I'll clean you both up and we can get out of here. What time do you reckon your Jethro might get home?'

'He's got a day off today. Was supposed to be here because of the kindness of his employer as I was due any day and we're so cut off up here, with it being remote and all. But instead of being with me, he's

[23]

chosen the pub. I reckon he could return at any time. He's been gone since last night after he kicked me down them stairs.'

'Now look here,' said Clara, putting on her best school mistress voice, 'you need feeding and cleaning up before we leave and if your Jethro turns up, well, you've got me here as well. My guess is he'll be a charmer in my company.'

Reluctantly, Lottie nodded and then she took the infant to her breast. Thankfully he began to suckle nicely after a couple of attempts.

'Right then, I'll leave the two of you to it and will be back as quick as I can.' Clara wiped her weary brow. The truth was she could do with a brew herself right now. She quickly plunged her bloodied hands into a trough of clean water intended for the livestock before wiping them on her dress. She was no longer concerned about her appearance – it was best that mother and baby were taken care of.

The front door of the couple's cottage was ajar, so with some trepidation she pushed the door and called inside for fear he was there.

'Mr McWhirter!' she called out, but there was no reply so she stepped inside. The first thing that struck her was how cold it was. There was no warm welcome or cosy fire blazing away in the hearth here. On the wooden counter she noticed a large black kettle. There was no sign of any tap inside the house, but to her relief when she opened the back door there was a water pump in the yard. She filled the kettle up, then set about lighting a fire. Why did things have to be against her? Even though the fire was set with wood, balls of old newspaper and coal it would take time to get the fire going. No doubt as Lottie was wanting to make her escape she hadn't banked on the fact that she would need that fire so desperately.

Clara located a box of matches on the mantel and struck one to ignite the kindling. There was a metal blower beside the fire which after a while she placed in front of it to draw the flames. Before long she had a nice fire going and was able to boil the kettle to make them a cup of tea and finally to wash both mother and baby.

'Do you have any clean clothes we can change you into?' Clara asked Lottie when she arrived back in the barn.

The woman laid down her cup of tea on the straw beside her. 'Yes, in the bedroom. You'll find some in the chest of drawers and there's my best shawl in the wardrobe.'

Clara's eyes searched for the baby to see he was asleep swaddled in her petticoats, sated from his feed.

'Now be sure you finish your tea,' Clara advised. 'I'll be back soon with your clothes and a warm blanket for the baby. Then we're getting out of here.'

The woman nodded, closed her eyes and laid her head back on the hay bale for a moment.

Clara worked as quickly as she could, rifling through cupboards and wardrobes to fill an old carpet bag she had found with the woman's belongings. Once that was full she shoved the rest into a couple of wicker baskets. There was hardly time to think clearly.

She was just escaping down the stairs when she heard voices outside. It was him, Jethro McWhirter, speaking with his elderly neighbour. What if the man was telling him that he'd heard Lottie cry out in pain? But then again, she'd thought the man was a little deaf anyhow; when she'd encountered him once in the post office, he'd seemed to have difficulty hearing what Mr Fothergill had to say to him, so maybe the conversation wasn't about Lottie's screams at all. Still, this gave Clara the good fortune to escape through the back door and into the barn.

When she returned, she roused the sleeping woman by shaking her arm.

'Lottie, quick, your Jethro has just returned.'

The woman's eyes flicked open and Clara could see the horror in them as Lottie jerked forward and pulled herself up into a standing position. She was on high alert, that much was evident.

'You've got a bit of time to get dressed as he's talking to your neighbour, but hurry nevertheless and we'll get out of here across the field.'

Lottie did as she was told, changing into a clean linen dress. Clara draped the woman's shawl around her shoulders. Lottie looked weak and shaky, but it would be safer for her to leave in that condition than remain with a brute who would cause her even more harm. She handed both baskets to Lottie while she lifted the sleeping infant to carry in one arm, using her free hand to carry the carpet bag. Thankfully, Clara hadn't brought too much from the house.

Stealthily they made their way out of the back door of the barn so they were not visible from the cottage, though it would be evident what had taken place here as the infant's afterbirth was left behind and a bloodied mess soaked the hay where Lottie had lain. Clara had managed to tie off the placenta with some string she'd found in the barn and had later snipped the placental cord with a pair of sharp scissors she'd cleaned with boiling water.

The walk to the village seemed never-ending with Clara glancing over her shoulder more than once to ensure they weren't being followed. If Jethro had been in their wake, she didn't know what she would have done. Lottie was in a frail condition, and she herself wasn't all that well built. What chance would they have against a six-foot something brute who was built like a stone wall?

Clara led her back to The Vicarage in such a way so that they would pass as few people as possible who might know them – fortunately, apart from passing a costermonger on his cart and a couple of elderly ladies, there was no one of note. As she opened the wooden gate, she blew a breath of relief. Safely home at last.

***

'Where have you been?' Emily wanted to know as soon as Clara entered the house. 'You've missed your interview and you look like you've been pulled through a hedge backwards!' she said as she gazed in horror at her sister's tattered and torn dress. Her mouth gaped open as she caught sight of the baby in her sister's arms and Lottie stood behind her.

The interview!

In all of the excitement and panic, Clara had completely forgotten about that! No time to dwell on it now though as both Lottie and the baby needed a bed. Noticing what was going on, Mama ushered towards them.

'Please come through and sit down, Mrs McWhirter.'

It was bitterly cold and Clara realised if Lottie didn't rest then she would be in danger of collapse, so she was thankful to Mama for taking charge of the situation. She led the woman through to the parlour where the baby was placed in her arms for another feed while Mama went to fetch Lottie some nourishing stew.

'I made her a cup of tea,' Clara explained as she sat at the kitchen table, 'but she didn't drink much as she fell asleep. Mama we had to get out of there fast as her husband was due home. She was already trying to escape as he'd kicked her down the stairs last night.'

Mama nodded. 'How awful, and in her condition too. You look like you need to rest yourself, Clara.' She patted her daughter's shoulder. 'So it was you who delivered the baby?'

Clara nodded. 'Yes.'

'Well done.'

'Well done for what?' Emily asked as she entered the warm and steamy kitchen, the stew bubbling away on the stove.

'It was Clara who delivered the baby.'

Emily's eyes grew large and round. 'Really? No wonder you missed your interview! What bad luck though.'

At that point, Clara couldn't have cared less. She just felt so sleepy. After they'd all had a good feed from the lamb stew with hunks of fresh bread slathered in salted butter, Mama said, 'Mrs McWhirter can have my double bed for time being as there will be plenty of room for her and the baby.'

Clara nodded gratefully. 'Well I can double up with Emily and you can have my bed for now, Mama.'

Emily scowled for a moment. She was a selfish sort in many ways and wouldn't like the thought of her sister sharing her bed, but this was an emergency situation as far as Clara and her mother were concerned so Emily had little say on the matter. Clara knew that she could butter her sister up by giving her something for herself. Maybe the gold pixie on the chain from Patrin? That might do it but being the sentimental sort she was she didn't really want to part with that, so she'd have to think of something else. Maybe she could give her one of her dresses and get Mama to alter it for her? Yes, that should do the trick. The turquoise one with the leg of mutton sleeves. She'd look pretty in that.

***

Lottie and the new baby – who she'd named Samuel – settled in well to the house and callers were kept away from the door just in case anyone should see them living there. If a parishioner knocked unexpectedly, Mama ushered them into the church next door where she took them to speak in what had been Papa's old office. Unfortunately, one visitor turned up and, noticing the kitchen door ajar, shouted in, 'Coo-ee! It's me, Mrs Masters. I've brought Lillibeth with me for a fitting!'

Oh no! Clara glanced at Lottie. 'You'd better nip upstairs,' she whispered, but as she did so she noticed the knob on the parlour door turn, and in walked Mrs Pettigrew with her gangly daughter by her side. Both were wearing the most ridiculous hats she had ever seen.

'Oh Clara,' Mrs Pettigrew began but then she noticed Lottie and the baby in the corner. 'I'm sorry, I didn't realise you had any visitors,' she said, her eyes widening. 'Hello, Mrs McWhirter. I didn't realise you'd had the baby.'

Mrs McWhirter nodded but said nothing, so it was up to Clara to fill in for her.

'Yes, it was just a couple of days ago. Lottie brought him along for a visit.'

'Should you be out then? Shouldn't you be in confinement?' Mrs Pettigrew said sharply.

Clara put on her sweetest smile. 'Er … Mrs McWhirter has just dropped by with a donation for the church. That's why she's visiting us today.'

Mrs Pettigrew wrinkled her nose as if she couldn't possibly believe that someone like Lottie McWhirter could afford to make such a donation, and of course it hardly seemed likely as she'd just given birth. Probably not one of Clara's best ideas but she'd said the first thing that came into her mind.

'Where is your mother, anyhow?' asked Mrs Pettigrew.

'She's over at the church at the moment, arranging the flowers.'

'Well didn't she tell you I had an appointment with her?' Mrs Pettigrew's nostrils were in full flare now. She was more than a little annoyed at being disregarded and told untruths to boot.

'No,' said Clara, which was the truth. 'She hasn't mentioned a word to me.'

'This just isn't good enough. I'll call back later so she'd better be here then! Come along now, Lillibeth,' she prodded the girl in the small of her back with her umbrella as if she was pushing her out of the door. She took one final glance backwards at the scene before her as if trying to make sense of it and then added curtly, 'Good day to you all!' before making a dramatic exit with her precious daughter.

'I'm sorry about that,' Clara said to Lottie, not know whether to laugh or cry.

Lottie shrugged and smiled. 'It couldn't be helped I suppose.'

Something that troubled Clara was the fact that now Mrs Pettigrew had seen Lottie and Samuel there, it wouldn't be too long before she'd be gossiping to her cronies about it, and that just wouldn't do.

'I'm sorry, Mrs McWhirter. I think it will be safer if I find somewhere else for you to stay if you don't want Jethro to find out you're here.'

'I suppose so, but where else can I go?' Lottie replied meekly.

'Just leave that to me,' Clara said with more conviction than she really felt. She was just going to have to find out if the gypsies were still around in the area.

Chapter Four

'What's going on here?' Mama asked as she entered the parlour. Lottie was stood with her shawl draped around her shoulders and one of Clara's old hats perched on her head. Baby Samuel was cradled in her arms while Clara had both the carpet bag and baskets in her hands.

'It's Mrs Pettigrew. She called earlier and reckoned she had an appointment with her daughter to see you,' Clara explained.

Mama shook her head. 'That woman! No, it was for tomorrow – she's obviously mixed up the days. But why are you leaving?'

'Mrs Pettigrew just walked into the house as the back door was left ajar. She saw that Lottie and the baby were here and she was so annoyed that you weren't here to attend to her that I fear she will tittle-tattle around the village and word will get back to Jethro.'

Mama frowned. 'Now that is a possibility. But where are you going to go?'

'I don't know yet. But I have to get them out of here.'

Mama chewed on her bottom lip in deliberation. 'I have an idea,' she said. 'She could stay at your Auntie Miriam's in Stonebridge for time being. It's still close by but far enough away for now until we think of something else.'

Clara nodded. Stonebridge was a few miles away but still in walking distance.

'We'll go there then. Auntie won't turn us away, I know she won't. We better set off walking now before it gets dark.'

'No, you won't!' said Emily who had just entered the room looking flushed from the cold air. 'I just caught what you said about having to leave here. Jake is in the kitchen as he's just brought me home with the shopping. I'm going to make him a brew and then he can take you all over to Auntie's house on his horse and cart.'

'Oh Emily, you do surprise me sometimes!' Clara said, smiling. Maybe she was wrong about her sister being so selfish when she could think of something like this.

Emily blushed. 'It just seems a sensible suggestion, that's all.'

By the time Jake had finished his cup of tea, darkness was beginning to fall. They set off for Stonebridge with Clara up the front of the cart alongside Jake and Lottie and the baby snuggled up under a couple of thick blankets on the back of it.

'I won't forget this, Jake,' Clara smiled at him.

'It's all right,' Jake winked at her. 'It'll be my good deed for the day.'

Clara nodded. Her sister could do worse than to marry Jake. The man was always there for her and often came to the family's rescue now Papa was no longer here.

'Gee up!' he shouted at the horse to get him started as Mama, Emily and the two younger ones stood at the gatepost waving them off.

It was a bumpy ride to Stonebridge, made worse by the ruts on the rough track along the way. Thankfully Samuel slept throughout, and Lottie seemed to sleep a little too for whenever Clara turned around to take a look at the pair the woman's eyes were closed or near closing. Though Clara knew that as the mother of a newborn baby Lottie would be able to rouse herself instantly if Samuel needed her. She was still on high alert, particularly as she had the threat of Jethro coming after them.

It shouldn't be like this. If Lottie had a decent husband, they'd both be home together now by the fireside with their baby enjoying their time together. There are much better men in this world than Jethro.

They were about a quarter of a mile from Stonebridge when a coach and horses almost collided with them, causing Clara's heart to thud with fear.

'That driver wasn't paying heed,' Jake said crossly as he brought the cart to a standstill by pulling on the horse's reins.

'No, you're right there,' Clara agreed. She turned around to Lottie at the back. 'Are you both all right?'

'Yes, that was a bit of a scare though.' And at that moment, as if on cue, baby Samuel began to air his lungs. Maybe it was the way the cart had to be brought up sharply or maybe he just needed a feed, but in any case he was now unsettled.

A gentleman was now leaning out of the coach window. 'Watch where you're going!' he shouted at Jake.

'Now hang on a moment,' Clara shouted back at him, not giving tuppence for who he might be for the safety of them all was at stake here. 'It was your driver who caused this, not ours. He was driving like a mad man. Maybe you'd better check to see if he's been drinking alcohol.'

Beneath the glow of the lamplight, although the gentleman's face was not as visible as during daylight, she could see and sense his anger at her retort.

'I can assure you, Miss, that my driver does not drink alcohol when driving this coach and is fully competent!' Then as if he had no more to say on the matter, he sat himself back down and the coach made off in the opposite direction to them.

'Well done!' Jake chuckled. 'Those nobs want telling and all! I think you might have been correct about the coachman's drinking – that gent had no more to say as you hit a nerve.'

Clara should've felt glad she'd put someone like him in his place, but it came to her in a flash that he was the same man who shouted at the elderly beggar the other day and tried to beat him with his cane. She had thought she'd recognised the voice. He was a cruel sort if ever there was one. Trust their luck to encounter him tonight of all nights.

When they arrived in Stonebridge, they located Auntie's cottage down a secluded winding lane that was edged with trees. An oil lamp was burning brightly on the window ledge in front of the lace drapes, and all looked warm and welcoming.

Hearing the noise from the cartwheels and everyone's chatter she came out to greet them, swinging a lantern in her hand.

'Why if it isn't my lovely niece, Clara!' she said with great excitement. 'And how come you're visiting me here at this hour of an evening? Not that you're not welcome of course, but I rarely get visitors.'

'I'm sorry about this,' Clara said, stooping to plant a kiss on her aunt's soft cheek. 'Mrs McWhirter has recently given birth to a baby boy and she was stopping with us as her husband is violent towards her. But, unfortunately, the biggest gossip in Foxbridge has got wind of this so I'm taking no chances in case her husband discovers their whereabouts. Mama suggested bringing both of them here if that's all right? Only until we can think of another plan.'

Auntie began to beam. 'Of course it is and both will be most welcome here. They'll be company for me. Now let's get you all inside.'

They stayed for a half-hour to settle both mother and baby into the cottage, and it wasn't long before Lottie and her child looked most at home seated on the settee as Auntie fussed over them all, bringing out her freshly baked mince pies and glasses of her elderflower cordial. Clara felt reluctant to leave but realised they had to get going; Mama would be concerned about them and Jake had to rise early in the morning for work. They'd taken up enough of his time as it was.

As they said their goodbyes on the doorstep, Clara promised she'd be back soon to check on them all. As she clambered on board the cart, soft powdery flakes fell from way on high. The sooner they got home the better as before too long the road between Foxbridge and Stonebridge could prove impassable.

***

The following day, Clara couldn't shake off the feeling of loss about missing her chance of an interview at Stapleton Manor. As she sat in the rocking chair gazing out of the French windows onto the snow-covered lawn outside, she found herself rocking faster and faster.

'For goodness sake, Clara,' her mother scolded, which was most unusual for her. 'You'll wear out the wooden floor!'

Clara brought herself back into the moment and stopped what she was doing before turning to face her mother.

'Sorry, Mama. I'm just so frustrated about missing my chance at that interview yesterday.'

'I realise that. What you did was a mighty fine thing helping to bring a new life into the world and helping that woman escape her cruel husband before she got another hammering from him. Believe me, I've seen that sort of thing with parishioners before. The husband goes quiet and even attentive when a new baby is born and then one day out of the blue he'll explode again. It might be an undercooked potato, not having his supper on the table on time, or just because he's drunk and thinks he can do what he damn well likes!'

Clara gasped a little. It was unusual to hear Mama using a curse word. Her mother closed her eyes momentarily as if reminding herself who she was.

'I apologise for saying that word, but not for the rest of it. If I were you, I'd take a walk over to Stapleton Manor while the snow's not too deep and ask if you might speak to someone there. Ask if the post is still open and explain why you couldn't attend yesterday.'

Clara blinked. 'Do you think that might work?'

'There's no harm in trying. What do you have to lose?'

Mama was right. She had nothing to lose whatsoever. *Only your dignity*, a little voice in her head reminded her.

So later that day she set off across the fields to Stapleton Manor with seeping trepidation in every step she took.

***

Standing at the end of the manor house driveway, shivering partly from the cold and partly from apprehension, Clara drew her cape firmly around her shoulders to keep the biting wind out. She had considered retracing her steps and returning to the comfort of her home and family, but what would that do for her? Make her a coward, that was what. She stared at the house with its grand wrought iron gates and elaborate pillars. The large grey building seemed far in the distance. It would take her a long time to even walk up the long driveway, never mind consider knocking at the door. And would it be proper to knock on the front door anyhow? She wasn't going to be a servant as such, but neither would she be a part of the family. Maybe it would be best to knock on the back door. But how could she even get through the front gates? They appeared to be locked. Then she noticed the small lodge house to the left which was partly hidden behind the trees. There was a sign at the gate saying to pull the bell cord for attention. No doubt it alerted the lodge-keeper and he would attend to her. Fancy living in a house that had another smaller house in its grounds?

She tugged on the cord and presently a small wizened man who walked with a shuffling limp came towards her. He looked as if in middle-age to her, but he may well have been older.

'Sorry, the master's not wanting to buy anything from you today,' he said curtly, sounding slightly out of breath in a way that made her wonder if she'd somehow disturbed him.

'I'm not selling anything,' Clara explained. 'I'm here about a job.'

'No one's mentioned anyone coming here for a job today,' he said, narrowing his eyes. 'Plenty of staff working at the big house already. There's no positions going that I'm aware of.'

'This is for the post of a governess. I should have attended yesterday but got unavoidably detained.'

He sniffed loudly, clearly suspicious that she had bad intent. 'I see. So, who should I inform that you've turned up a day late, then?'

She didn't much care for his sarcastic tone of voice, so she glared at him. 'I don't rightly know to be honest. I was supposed to see Lord Stapleton,' she explained.

'I'll tell you what I'll do,' he said after a while with a note of sympathy in his voice. 'I'm not supposed to let unsolicited callers into the grounds, so I'll escort you up to the house myself and we'll ask for the housekeeper, Mrs Montgomery, to see if she can sort this out. How does that sound?'

Suddenly he had a twinkle in his blue eyes which made him look less formidable and Clara found herself relaxing and smiling at him.

'Well, Mr…?' Clara trailed off, realising she hadn't a clue what this man's name was.

'Snelgrove.'

'Mr Snelgrove. I've come this far so I might as well try to speak to the housekeeper. I appreciate you trying to help me.'

He nodded. 'I have to warn you though, Miss…?'

Now it was her turn to fill in the details. 'Miss Clara Masters.'

'Miss Masters, I have to inform you that governesses don't last very long here.'

She quirked a brow. 'And why would that be?'

'I'm not at liberty to give any details, but since the passing of the lady of the house they have become a difficult family to work for.' He tapped the side of his nose. 'If you get me drift.'

She thought she did get his drift very well indeed and she asked herself if she should be here at all. But instead, she found herself saying, 'I'm willing to accept the risk.'

He looked her up and down as if appraising her and then clucked his teeth.

'Very well, Miss Masters. Please follow me.'

The walk up the driveway seemed never-ending. She swore she could have walked from Foxbridge to Crownley in the time this was taking. Mr Snelgrove made no conversation along the way which made things feel awkward between them. Now she was more concerned than ever that she might have disturbed him and he was irritated by her intrusion, but then unexpectedly, he said, 'I'll take you to the back door of the kitchen and ask Cook to see to you. She'll probably send one of the kitchen-maids to fetch Mrs Montgomery. Will that be all right for you?'

'That will be fine, thank you. And I'm sorry for my intrusion, Mr Snelgrove.'

'It's no bother, miss. And good luck. I mean that. If you want the job then I hope you get it but be prepared to use a bit of mettle and stick up for yourself from time to time.'

She nodded nervously. Mr Snelgrove led her to the large wooden back door where he opened it a fraction to have a quiet word with Cook, who looked her up and down. Oh dear! Was this another one she'd disturbed? No doubt Cook might have been preparing dinner for the family and could do without her intrusion. But instead Cook smiled broadly.

'Come along, dear. Come and have a nice cup of tea with us in the kitchen. We're just on a break before dinner, then Maggie, one of me maids, can fetch the housekeeper for you.'

Clara nodded gratefully, deciding that maybe the staff here wouldn't be too bad after all.

***

'And then the man turned up at the back door with a box in his hands. I said "'ere what you got in there, fella?"'

'Did yer, Cook?' asked the kitchen-maid Maggie.

'She did an' all,' said the young man named Billy. Billy seemed to be like a general dogsbody around the place. A gofer, as her father would have called him – a go for this and a go for that. 'Wait till she tells you what happened next!' Billy could hardly contain his mirth as he began to laugh so hard that he clutched his sides.

'Well,' said Cook with a solemn expression on her face which made Clara wonder what on earth had happened. 'I says to him again, "What you got in there?!" And do you know what he said?'

'No?' Maggie was on the edge of her seat in anticipation.

'Go on, tell the girl,' chuckled Billy.

'Well, he replies, "I got your Christmas bird, missus!" I thought to meself, a fourteen-pound turkey would never fit in that bloomin' box. So I asks him to open it and out flew a yellow canary!'

'She thought he were poulterer, see,' explained Billy, 'but it were one of them door to door salesmen trying to sell a canary.'

'Aye, fancy me thinking that and I was expecting Mr Mullard. But that fella I found out was a travelling magic act. I don't think he was really serious about selling the canary. Or maybe if he was, he had hit on hard times!' Cook threw back her head and a deep throaty chuckle emerged that threatened to choke her.

Soon they were all laughing around the large pinewood table, but the laughter ceased as a woman in a black damask dress with a white frilled collar stood at the head of the table glaring at them all. The silence felt uncomfortable and then she spoke.

'Shouldn't you all be back at your work now?'

'No,' said Cook firmly, 'we still have a few minutes to go.' She stood and, drawing herself up to her full height to face the woman, said, 'This young lady here is Miss Clara Masters. She missed her interview yesterday and wondered if the master could see her this afternoon.'

Mrs Montgomery sniffed and stared at Clara, her brown beady eyes watchful and alert. 'Why did you miss yesterday's appointment?' she asked sharply.

'I delivered a baby,' Clara explained, hearing Maggie gasp beside her in awe of what she'd done.

'A baby? Are you a midwife then?' She quirked an astonished brow.

'No, Mrs Montgomery. I was passing a farm cottage and the lady of the house went into labour. There was no one else around so I delivered the child.'

'And are both mother and child all right?' asked Cook with a concerned look on her face.

'Yes, thankfully.'

'Well that's to be highly commended, don't you think, Mrs Montgomery?' Billy smiled.

The housekeeper nodded. 'Exceptional circumstances indeed. I shall have a word with his lordship to see if he can see you in a moment.' She turned on her heel and left the kitchen.

'I think you've impressed her. There's not many that can do that!' Cook chuckled.

Mrs Montgomery returned a few minutes later with a smile on her face and Clara noticed Cook nudging Maggie as if to say, 'Look at her!'

'Lord Stapleton will see you in the drawing-room in ten minutes. If you'd like to freshen up I can show you to the servants' rest room.'

Clara felt her stomach flip over. 'Yes, thank you. That would be a good idea,' she said. Then she nodded at the kitchen staff and thanked Cook for the welcome cup of tea before setting off with the housekeeper.

***

Staring at herself in the mirror above the vanity unit in the small rest room, Clara studied her face.

Do I look like someone who can be a governess to this gentleman's children? she asked herself. *Will he take to me? Or will he be angry that I didn't show yesterday? Nevertheless, he is seeing me so the position cannot be filled.*

She quickly tidied up her hair, removing and replacing several hair pins to form a neat chignon knot at the back of her head. She hadn't worn her bonnet and now wondered if she should have for the interview, but she had arrived here at a moment's notice after all. Her dress looked respectable and was quite new so she didn't look too shabby, and her black leather boots were highly polished. There was a light knock on the door.

'Are you ready now, Miss Masters?' Mrs Montgomery asked

Clara took a deep, composing breath before replying, 'Yes, I am. Thank you.' Then she opened the door and followed the woman down the long corridor which displayed what appeared to be a gallery of family portraits. The speed the woman walked meant she didn't have time to study them, but if she was fortunate to get the job then she surely would. As the housekeeper walked along at a brisk pace, Clara heard the clinking of the keys on the chatelaine silver chain she wore around her waist. Mrs Montgomery stopped abruptly outside a dark walnut wooden door and rapped on it three times.

'Enter!' boomed a male voice from within.

Clara swallowed hard as Mrs Montgomery swung the door open.

'Miss Masters is here to see you, m'lord,' the housekeeper said.

The man was standing with his back to her looking out of the leaded windows. She could see he filled his dark green velvet jacket very well. He had broad shoulders and from the back of his head she could see that his hair – of which there was plenty – was shiny and black.

He turned suddenly, causing her to gasp with shock. Those dark eyes, that aquiline nose, the strong chin – she'd recognise him anywhere. He was the same gentleman who had tried to strike the old man at the market with his cane and the self-same man who had shouted at them when his driver had almost run them off the road that night on the way to Auntie's house.

Her legs felt boneless and she wished she could turn around and walk away before it was too late, but he was already appraising her with a look in his eyes which said to her, 'You'll do very nicely, m'dear.'

Chapter Five

Clara blinked several times. Was this really happening to her? Surely this had to be a bad dream and she'd wake up any moment now? She felt rooted to the spot, partly with fear and partly with interest at just what this man had to say.

'Please take a seat, Miss Masters,' he instructed, then looking at his housekeeper said, 'You may leave us now, Mrs Montgomery.'

Mrs Montgomery nodded, turned on her heel and left the room.

Clara took a seat and Lord Stapleton sat opposite her behind his large carved oak desk. He shuffled through some paperwork and then put on a pair of what she assumed were reading glasses.

'Damned plebs,' he muttered under his breath, which she didn't know if she were intended to hear or not. 'Paperwork, paperwork and more paperwork! When will it ever end?' And then as if just realising she were sat in front of him, he said, 'So, it's my understanding you were to have attended an interview here yesterday but were unavoidably detained due to having to help deliver an infant?' He peered over the top of his spectacles which made her feel uneasy, as if he thought she were about to create some excuse, even though what he'd relayed was absolutely true.

She cleared her throat before replying. 'Erm, yes, your lordship. It wasn't expected and there was no one else around. If I'd run to the village for assistance, by the time I'd have returned the woman might have given birth all on her own.'

'Yes, yes. I can understand that and as excuses go, it's the best one I've heard yet,' he chuckled.

Who on earth did he think he was making light of this? She felt her hackles rise as she gritted her teeth.

'The mother in question had been beaten up by her husband only the night before, so I don't think this is a laughing matter at all!' she said without prompting. Lord or no lord, Clara was about to get up and walk out on the man, but then he looked at her and his face fell.

'I am sorry, I didn't wish to make light of it. You see, there was one young lady who attended an interview here yesterday who was almost an hour late. Poor time keeping is something I cannot abide. After all, wars would not be won if the enemy was kept waiting!'

'I don't see how what you're saying has anything to do with anything,' she said crossly.

His voice took a more serious tone. 'What I mean to say is the young lady then went on to create all manner of excuses as to why she didn't arrive on time. She blamed her mother for not waking her up in time, she blamed the poor weather and even her mode of transport. It became obvious to me that she'd either simply decided to attend at the last moment or had been forced to by her parents.'

Clara nodded.

'So you see, it was refreshing then to hear of a genuine excuse that was so big and bold that it simply had to be true!'

Clara found herself relaxing. *At least he does have a sense of humour, even if he is prone to fits of temper,* she thought.

'Now then, I'd like to hear a little about yourself,' he asked.

'What would you like to know, sir?' she said, taken aback. She hadn't anticipated this.

'About your circumstances. Your family?'

'I see.' She took a deep breath in and let it all out again, knowing this was going to be painful for her. 'I live with my mother, two sisters and younger brother at the vicarage of St. Bartholomew's church in Foxbridge. My father, who was the local vicar there, died quite suddenly a few months ago. Now we will have to move as there are plans to appoint a new vicar shortly, so my circumstances have changed. I noticed your advert to take care of two daughters aged twelve and thirteen and a son of eight years old, and thought I'd apply for the position.'

'I understand,' he said thoughtfully as he steepled his fingers on his desk. He didn't even mention the death of her father. How callous of him not to understand how painful this was for her. 'And what makes you think you'd be the right person for the position?'

'Well I'm good with children for a start. Not just as I have younger siblings but because I have several years of experience teaching in the Sunday school.'

He nodded but was silent. What was she to say now? She hoped he'd fill in the gap but instead he just kept looking at her. If he carried on then she might begin to cry at the thought of her very sad circumstances, so she decided to turn the tables and ask him a question. She realised this might sound impertinent, but she felt she had little to lose.

'So, could you tell me a little about the children that I might end up having in my charge?'

His eyes widened as if he was a little taken aback at her being so upfront. He let out a little sigh, which surprised her.

'Amelia is the eldest. She's thirteen years old and if I'm honest, she can be a little madam to deal with. She's bossy and brassy and bold.'

He chuckled. 'She fears nothing and is a little like yourself!' His eyes were shining now as she felt the heat infuse her face. 'Danielle is twelve years old and nothing like her sister. She's quite introverted and has her face forever in a book. I worry about her sometimes. James is eight years old and a little powerhouse of a person. He's so full of energy that he needs reining in sometimes as he'll hardly sit still and concentrate.'

'And how has their mother's death affected them all?' Clara asked sympathetically, but as soon as she'd uttered the words she regretted them. From the way Mr Snelgrove had spoken, Lord Stapleton hadn't lost his wife all that long ago.

'How do you expect?' he replied curtly. Changing the subject, he carried on, 'I see from your letter that you play the pianoforte?'

'I do indeed,' she smiled, feeling this was something she'd like to discuss. But then his manner changed abruptly.

'For the time being there is to be no music whatsoever in this house. You are to teach them reading, writing and arithmetic, and use of the globes. It's permissible for you to supervise them for their daily exercise, but there will be no dancing or any other such frippery. Understood?'

Open-mouthed, she nodded. How dreadful for those poor children. And as she looked around, she realised apart from Cook speaking of a turkey earlier, she had so far seen no other sign of the festive season in the house.

'Am I permitted to meet the children beforehand, providing you offer me the position?' she asked hopefully.

Lord Stapleton shook his head. 'They're not here at the moment as they're spending time with their aunt in Scotland. They won't return until the New Year, which is good for you as you'll get to spend your final Christmas with your family at The Vicarage.' She nodded. 'Make sure it's a special one as I do understand what it's like to lose someone,' he added, taking her by surprise.

'Thank you, sir.' It was clear that she had the job as governess, but now she wasn't certain whether she was happy or sad. Lord Howard Stapleton was certainly an enigma; at times he seemed gruff and guarded, but at others he did seem to have a heart in there somewhere.

'Right, that's settled then. You shall commence your duties on Monday the 4th of January. If you could move your belongings in here a couple of days before then, that would be fine.'

She nodded. 'I appreciate that, sir.'

He smiled broadly. 'I'll ask Mrs Montgomery to show you where your quarters shall be and the schoolroom, then I'll arrange for my coach to take you home.'

'Oh, I don't want to put you to any trouble,' she said, trying to show how accommodating she was, but in truth it had been a long hard slog to get here in the first place.

'One of those, are you?'

'Pardon, sir?'

'A martyr. A martyr to the cause, whatever the cause happens to be. Now listen here, you cannot walk all that way back to Foxbridge. It looks like there will be more snow to come tonight, so do as you're told, young lady.'

She didn't much care for his tone, but then he smiled again. She was going to have to keep on her toes with him as she could not be sure if he were pulling her leg or whether he was being deadly serious.

***

The housekeeper opened the door on the top floor of the house, the floor just beneath the attic.

'This floor will be all your domain, Miss Masters,' she said.

Clara gulped. There was a fair-sized sitting room which housed a small sofa and armchair, a fancy fireplace, a table and chairs and a beautiful oriental rug with a striking peacock embroidered into its design. She'd never seen anything so beautiful. Across the way was a tall, arched window which looked down onto the back of the property where she could see a field and some sort of lake, and beyond that a wooded area. Then offset from the sitting room was a small bedroom with the bed nestled within a curved mahogany bedstead, over which was laid a patchwork quilt of many colours. Then there was a matching mahogany washstand, wardrobe, and dressing table. And it was all hers. Even the lace curtains were beautiful.

'I'll just show you the school room and rest rooms for the children,' Mrs Montgomery said curtly, not asking whether she liked the quarters or not. A thought occurred to her that maybe the woman was envious of her new position here.

Clara fell in love with the schoolroom. Its several windows gave it a light and airy feel. In one corner was a blackboard and easel, in another was a double bookcase of children's books, a large globe and a big box of toys. There was even a wooden rocking horse. Several colourful rugs were scattered here and there and to the other side of the room were the wooden desks. Three for her charges and a large one for herself as governess, she concluded. Clara drew open one of the drawers and recoiled in horror to see a willow cane there.

'I … I'm not expected to use this, am I?' she looked at Mrs Montgomery, whose eyes widened.

'I'm afraid so, Miss Masters. His lordship says, "Spare the rod and spoil the child" just as it reads in the Bible. Believe me, you'll need that cane with some of the antics those children get up to. That's why no governess ever lasts for long here. I'd keep looking in the newspaper for other suitable positions if I were you.'

'Mrs Montgomery, I am not one to give up. I have helped to bring up my younger brother and sister and taught at the Sunday school and never, I repeat never, in all of that time have I felt the need to raise my hand or a cane to a child. Never. Not even once!'

The housekeeper's stance stiffened. She was annoyed, that was for sure. Mrs Montgomery obviously wanted her to fail at the first hurdle. Well, Clara was having none of it. If anything, it made her more determined than ever to do a good job here.

'The coachman has been summoned at his lordship's behest. You'll find him waiting at the main entrance for you,' she said stiffly. Then she brought her beady gaze to meet Clara's eyes. 'One more thing. You are not permitted to take your meals with the other servants and are to maintain an adequate boundary between them and yourself. You are to take your meals in your quarters at all times, understood?' The woman's top lip twitched. Clara had got under her skin with her frank manner of speaking, but she wanted it to register with the woman that she did not intend to physically punish any of his lordship's children.

Clara nodded in acknowledgement. So, here at this house she was neither servant nor master. What would she be here then really? *Bewildered*, a little inner voice whispered in her ear.

***

The coach dropped her off outside The Vicarage and she thanked the driver. She wondered if he was the same man who had crashed into Jake's horse and cart on the road to Stonebridge, but she didn't think he was. This man had not a whiff of alcohol about him as he helped her down the coach step. To be truthful though, it had been dark that night so she just couldn't be sure whether he was the same man or not.

Hesitantly, she opened the wooden gate and made her way across the path that cut through the garden. She skirted the outside of the house until she came to the parlour window. Peering inside, she saw Emily and Jake kneeling by the fireside; they were laughing about something and from the way they were now gazing into one another's eyes, Clara knew she had witnessed something special. She remembered Emily had mentioned something earlier about roasting chestnuts that evening, so she surmised that's what they'd probably been doing. She didn't want to intrude on their moment, so she let herself in through the back door to find Mama cooking over the stove and Meg and Edmund sitting at the kitchen table eating hot buttered crumpets. The whole house seemed a perfect Christmas scene and in some ways made her feel like an intruder this evening.

Mama glanced up from the pan she was stirring with a wooden spoon. 'It's stew with dumplings tonight,' she said.

Clara nodded. 'It smells delicious.'

Her mother stopped what she was doing and laid down her wooden spoon on the counter. Then she turned to face her daughter.

'How did your interview at the big house go?'

'It was interesting, put it that way.' Clara huffed out a breath. 'But I have secured the position.'

Mama's face broke out into a big smile. 'That's wonderful! But why didn't you say so as soon as you walked in through the door? Aren't you happy about it?'

'I have mixed feelings, Mama. As soon as I saw Lord Stapleton's face I recognised him as the angry man who was in that coach that nearly ran us off the road on our way to Auntie's house, and the same man who struck an elderly beggar with his cane on the common when he asked him for money a few days ago.'

Mama chewed on her bottom lip. 'To be fair,' she said stroking her daughter's shoulder, 'that wouldn't have been his fault if his driver were inebriated, would it? And from what you told me previously about the old man, he had been pestering him for a long time.'

'Yes, but still there are ways of treating folk. And he didn't need to shout at us all in that manner while we were shook up when his coach collided with our cart,' Clara rebutted.

'Maybe he was shaken up himself, have you considered that? Your father always said there are two sides to every story.'

She nodded. Her mother and father were right, of course, and thankfully the driver who'd brought her home mightn't be the same man. She'd have refused to have got into the cab if she'd smelt the slightest whiff of alcohol on his breath. His lordship probably had a couple of different drivers, come to think of it.

'Go and get yourself ready then, Clara. The children have had their tea and Emily and Jake will join us.'

Clara smiled, forgetting her earlier irritation. 'They're getting close, aren't they? I just saw them through the parlour window.'

Mama nodded and smiled. Clara realised her mother was secretly hoping her daughter would marry the lad. They would make a good match too, but Emily didn't seem that bothered. She was being all lovey-dovey with him at the moment but knowing her sister he could turn up here again another day and she'd be offhand and complacent with him. On more than one occasion Clara had noticed a hurt expression in his eyes. She wondered if her sister was just using Jake, but whatever was going on there she realised she mustn't interfere.

Clara watched the others during supper. Meg and Edmund were supposedly in their beds upstairs, but from the bumping emanating from the ceiling Clara knew they were playing around. But where was the harm in it? There was no school for them tomorrow as it was the end of term. *Let them enjoy themselves*, she said to herself.

'You're quiet, Clara?' Emily said as she helped herself to second piece of bread and butter. 'You ought to be celebrating now as you've got that job. Not everyone could get it … I couldn't for sure!'

Clara smiled. Maybe she should have been over the moon, but she felt so uncertain about her new employer and the children she had yet to meet. Apart from Mrs Montgomery, the rest of the staff appeared friendly enough, but when would she encounter them if she were not allowed to dine with them? She realised she might well have a lonely time ahead of her. Maybe that was another reason previous governesses had not lasted all that long.

'It's still a shock for her,' Mama said, guessing her eldest daughter had some misgiving and taking the chance to intervene.

Clara hesitated for a moment and glanced across at Jake who caught her eye.

'The man whose coach almost ran us off the road on the way to Stonebridge the other evening, he's my new employer,' Clara explained.

Jake dropped his spoon with a clatter into his bowl of stew. 'I … I'm sorry, Mrs Masters,' he said, nodding his head to Mama. 'That man was very angry that night, Clara. I didn't like the look of him.'

'I know,' Clara shook her head. 'I saw him get angry another time too with an elderly fellow at the common, but I think he has another side to him.'

'He's grieving as his wife has passed away, I expect,' Mama said sagely.

'That's no excuse to be rude and nasty though!' Emily said, tossing her vibrant auburn curls as she shook her head vigorously. 'We're not like that, not one of us, and we've all lost Papa!'

It was true and Clara couldn't deny that fact. Not one of her family would be nasty because they were simply heartbroken that Papa was no longer here.

Chapter Six

Christmas Eve dawned and Clara rose from her bed early to make it to the marketplace. She'd need to get in all the food supplies for Christmas Day so she took Meg and Edmund along with her to help carry the baskets home. Meanwhile, Mama was already baking her well-loved mince pies, a couple of batches of bread and was boiling a large ham on the stove for their Christmas Eve tea.

Emily was giving the house a good spruce up as Mama had said it was possible visitors might call in unexpectedly as it would be their final Christmas living there. Mama had wanted to invite her sister over with Lottie and the baby, but Clara thought it too risky. So far they hadn't seen Jethro McWhirter anywhere and he certainly hadn't knocked on their door as of yet, but Clara had a feeling he was out there somewhere waiting to pounce. Mrs Pettigrew would surely not have kept that nugget of gossip about Mrs McWhirter and the baby being sighted at The Vicarage to herself.

Clara sighed deeply as they approached the marketplace. It was already crowded at this hour of the morning. Everyone must have had the same idea about getting there early before things sold out as they surely would that day. She nudged her way through the crowds, jostling the elbows of well-dressed men in top hats and smart frock coats and women in fur edged capes with fancy hats, as well as those of a lower social class who, even of a lower standing, were dressed as best as they could for a special day. It was so crowded that she warned the children to stay close to her side.

'If we lose one another,' she said, 'we'll meet up at the front of the church.'

Meg and Edmund nodded obediently, but she knew they'd rather be back home playing in front of the fire rather than going shopping with her, so it was with some surprise she noticed something to keep them amused. A Punch and Judy show was taking place to the left of the church. Quite a crowd had gathered to watch Mr Punch and Judy playfighting with a string of sausages before a crocodile came along and snapped the sausages up in front of them – how the children laughed! A man in a straw boater hat who carried a wicker basket over the crook of his arm mingled amongst the crowd selling pokes of peppermint and Bentley's Chocolate Drops to the children and their parents. *Whoever had that idea has a captive audience*, Clara thought, smiling to herself. It was one way to keep the children amused as the adults shopped at various colourful stalls.

'You both go and watch the show,' Clara addressed her younger siblings. 'Here's a couple of pennies for sweets, but you'll have to help me carry the baskets afterwards as they'll be too heavy for me to cart home on my own.'

Both nodded enthusiastically and ran off in the direction of the puppet show, leaving their baskets with Clara. She began to browse the various stalls and found what she was looking for: a hunk of cheese; a large pat of butter; some pickle preserve to go with the ham her mother was cooking; a selection of apples, oranges and nuts; a link of pork sausages; a quarter of tea, and a selection of penny buns. She was about to turn around to go over to where her brother and sister were watching the puppet show when something caught her eye. It was a gypsy caravan, and not any old one either. It was Patrin's! Feeling excited she decided to leave the heavy baskets there with Meg and Edmund, along with a warning not to let them out of their sight as there were often light fingers at work around the marketplace. They both nodded happily as they wanted to see the end of the show, so she set off for the caravan. Patrin's sister was sat on the steps. For a moment, she thought the young girl wouldn't recognise her but then she greeted her warmly.

'You spoke to our Patrin, didn't you? A few days back?' his sister asked.

'I did indeed. Is he around?'

She shook her dark lustrous curls and as she did so her gold hooped earrings caught the morning sun. 'Ah no, well what I mean is, he is around here but he's busy.'

'Oh?'

'He's in that boxing tent over there?' She pointed to a large tent with a yellow and red striped canopy covering its roof. 'He's sparring to get a bit of practise in at the moment. In a couple of days he said he's going to take on any man in this village. He's not been beaten yet.'

Clara frowned. 'Sorry, but what does he, or they, get out of it?'

'If they knock him down on the canvas then they get a purse of five sovereigns, but if he knocks them down he gets the glory of still being the undefeated champion!' she said proudly.

'Oh, I see. I'd better leave you to it then.'

'Aw,' the girl frowned momentarily. 'Why don't you come into the caravan for a while? I've got a pot of tea brewing here,' she pointed to the small fire she had going to the right of the caravan with a large blackened kettle suspended over it. 'I can tell your fortune if you like?'

Clara gasped. She'd never had her fortune told before. Emily would have jumped at the chance, but she wasn't sure. Then again, what harm could it possibly do?

'I will then, if you're offering. Thank you.' She expected the girl would ask to have her palm crossed with silver like she'd once read about in a book, but she had plenty of money on her. 'I better just explain to Meg and Edmund. They're my younger siblings. They're watching the Punch and Judy Show.'

'Aye, well you go on then and I'll get the tea ready for us by the time you return.'

Meg and Edmund were only too happy to stay a while longer. She told them if the show finished to come and get her from the caravan and they both nodded in agreement. When she returned to the caravan the doors were wide open but there was no sign of the girl. Tentatively, Clara climbed the wooden steps and called out, 'Hello?'

There was no answer. *Maybe she's been called away?* Clara thought, but then the girl arrived breathless behind her and said, 'Please go and sit inside. I just ran over to the boxing tent to tell Patrin you are here.'

Clara felt her cheeks infuse with heat. Why would the girl do that?

'Oh, you didn't need to do that, but thank you,' Clara replied. It would be helpful, though, as she needed to speak to him about Lottie and the baby getting away to a more permanent place of safety.

'There's no need to thank me, miss,' she said. 'He said after the last time you spoke that if I was ever to see you again to let him know.'

That's curious. Why should Patrin want to seek me out?

'Well thank you for going to the trouble,' she said.

'Ah, 'tis no trouble at all now. He'll be over in a few minutes after we've had time to have a cup of Rosie Lee and a chat.'

Clara nodded, knowing full well that the chat meant the girl telling her fortune.

'Sorry, I don't know your name?' she asked.

The girl shook back her dark curls, her vivid violet eyes shining brightly, and said, ''Tis Florica, but everyone calls me Flori for short.'

Clara smiled. 'Florica is a beautiful name. I've never heard of it before.'

'Only me Ma and our Pa used to call me by the full name, sometimes Patrin too if he's annoyed with me,' she giggled.

Clara couldn't imagine anyone being annoyed with the beautiful creature she saw before her. She guessed the girl was about thirteen or fourteen.

They seated themselves on the two low wooden chairs that were inside the caravan, a small table in front of them. It was then Clara noticed the crystal ball. She'd only ever seen one in a book before. Clara noted how clean everything looked; Flori obviously took pride in keeping the caravan spruced up. Beside the crystal ball were two steaming cups of tea.

'Drink your tea as we chat,' she said, 'and I'll read your tea leaves first.'

They chatted in general about the upcoming festivities, but all the while Clara was aware of the fact that Patrin would be here soon. She was grateful for the cup of tea to soothe her jangling nerves and moisten her dry lips.

'Now then,' said Flori with a smile as she took Clara's teacup from her hand. She flipped it upside down on its saucer and rotated the cup three times, before turning it right side up. 'I'm going to read your tea leaves.'

Clara's breath hitched in her throat. Did she really want to know what was in front of her? After all, if someone had forecast her future this time last year she might have been warned of her father's impending death which would have frightened her and ruined her final months with him. Some things were best not knowing.

Flori held the teacup in her hand and peered inside. 'I see changes afoot,' she said solemnly. 'Big changes.'

That much was evident to Clara. After all, she was taking on a new position as a governess to work for a family she didn't know, which would involve moving into their stately home.

'What sort of changes?'

'With regards to relationships, I see a new man coming into your life. This man is out to do you good, but then, wait, there is a young woman…'

Clara was inwardly shaking her head. Surely this was some sort of contrived thing? Flori and Patrin were trying to trick her, maybe?

'There is a man you fear but he is not out to harm you. However, the young woman will. This is a warning for you. I'm sorry your tea leaves don't hold any better news for you, but I don't feel I can tell a lie.'

Clara felt a shiver course her spine as she wished she hadn't encountered the girl, but then Flori said, 'But don't fear, this is only a warning for you. It doesn't necessarily mean anything bad will happen. Just keep your wits about you and it won't.'

Clara let out a little breath of relief. 'Thank goodness for that. Do you see anything else in the leaves?'

'No, the warning is so strong that I can't see anything else. That happens sometimes. I'll try the crystal ball instead.' She placed both of her hands on the ball and closed her eyes for a moment, almost as though she were in a trance, and then she peered inside the ball. 'I see a swirling mist,' she said.

'A mist?'

'Yes, and there's someone walking through it. A man.'

'Is he one of the men you spoke about earlier?'

'No, this man is much older. He's a good man, everyone likes him. He's smiling now and tipping his hat to me. Wherever he is, he's happy, but I get the feeling this man looks over you.'

Clara's heartbeat quickened. 'I think I might know who he is,' she said excitedly.

'He's dressed in black. He might be an undertaker?'

'No, not the man I know.'

'Wait a minute, I see a white collar. He's some sort of man of the cloth.'

'That's him!' Clara felt like grabbing the crystal ball from the girl and peering inside. 'Please can I see him?'

Flori shook her head. 'I'm so sorry,' she explained. 'Only I can see him as I interpret these things, it's a gift that not everyone is blessed with. Please try not to interrupt as I might lose him all together.'

'I'm sorry.' Clara's eyes were beginning to mist with tears as she waited on tenterhooks to hear what the girl had to reveal next.

'He's still here and he's trying to give you something. It looks like a red rose.'

'Yes! Yes!' Clara said. 'He grew them in our garden. He was fond of his roses.'

'You have no need to fear as he will always be around you, especially when the roses bloom every year,' Flori said softly.

A tear trickled down Clara's cheek. She took a clean handkerchief from her reticule to mop it up.

'Your father is leaving now, and I see a woman. She's in danger. It's not you. She has a baby in her arms.'

'Lottie! How is she in danger?'

'I see her lying at the foot of the stairs covered in bruising.'

'But that's already happened, that's why she was trying to get away from her husband.'

Flori looked at her with trepidation in her eyes. 'This is definitely the future. She's in more danger from her husband, she needs to go far away … but this is only a reflection of what might happen. Another warning.'

This was one warning too many for Clara who now she wished she hadn't come at all.

'I think I'd better leave,' she said, reaching for her coins to pay the girl.

Flori held up her vertical palm. 'No money, please. I do this as a favour to you. These warnings I've given you are unusual, I know, but at least you should have some comfort in connecting with your father once again.'

Clara nodded. That was something at least.

'Please don't rush off, I have one more thing to tell you,' Flori said.

'Go on.' Clara decided if it was another warning or bad news she just as well hear it.

'Your family fortunes are about to change. I see your family living in a smaller house, but they will be happy there. But for some reason, you aren't with them.'

'No, I will be living elsewhere soon.'

'There is also a marriage on the cards.'

'But I've no intention of marrying anytime soon and there is no one…'

'It might not be yourself. That's all I know is I can see a wedding, a spring one as there are apple and cherry blossoms.'

'That's curious. I can't see our Emily marrying soon. But wait a moment, Mrs Pettigrew's daughter is due to wed, maybe it's her?'

'I don't think so, this is either you or someone close to you,' Flori confirmed.

Lillibeth Pettigrew is definitely not someone I would have considered close. How strange, Clara thought.

There was a sharp knock on the caravan door which startled both women. The warnings had been enough, but now this?

The door opened and Patrin stood there shirtless, his skin slick with perspiration. His torso was very muscular, she noticed. Flori rose from her seat and went outside the caravan to have words with her brother.

'You might have put your shirt back on,' Flori scolded him, her words carrying through the open door to Clara. 'Particularly when there's a young lady here!'

She heard him chuckle. 'Well, I don't think the lady will be minding too much, particularly when she's seen me in this state afore now.'

Clara's cheeks seared with embarrassment as realisation crept in. There was the time she'd spied on the gypsies in the woods and he'd stripped off to the half to wash himself.

'Please put this on,' Flori said, returning to the caravan and opening a cupboard. She rolled her eyes in a good-natured fashion at Clara and handed her brother his flannel dressing gown.

He put it on without murmur or complaint. Clara smiled to herself. *She might well be a young girl, but she knows what she wants and how to get it.*

Flori turned in Clara's direction.

'I'll leave you both now as my brother would like to speak to you. Would you prefer to speak to him inside the caravan or outside of it?'

Clara chewed her bottom lip and thought for a moment. It wouldn't be deemed proper for her to be left alone with Patrin unchaperoned in this caravan, and someone might see her leaving him afterwards, so she opted to speak outside. Whatever he had to say to her couldn't be that secret as, after all, she barely knew him, although she felt in some way that she had known him for years. She followed Flori down the caravan's wooden steps and watched her leave to go off in the direction of the market stalls, then she glanced up at Patrin's beaming face. He did look pleased to see her, but then she noticed a slight swelling on his cheekbone.

'Hello. What happened there?' Instinctively, she reached out to touch it and he winced. It was most unusual for her to be so intimate with someone she didn't really know, and that scared her somewhat.

'I had a good sparring partner,' he chuckled. ''Twas one of the other gypsies, Thomas. I'm going to have to watch him or he'll steal my title as the best bare-knuckle fighter in these parts.'

She nodded. 'Is that what you'll be doing in the tent afterwards?'

'Yes. But keep it quiet as we should be using Queensbury rules.'

'What are those?'

'The Marquess of Queensbury Rules were brought in so that boxing gloves have to be worn, and the count to ten rule has be to used when someone's knocked out.'

'For safety reasons then?'

'Yes.'

She shook her head and tutted at him. 'Then why do you carry on with the bare-knuckle fighting?'

He shrugged his shoulders. 'Seems to be what attracts people most. They like the idea of a little illicit gambling and witnessing something they shouldn't. It draws in the crowds and it's in my heritage. The men in my family have all been bare-knuckle fighters. My great grandfather was a champion in these parts,' he said proudly. 'He was known as Fearless Finbar. People came from miles around to watch him and he was never, ever defeated.'

'You sound proud of him,' Clara smiled to see the pride in his eyes as he spoke.

'I am. He's no longer on the earth plane with us. He died a few years back, but he'll always be remembered. He even took on men who were years younger than him and beat them!'

Clara frowned as the winter sun was getting stronger behind him and dazzling her eyes. She shielded them with her hand before asking, 'Is that what you'd like? To be remembered?'

'For sure I would. This is in my blood. I intend boxing like this until the day I die!'

A cold shiver ran down Clara's spine as she studied his face.

'What was it you wanted to see me about? I don't have much time as I expect that puppet show where my brother and sister are waiting will finish soon.'

'I was going to ask you if you know of any work going for myself and Flori? We would like to remain here throughout the winter instead of moving on with the others. It's a long story but there's been a bit of a fall out in the family and we both can't bear my cousins arguing between themselves and causing strife no more.'

'Oh.' She hadn't been expecting that answer, and it scuppered her plans now to ask about him taking Lottie and the baby with them in their caravan. 'I can't say I know of anywhere as I've been looking for work myself. Our family fortunes have changed since the death of my father.'

'I am most sorry to hear that,' Patrin said gently. He looked into her eyes and she saw genuine sympathy there for her. 'Where will you be working?'

'At a manor house as a governess to three children.'

'That's nice. And yer'll have to live in there?'

She smiled and nodded. 'Maybe you could ask at one of the big houses if they're looking for anyone. What can you do?' she asked.

'Just about anything to be honest with you. I'm good at gardening, as a handy person, I can even sharpen knives and cook too!' He laughed. 'And I'm definitely good with horses.'

Her gaze was diverted to the strong looking white horse which was tethered to a wooden post.

'Do you have any references though?' she asked.

He shook his dark curls. 'No, as we move from place to place, I don't have any.'

'Anyone who can vouch for you and your conduct?'

He looked thoughtful for a moment as Clara glanced at the Punch and Judy stall to see if she could spot Meg and Edmund, but there was no sign of them. She sharpened her gaze, looking over the remaining children and realising that they were nowhere to be seen.

'Oh no!' she said as fear clutched her insides.

Patrin's eyes widened. He placed both of his hands on her shoulders.

'What's the matter?' he said, gazing into her eyes as she felt in a stupor for a moment.

'My brother and sister, they've gone! I told them to wait there for me, but I can't see them anymore.'

'Come on, I'll help you find them,' he said with great confidence. She followed him over to where the puppet show was packing up for a break. The man was now collecting coins in his straw hat for the performance.

'Punch 'n' Judy will be back here in one hour!' he shouted at the crowd.

'Bart, have you seen a boy and girl?' Patrin asked the man.

Bart chuckled. 'Seen loads of them this morning.'

'Please sir, my brother and sister were sitting here earlier throughout the show, they had a couple of baskets with them. My brother has red hair and my sister has fair hair.' She paused as she remembered something. 'My brother had a toy wooden soldier with him.'

The man smiled. 'I remember them now, they disappeared all of a sudden. I thought I heard someone calling them.'

Clara's legs became boneless as she felt giddy with fear. Who could have called them? She scanned the market crowd but it had grown since the last time she'd stopped by at the stall. Then she felt a reassuring squeeze of her hand from Patrin.

'We'll find them,' he said, nodding at the puppeteer. 'Bart, keep an eye out and if they return then keep them here.'

The man nodded back at him, his face solemn now as if he feared where they'd got to, too.

As they pushed their way through the bustling crowd, Patrin kept hold of her hand. Over the chatter of the market goers Clara could hear the shrieks and giggles of a young girl. She was sure it was Meg's laughter carrying on the breeze, and then she heard Edmund laughing too. There was no doubt about it.

'I can hear them,' she said with tears in her eyes. 'Over there!' she pointed. Patrin elbowed his way through the throng until they arrived at a wooden signpost which read "Test your strength here". Josiah Whitman was standing there shirtless, a contraption around his neck with a seat on either side upon which sat Meg on the left and Edmund on the right. He was lifting them into the air and both children appeared to be loving it, but Clara felt her hackles rise with anger.

'What do you think you're doing?' she yelled, glaring at the man. 'Please put my brother and sister down right now!'

Quite a circle of people had gathered and Josiah looked at her with great amusement in his eyes.

'How did you get hold of them anyhow, they were at the puppet show?' she continued.

Edmund looked at her and said, 'Please don't get angry, our Clara. Josiah just spotted us and asked us to come here for a moment to help him win a prize.'

Clara found it hard to remain angry with the children, especially as Meg's bottom lip was now quivering and she appeared as if about to burst into tears. The stallholder helped Josiah remove the yoke from around his neck and the children were placed firmly on the ground once more. The crowd cheered, impressed with his show of strength. It was then that Clara noticed Patrin glaring at Josiah.

'You did wrong there, fellow me lad!' Patrin shouted at him. 'You worried Clara about them. She'd told them to stay put at the puppet show until she collected them.'

'We didn't mind!' Edmund said brightly, but Patrin ignored him to carry on sizing up to Josiah. Josiah glared back.

'Ain't you the fighter who's going to be in the tent on Boxing Day?' he asked.

'I am.'

'Then I think we'll meet up and settle our differences then,' Josiah snarled.

'That's fine by me,' Patrin replied, continuing his menacing stare.

Josiah grinned. 'Me too. Maybe we could do so in that boxing booth of yours tomorrow?'

'Just come along and I'll take you on any time. I'll take great delight in knocking a big lump like you flat out on the floor!' Patrin declared, beginning to invade his space as he brought his face close to Josiah's. Clara was about to step in between the two men to break the impasse when Meg distracted them all by crying very loudly, the tension clearly rousing her emotions. The crowd began to walk away and the stallholder paid Josiah several coins into his filthy looking palm. Maybe the man hadn't changed as much as she'd thought. Money came first as always for him. Finally, Josiah broke the standoff and began to walk away, jingling the coins in his pocket as if to torment Patrin, who let out a long, composing breath.

'If you just give me a chance to change into a clean shirt and my jacket, I'll help you home with your shopping,' he said, glancing at the abandoned wicker baskets on the ground. Clara nodded in appreciation. Christmas Eve was turning out to be entirely different to previous ones. Now there were two men at one another's throats, and she feared she and her family were the cause of it.

Chapter Seven

By the time they'd arrived home, Meg had ceased sniffling and
Edmund had stopped complaining about having to leave the attractions
at the marketplace. Now he was enthralled as Patrin had hoisted him
high upon his shoulders and was singing "The Grand Old Duke of
York" to him while Edmund bounced his toy soldier up and down in a
rhythmic motion to the song.

'Good heavens! What's going on here?' Mama was at the door to
greet them all with a bemused expression on her face.

'I've brought both the shopping and the children home safely,'
Clara said.

Mama's hand went to her throat as if frightened. 'You said that as if
something happened.'

'It did, but all is well now,' Patrin reassured. He helped Edmund
down from his shoulders and onto the path safely beside him. Mama
shot Patrin a curious look, clearly wondering who the stranger before
her was.

'This is Patrin, Mama. He helped us home with the shopping.'

Mama glanced at the laden baskets that Clara and Meg were
carrying inside and raised a questioning brow.

'Patrin was helping us until we got up the hill, honestly, Mama,'
Meg blurted out.

'Yes,' said Clara as she brushed past Mama to enter the house, 'he's
been very good but Edmund was upset as I rushed him from the
marketplace, so Patrin hoisted him on his shoulders to stop him from
crying.'

Mama nodded gratefully, knowing full well what her only son could
be like at times.

'You don't mind if Patrin joins us for a cup of coffee, do you
Mama?'

Mama smiled. Clara realised her mother could hardly refuse in front
of the man, but being the charitable person that she was she wouldn't
have refused anyhow. Soon they were all seated around the kitchen
table as Meg and Edmund went off to play in their bedrooms.

'So, that Josiah Whitman had purposely lured the children away
from the Punch and Judy show?' Mama blinked several times,
incredulous with what had occurred.

'Yes, it appears that way,' Clara said. She took a sip from her
coffee cup and set it down in its saucer again. Coffee was usually a

treat in the home; they rarely drank it throughout the year, but for some reason did so at Christmastime.

'But I thought you were going to keep an eye on them?' Mama frowned.

'I did, but they wanted to watch the show so I told them to stay there while I shopped and they promised to do so.'

'I'm sorry, Mrs Masters,' Patrin butted into the conversation. 'It was partly my fault as I told my sister if she ever saw Clara again to tell her I wished to speak to her.'

Clara smiled. 'It's not your fault, nor your sister's, it was just circumstance and opportunity for Josiah. He's a wrong one.'

Mama shrugged her shoulders. 'Your father tried to help that young man so many times,' she sighed heavily, 'and where did it get him? Josiah let him down on more than one occasion. He even caught him pilfering coins from the church collection once.'

Emily entered the kitchen and eyed Patrin curiously. 'Who's this?' she asked outright.

Mama glared at her. 'Don't be so rude, Emily. This is Patrin. He helped Clara home with the shopping.'

'Hello, Patrin,' Emily said in a forward fashion as she batted her eyelids at him. 'I feel I know you from somewhere.'

'You should do,' chuckled Clara. 'Remember we used to watch the gypsies in the woods?'

Emily's face flushed beet red. She obviously hadn't made the connection.

'What's this?' Mama looked at Clara.

'Sorry, Mama. Whenever the gypsies were camped in the woods we used to sneak off and watch them as we loved listening to their singing and watching their dancing.'

'Oh my goodness, thank heavens your father isn't alive to hear this.' Turning to Patrin, Mama said, 'I'm sorry, Patrin. No offence meant, but it's unbecoming behaviour for two young ladies to hide in the woods to watch people.'

'It's all right, Mrs Masters. No offence taken. None whatsoever.' He shot Emily a wicked glance and winked at her, causing her to blush even more. Emily said nothing further about the matter and poured herself a cup of coffee from the pot before joining the others at the table.

'So,' Mama said, 'what are we going to do about Josiah? I can't have him kidnapping my children like that.'

'Who's kidnapped Meg and Edmund? I thought they were in their bedrooms?' Emily's eyes widened.

'Oh, it's nothing,' Clara shook her head. 'I don't think it will happen again. They were watching the Punch and Judy show and he took them to the "Test your Strength" stall so he could lift both at the same time in some sort of contraption the stallholder put around his neck.'

'It was like a harness for my horse, Leander,' Patrin explained. 'He's a big shire horse. Anyhow the contraption went over the neck like a yoke and had a seat either side.'

Emily scowled. 'He's a show-off, that Josiah. Likes to think he's the toughest man in Foxbridge.'

'He ain't fought me yet!' Patrin declared. Then realising he might have alarmed Mrs Masters, he turned to her and said, 'Not to worry, missus. I meant in the boxing ring … I'm a fighter you see.'

Mama nodded but her face was a picture. If Papa was here now, Clara didn't know what he'd say or do as he had been such a peaceable man with a soft spot for Josiah.

Finally, Patrin rose from the table. 'Well, if you'll all excuse me, ladies, I'd better be getting back as my sister will wonder where I've got to. I've got more sparring in the tent this afternoon ahead of the Boxing Day attraction.'

'That's so funny!' Emily giggled. 'A boxing match on Boxing Day.'

'Aye, I suppose it is.' Patrin quirked a lopsided grin at her, then his face suddenly took on a guarded look. 'Won't be so funny though if Josiah steps into the ring with me.'

Clara noticed Mama shiver beside her and she hoped Patrin hadn't created a bad impression of himself towards her. She didn't want her mother to think of him as being a violent man as it went against all her principles.

'Thank you for the refreshment, Mrs Masters.' Patrin stood, then nodded at her mother and replaced his flat cap firmly on his head.

'You're very welcome, Patrin,' she said kindly. 'Emily, would you be so kind as to show Patrin out?' Her eyes were shining as she looked at the man. No, Mama had taken to him herself. Clara need have no fear there.

'Ladies,' he said with a theatrical bow and followed Emily from the room, leaving Clara and her mother unable to speak for a moment as he departed.

'Well, this food won't make itself. I need to finish off cooking the ham and bake another batch of mince pies,' Mama said finally. She turned to Clara, 'You managed to purchase some extra flour and a pat of butter, I hope?'

Clara nodded. 'Yes, the butter is in the pantry and the flour is in the usual cupboard. I've put everything else away, Mama.'

While their mother busied herself, Emily beckoned Clara into the parlour and closed the door behind them. A glowing fire was drawing in the grate and Clara was grateful for it too because although it had been sunny earlier, now there was a distinctive nip in the air outside. As she gazed out of the window, she noticed the earlier sunshine had now disappeared and had been replaced by a slate grey sky overhead, an ominous sign that snow was imminent. She stretched out her fingers and warmed them by the fire before sitting herself in one armchair as her sister took the one opposite, plonking herself down in it with a loud sigh.

'So, how did you meet the gypsy fella?' Emily asked.

Clara smiled. 'It was when I was in the marketplace a few days ago. He was playing a fiddle outside the church and his sister was dancing with a tambourine in her hand. I stopped for a while and he came over to speak to me as he recognised me as watching him in the woods. Of course, I had no idea he'd ever seen me before.'

Emily harrumphed. 'Well, I don't remember him even though he seemed to know me.'

'I think he's just teasing you. I went back there alone several evenings on the run to watch the troupe after that time we went there together.'

Emily shook her head. 'But why would you do something like that, Clara?'

Clara shrugged her shoulders. 'I suppose I was just fascinated with them all, with what they did. I loved watching them eating and drinking around the campfire and later they sang songs and danced. It was mesmerising.'

Emily looked at her sister as though she were dancing with the fairies herself.

'Hmmm,' she said as a slow smile appeared on her lips.

'Please don't look at me like that.' Clara shook her head.

'Like what? Like I'm someone who thinks it was more likely that you'd taken a fancy to Patrin?'

Clara could hardly tell her sister that, yes, it was exactly that. Ever since she'd watched him stripped off to the half washing himself, she'd been utterly fascinated with him and she really didn't know why. It didn't seem proper either, so she could hardly share that with her sister.

Before Clara had a chance to protest, Meg came rushing into the room. She stood looking at Clara for a moment, her bottom lip all of a quiver.

'Please can you tell Edmund. He's taken Miranda and hidden her from me!'

Miranda was Meg's favourite doll, but for some reason Edmund liked to hide it and torment his sister from time to time. Clara knew he was doing it to seek Meg's attention as he hated it if she went off to read on her own and didn't want to play with him, but being that much older than he was she sometimes liked her own space.

Clara shook her head and almost laughed. Sighing, she got out of her comfortable armchair.

'Right, we'll sort this out once and for all but if he returns Miranda to you, will you promise to play nicely with him, at least for a while?'

Megan nodded solemnly, and Clara realised she'd have a lot more of this when she became a governess at the big house.

***

That night there was a feeling of peace in the house. After they'd been to the Christmas service at the church, Mama had served up the baked ham with boiled potatoes, a chutney she'd made and the pickle Clara had purchased from the market. Then they had tucked into hot mince pies with fresh cream before lighting the special festive candles on the mantelpiece and the tiny candles on the Christmas tree.

'I love this time of the year,' Emily said as they watched Meg and Edmund hang their stockings over the mantelpiece with high expectations of what Father Christmas would leave for them during the night.

Clara smiled contentedly as she sipped her cup of hot cocoa. It was comforting them all being together, but in the pit of her stomach was the niggle they were putting off the inevitable. She glanced at her father's favourite wing-backed armchair in the corner. Somehow they found it hard to use it because it had been his, but of course there were occasions like this evening when they were all in the same room together that it had to be used. Now Mama was sitting in it, embroidering a cloth that she wanted to finish by the morning to donate to the church before they moved out. There had been no luck finding another place for the family to live as yet, but Mr Fothergill at the post office had put a card in the window for them that read:

"Respectable family wish to find a house or rooms to let at a reasonable cost. Please contact Mrs Masters at The Old Vicarage, Rodden Row, Foxbridge."

As of yet, the church had not told Mama that the family had to leave the house, but she realised it would be needed for the new vicar in the near future so she considered it best to vacate as soon as possible. There was an increasing feeling that life would never be the same again for any of them.

Chapter Eight

'Oh look at that, Edmund!'

'Whehee! Let's go play!'

Clara was woken by shrieks from Meg and Edmund early on Christmas morning but it wasn't just because Father Christmas had filled their stockings with little gifts, pink sugared mice, nuts, tangerines and shiny coins – it was also because it was snowing outside. She yawned and blinked for a few seconds before setting foot out of bed, then drew back her bedroom curtains to see the snow which had fallen during the night covering the ground in a white glistening blanket. The sky was still leaden and it appeared as if it would snow for hours to come yet. Thankfully, they lived beside the church so could make it to the Christmas service. The vicar who was covering, Reverend Barnett, was lodging with an elderly lady in Rodden Row, so they didn't have too far to walk either. But apart from those living in the Row and maybe neighbouring Laburnum Lane and Abbots Acre, Clara had no clue how anyone else would make it to church on Christmas Day.

She quickly washed and dressed and made it downstairs to the kitchen where Emily was stirring a big pan of porridge with a wooden spoon. Mama was seated at the table and somehow she'd encouraged both Meg and Edmund to seat themselves beside her.

'No, now listen both of you,' she was scolding in a playful fashion as she wagged her index finger at them. 'Eat your breakfast first, then you can get dressed in your warmest clothes and build a snowman before we go to church.'

Both children smiled at her, although Clara could tell how impatient Edmund was as he kicked his legs under the table while his top half remained calm and collected, like a swan. It seemed the only way he could contain his excitement, though Meg was happy enough as she was dressing Miranda in a new outfit at the table. Mama had stayed up during the night to make the shiny new dress of blue taffeta silk and white lace. Clara guessed they were offcuts from the ball gown Mama had recently made for Mrs Downing, the farmer's wife.

'Do you like Miranda's new dress?' Meg asked. Her pretty hazel eyes were trimmed with large dark lashes. Clara knew she was going to be a beauty when she grew up.

'I do indeed,' said Clara, then she pecked her mother on her soft downy cheek before seating herself at the table opposite her. 'Merry Christmas, Mama,' she said.

Emily looked at them. 'Are you all ready for this porridge before it becomes a gloopy mess?' she asked and then chuckled.

They all knew what Emily and her porridge were like and they didn't want to chance it any longer – the last time she'd made it she'd burned the saucepan and it had taken ages to scrub clean again.

'Yes,' said Mama. 'We're ready. Please dish it up and come and sit down yourself.' Then turning to Clara, she said, 'Can you wash up afterwards, please?'

Clara smiled and nodded. If there was one thing about Mama that she had realised a long time ago it was that she liked to see fair play. If one daughter cooked, then the other washed the dishes. She even had Meg and Edmund helping since Papa had died. Edmund collected sticks and carried small buckets of coal for her, whilst Meg was a dab hand at black leading the grate or sweeping the kitchen floor. Both youngsters' help saved the rest of them an extra chore here and there.

Later, after Clara had wiped the dishes and slotted them away in the cupboard, she laid down the soft cloth she'd been using and watched through the window as the children built their snowman. Majestically, it towered above them as they reached up to drape an old black scarf of hers around its neck. Mama had given them an old top hat that had been left behind by one of her customers who never returned for it. The snowman's eyes were made from two pieces of coal and a pointed nose from a large carrot. All the things would be reused afterwards, of course, as they couldn't afford to throw anything away these days. Papa had often loaned items in the past, like his bowler hat or his old tweed jacket, for previous snowmen, but now it didn't seem right to use those things.

When they were all changed into their best clothes and ready for church, Mama warned the children not to throw snowballs at anyone outside as it wasn't the proper thing to do. But she needn't have worried as aside from themselves, only the vicar, his landlady and a few other folk from the neighbouring houses and cottages showed up to the Christmas Day service. Even the organist, Mr Price, hadn't managed to make it, so Clara stepped in to play the piano instead. She wasn't sure of all the music so the Reverend Barnett kindly allowed her to play some Christmas carols that she knew well, which Clara was most grateful for. His Christmas message was about keeping the peace, particularly during the festive season, but Clara thought his sermons weren't as inspiring as her father's had been. She shed a few tears reminiscing on the same time last year when they were all at church together, seated proudly in the front row as the congregation sat there spellbound, hanging on to Papa's every word. The Sunday school had performed a Nativity where Meg had played the part of Mary and Edmund a shepherd boy. Mama had sat there with tears coursing down both cheeks. Back then they'd all had a future together and there were no concerns about money, putting food on the table or keeping a roof over their heads. Little had they all known then that this Christmas Day would all be so different.

There was a delicious aroma of roast goose permeating the air as they all trooped into the kitchen at The Vicarage after the service had finished.

'I can't wait to eat my Christmas dinner!' Edmund said, rubbing his tummy in anticipation.

'It'll be about a half-hour or so,' Mama replied as she removed her best bonnet and placed it on the table. The others all followed suit, disrobing and hanging up cloaks, jackets, bonnets and caps.

'Before we prepare ourselves for dinner, I think we need to carry on with Papa's tradition of sipping a glass of sherry beforehand,' Clara said, looking at their mother.

Mama nodded with tears in her eyes. It was the only time of the year that their parents had allowed the younger members of the family an alcoholic beverage, and even then it was just a half a schooner each. Papa had been wise realising that the large feast they were about to indulge in would absorb all the alcohol they consumed. That way, the young ones didn't feel too left out of the festivities.

'I'll fetch the sherry from the parlour.' Emily headed off out of the room while Clara found five small schooner glasses to pour it in to. Quite soon they were all sitting around a crackling fire in the parlour toasting everyone's good health and remembering Papa and the things that he used to say. As well as a lot of laughter, there was also a tear shed here and there for how things had turned out for them all. Papa's loss was felt that Christmas Day as keenly as the day his coffin had been laid into the ground. Maybe even more so.

***

They were just finishing off the plum pudding when there was an urgent rap on the front door.

'Now who can that be?' Mama asked crossly, annoyed at being disturbed today of all days. 'I hope it's not that Mrs Pettigrew,' she mumbled under her breath as she went off to answer it.

Voices were heard at the door and then Mama shouting, 'Oh, no, surely not!'

Clara leapt out of her chair for fear of what was wrong. 'What is it?' she asked as she approached. Mama was stood in the hallway with the door wide open, and on the other side stood Jake, his face ashen grey.

'It's Mrs McWhirter,' he said breathlessly. 'I just went to take the Christmas cake your mother made to your auntie's house for them, when Mrs McWhirter answered the door. She told me her husband had found out where she was living and had wrestled the baby from her arms. He knocked her flying to get to his son! All she was doing was weeping and wailing while I was there, calling out for Samuel she was. She was fair near going demented with grief for the child. It were pitiful to see.'

'Oh, poor Lottie,' Clara said sadly as she shook her head. 'No wonder she's going out of her mind. What a cruel thing to do, to steal a suckling child away from his mother. Her husband is nothing but a drunk. I have no idea how he can look after the child. We have to find young Samuel before it's too late.'

Mama frowned. 'Maybe it's already too late,' she said sombrely. 'Look at the weather. How on earth did you manage to get there and back in this, Jake?'

'It happened yesterday before the weather took hold. I've only just managed to make it here this morning.'

'Oh my goodness!' Clara said. 'Then maybe you are right Mama and we're already too late, but we have to try to find the baby. Considering the weather and who has him, I don't hold out much hope. What's the pathway like to the McWhirter's farm cottage, Jake?'

'Pretty impassable, I'd say. I don't think the horse would make it. It would have to be a strong horse to do that.'

An idea was beginning to form in Clara's mind. 'There's only one horse I know around these parts that might be strong enough to get there,' she said firmly.

'And whose horse might that be?' Mama blinked in astonishment.

'Patrin's. He has a strong shire horse called Leander. I bet that could get someone up to the McWhirter cottage!'

'That's all very well and might be true enough,' said Mama, 'but how do you know where to find him?'

'He's staying near the marketplace in Crownley as there's a boxing match due there tomorrow in the big tent. Or should I say, was,' she said, chewing on her bottom lip and looking at her mother.

'But that might mean of course, due to the weather, he's moved on someplace,' said Jake.

'I doubt you'll find him then,' Mama replied sadly.

Emily came scurrying into the hallway. 'Didn't he mention something about staying on Farmer Downing's land when he was here last?' She looked at them quizzically.

Clara turned to face her sister. 'Did he? I didn't hear him say that. I just assumed he had set up camp at the marketplace because the caravan was there.'

'I'm positive that's what he said. Maybe he told me when I showed him out,' Emily smiled. 'Jake, can you take us there to find him?'

'Yes, of course.' Jake nodded at them, even though he looked thoroughly exhausted himself.

Clara looked at her sister. 'You stay behind, Emily. I'll go with him. There's no point in us all freezing to death in this weather.'

Emily sighed.

'Clara's right,' Jake smiled at Emily. 'I'll be back if we find him and then I can give you your Christmas present.'

Emily's eyes widened. It was evident she'd rather stay behind in the warm now she knew she had a special gift waiting for her from Jake. If the circumstances hadn't been so dire or warranted fast action, Clara would have laughed there and then.

'I'll just change into my boots,' she told Jake.

'Take your warmest cloak and a couple of blankets as well,' Mama advised.

Clara nodded and then rushed off to collect her things. Who knew what would face them if and when they found Mr McWhirter and the baby?

'

Chapter Nine

Farmer Downing's farm was on lower land than the McWhirter's cottage, but not too far away from it. Luckily the road from Foxbridge to Crownley was still passable with care, but Jake's horse wasn't capable of taking the steep rocky pass even if the weather conditions were good.

As they pulled up outside the farm, Clara heaved a sigh of relief to see Patrin and Flori's snow-covered caravan parked near the old barn.

'I'll go and knock to see if Patrin's there,' Clara said.

Jake got out of his seat and helped her down from the cart. Her feet immediately sank into the icy fresh snow as she made her way to the van, carefully climbed the steps and knocked on the door. There was no answer, so she called out, 'Patrin! Patrin!' which brought the farmer's wife, Elsa, to the kitchen door of the farmhouse. She opened the top part of the door.

'Who's wanting him?' she shouted back as she puffed out clouds of steam.

'It's me, Mrs Downing. Mrs Master's daughter, from The Vicarage!'

Now showing recognition, the woman smiled at her and waved. 'You both better come in as he's inside with his sister. He's helping us out here for a while to pay for his keep. Couldn't be letting them both sleep in the caravan in these conditions, so I've given them a bed each here. They're just having a hot drink in front of the fire as they've been helping to rescue some livestock from the top field.'

She unbolted the door to allow them to pass inside. They both wiped their feet on the rough coconut matting that served as a doormat. The kitchen was steamy with a delicious aroma of sage and cinnamon, and Clara could see from the bubbling pots on the hob that Mrs Downing was preparing a Christmas dinner. No doubt she was cooking later in the day due to the work that had been going on. It was easy to lose livestock in these conditions, and the farm animals came before any festive feast for the Downings. They were their livelihood, after all.

The woman led them into the living room where Patrin was on the rug by the fire with his feet stretched out as if warming his toes, his hands cradling a cup of what appeared to be cocoa. His sister was seated at the table polishing the silver cutlery ahead of dinner. They both looked up as Clara and Jake entered.

'Well happy Christmas to you both!' Patrin greeted them with a smile, then he laid down his cup on the fireplace and sprang to his feet. 'What brings you to these parts? I'm guessing it's not a social visit?'

'I'm afraid it's not,' Clara said solemnly while Flori stopped what she was doing and set down the fork she'd been polishing to gaze at the pair.

'Remember I mentioned a lady whose baby I'd recently delivered?' Clara looked at Flori who nodded wordlessly, remembering the fortune she had told Clara.

She nodded wordlessly.

'And how the poor woman was treated badly by her husband?' Clara continued.

'Aye, I do.'

'Somehow or other her husband discovered where she was staying and ripped his baby son from her arms. We need to find him as he's a dangerous man. Not only with his fists but he drinks too much. I fear for the life of the child.'

Before Clara had a chance to say anymore, Patrin started to put his boots on and then he grabbed his coat.

'What can I do?' he asked looking into her eyes.

'Your horse, Leander. Do you think he'd be strong enough to take us in Jake's cart up the mountain to the McWhirter cottage? It's a very rocky path, mind.'

'I should say so,' Patrin said smiling proudly, 'he's the strongest horse we've ever had. Never known him to fail yet.'

'Good,' Clara said. Then she turned to Mrs Downing and, glancing at Flori, said, 'I am sorry to disturb your Christmas day. Where is Mr Downing?'

'He's still in the field, he won't be long. He won't expect his dinner for a couple of hours anyhow as he's worn out. He's been up since the crack of dawn, so don't worry about disturbing us, lass. The baby's far more important.'

Clara nodded as a tear coursed her cheek. The kindness of people got to her at times like this. But how could Mr McWhirter have known that the baby and his wife were staying with her aunt at Stonebridge, anyhow? That part didn't make much sense to her, but before she had a chance to think on it any further Mrs Downing was taking her by the arm and guiding her to the kitchen, where she poured her a hot toddy.

'Here, you look perished already so you'll need this before you go. It will take a minute or two for the lads to attach the horse to the cart.'

Clara did as she was told. Although the need to get to the baby was making the blood pump around her body and causing her heart to fire fast, her brain felt numbed by it all.

Before long, she and Patrin were on the cart heading up the hill as Jake remained at the cottage to keep the load light. It was thought that it was best for Clara to go as she knew about babies and Jake didn't, but it would have been a help to have had him there nevertheless in case Mr McWhirter put up a fight. He was strong as an ox that one, but so was Patrin and he was younger too. She felt protected beside him as the cart ploughed its way through the deep snow.

Clara was chilled to the bone and her teeth chattered even beneath the blankets she'd draped over them both, but Patrin kept speaking to her to keep her alert. What on earth would happen if they were to get stuck in a snowdrift here? She had heard of people being found dead on the mountain in severe weather.

As if to allay her fears, Patrin turned to her and said, 'Now don't you worry. I know this mountain well as I used to live on it with my family as a young lad. If we get stuck there are a couple of shepherd's dig outs we can use for shelter.'

In all the worry she had almost forgotten that he was used to living off the land and might well have endured these sorts of conditions previously. She looked at him and forced a smile – it was of some comfort at least.

'And don't forget, Patrin said cheerfully, 'Mrs Downing has packed some provisions for us.' It sounded as if the woman was expecting them to get stranded for a couple of days, but then again of all people she would understand the dangers of the mountains in these parts, especially where her livestock were concerned.

'What if we don't find the baby though?' she said with a resigned sigh, her brow furrowing.

'Ah, don't you be talkin' that way. We'll find the baby for sure. Where else can the man have gone to anyhow? Nobody around these parts would want to take in a man who had kidnapped his own kin, ripping him from his mother's breast. No one at all.'

Clara nodded. That was probably true, but she feared the atrocious weather conditions right now as a strong gust brought an explosion of swirling snowflakes into their faces. A blast of the north east wind she guessed, and she shrugged to stay warm beneath her cloak and blankets.

'Never mind,' said Patrin as he touched her knee. 'We might have to get cosy together in one of those shepherd's huts!' He threw back his head and laughed.

What was she getting herself into? She hardly knew the man. Maybe she should have encouraged Jake to take her place, but then she reassured herself she was here for the baby. The truth was she had felt a bond with the poor mite after she'd delivered him. She couldn't explain it really as she'd never had much of a mothering instinct before now, although she loved her siblings dearly and was fond of the children at Sunday school.

'Gee up, boy!' Patrin shouted. Leander puffed out clouds of steam as he continued to plough his way uphill.

At the top of the mountain Clara hazarded a glance at the farm and the village below, but everything was obscured in a storm of swirling snowflakes. If they did become trapped up here, how would she ever find her way back home? Her heart plummeted at the thought of it all.

'C'mon,' said Patrin, 'we're nearly up the top now, and it won't be far to go before we get to the farm cottages. I don't think we should stop yet as Leander still has plenty of go in him.'

'But how will you know where to go? We can hardly see our hands in front of our faces.'

'The horse knows the way. I used to deliver potatoes up here to the cottages when I was a young lad. I could do it with my eyes shut.'

Clara hoped he was as confident as he sounded.

As the cart bounced over a hard rut, she heard someone cry out, 'Help!' It was unmistakably a man's voice.

'We're coming! Hold on!' shouted Patrin.

As they drew near to the voice, Clara noticed a figure lying in the snow. It was Mr McWhirter. He held his outstretched hands up to them as if expecting them to pull him on to the cart. A scattering of snow covered his body and Clara thought if they hadn't arrived just at that moment, soon he'd be buried in it.

'Where's the baby?' Clara asked angrily, unconcerned for the man's condition.

'He's back at the cottage,' he groaned.

'Then what are you doing out here in these conditions leaving him to fend for himself?'

'Believe it or not, I was looking for help.' He looked up at her with sad eyes, but they did nothing to dampen the fire in her.

'You should not have taken that baby from his mother in the first place. You deserve to freeze to death out here after what you did to your poor wife, a pregnant woman and all.'

To her horror, the man put his hands to his face and began to weep. He didn't look so scary now and she began to feel a sliver of compassion for him. She turned to Patrin.

'Can we help him up on the cart and get to the cottage to rescue the baby?'

He nodded soberly and she realised he probably had the same thoughts as herself about leaving the man to suffer his soul to the elements. They clambered down from the cart and Patrin helped to lift the man on the back of it, even giving up the blankets covering them to keep him warm. It would have been on Clara's conscience forever if they left him to die but every second they spent on him was a second away from the baby. It felt a long pull over to the cottages and Clara's fingers were so blue with the cold that she had to blow on them to keep them warm.

'It won't be much longer now,' Patrin reassured. 'We can get a fire going at the cottage if there's not one going already.'

Clara found it impossible to be as positive as she feared finding a sick or dead infant when they reached the place, or maybe not finding Samuel there at all. After all, how could they be sure the man was telling them the truth?

By the time they pulled up at the cottage, Clara's feet were like two lumps of ice and if she stayed out much longer she thought she'd faint and never regain consciousness. The weather seemed far worse up here high on the mountainside. She was cheered though to discover that there was already an oil lamp lit on the windowsill which told her that Mr McWhirter had meant to return to his home and hadn't intended heading to the village to get merry with pints of ale.

Patrin tried rattling the front door but it wouldn't budge. He dashed to the back of the cart.

'The door's locked man, have you got a bloody key?'

Mr McWhirter, who was still lying down beneath the blankets, groaned.

'It's in me jacket pocket,' he mumbled, but he appeared too tired to make the effort to retrieve it and hand it over to Patrin so Patrin searched his pockets for it. Triumphantly he held the silver key aloft for Clara to see.

There was not a moment to waste, so while Patrin tried to sort out getting the man into his own home, Clara snatched the key off him, unlocked the door and went in search of the baby. There were the embers of a small fire in the grate and a bucket of fresh coal beside it, so they'd be all right for heat for a while. Maybe they could boil a kettle on it to drink tea to warm them up, she thought as she chewed on her bottom lip. *But where is Samuel?*

Then she heard the infant's cries from above her. From the shrill sound he was making, she guessed his lungs were healthy enough. She ran up the stairs and discovered him in a makeshift cot made out of the top wooden drawer from a chest beside the bed. He was well wrapped up in blankets but somehow as he'd struggled – no doubt in search of his mother's breast – the main covering blanket had ended up almost over his head and it seemed to be that which was distressing him most of all. She knelt to draw back the blankets and lifted him into her arms. Then taking the top blanket she wrapped it well around him, swaddling the infant as she soothed him. He probably needed feeding and changing but for now the most important thing of all was for him to have human contact as she guessed his father might have been away from him for some time.

'There, there,' she soothed as she rocked him in her arms. 'You're quite safe and we're going to get you back to your mother, little darling.'

But as she looked out of the window down onto the village below all she could see was a swirling cloud of snowflakes which would make leaving here tonight impossible. She heard the front door slam shut, followed by a series of thuds and groans coming from Patrin as he staggered inside unsteadily with Mr McWhirter.

She shouted from the top of the stairs, 'I've found the baby!'

'Good!' Patrin yelled back at her. 'I'm putting Mr McWhirter to lie down in front of the fire for time being for him to warm up.'

'I'll be there now!' Clara shouted back. She took baby Samuel downstairs with her, feeling his soft head beneath her chin as she cuddled him.

'It suits you,' Patrin smiled at her as she entered the living room.

'Pardon?'

'Motherhood. You look right at home cuddling the baby.'

She smiled. 'I've plenty of experience with the young ones in our house over the years.'

Before too long they had Jethro McWhirter changed into dry clothing and sitting in an armchair by the fire with an eiderdown draped over him. Patrin had thought he'd need to recline as he was so weak, but as soon as he began to warm up the life returned to his body and the earlier blue tinge to his skin became pink and healthy-looking. Clara made them all a cup of tea and Patrin banked up the fire.

'What on earth were you doing, man?' he asked him.

Jethro shook his head. 'I thought I'd head to the village for some help,' he explained. 'I soon realised that I couldn't care for the baby on me own. I thought Nellie Bradshaw might 'elp out, see, for a few shillings.'

Nellie Bradshaw was an elderly woman with hardly a tooth left in her head who was well known for delivering babies in the area. People knew she was wise and trusted her words and ideas.

'I see,' said Clara. 'But what have you been feeding your son?'

'Goats milk. There's some in the jug in the pantry,' he explained.

'Goats milk? But he needs his mother's milk.'

He nodded. 'Aye, well I realise that now, but it's all I have here so it'll have to do until we can return the baby to his mother.'

'So, you admit now you did the wrong thing in taking him?'

'Aye, I do,' he said solemnly.

The way the man spoke told Clara that he was regretful. *But is he regretful about hurting his wife?* she thought. After all, she'd seen the bruises for herself.

'What about the other thing you did?' she questioned.

Blinking in astonishment he said, 'Sorry, I don't know how you mean?'

'Hurting your wife. I saw the bruises. It was me who helped to deliver the baby when you were supping ale!' She spat the words out at him.

'What bruises?' he asked, mystified.

'She was covered in them after you knocked her down the stairs.'

To her horror, he brought his hands to his face and began to weep like a little boy. When he'd composed himself, he said quietly, 'I had no idea. I must have been out of my mind on the drink. But it's no excuse,' he sobbed pitifully once again.

'Then when this is over, you must come with us to return your son to your wife and make amends to her,' she found herself saying. 'If you are a man of your word then you need to lay off that stuff, for the sake of both your wife and child.'

He nodded.

Patrin exchanged glances with her. 'I'll help him upstairs to bed,' he whispered.

Clara took the edge of coldness off the goat's milk by placing a cupful from the jug in a pail of hot water shallow enough to cover the sides of the cup. How could she feed him though? She found a clean piece of muslin which she dipped in the cup and allowed the drops to fall into the infant's mouth. It was better than nothing until they could get him back to his mother.

Patrin returned a few minutes later.

'McWhirter's tucked up in bed and I've lit a fire in the bedroom grate.'

'Oh Patrin,' she said as she choked back tears, 'we need to get this child to his mother.'

'Aye, I know that but we daren't go tonight. It will be dark soon as there's no let-up to this snow. I'm just going to stable Leander in the barn, feed and water him and then I'll be with you and we can see if there is something to eat here.'

She smiled at him and one of her tears fell onto the baby's cheek. She brushed it away with her hand. What chance did he stand if they didn't reunite him with his mother soon?

***

Patrin had been right when he'd said they couldn't leave that night as the conditions only worsened. After changing the baby into a makeshift napkin made out of a piece of towelling she'd cut in sections, she settled him back into his wooden drawer crib. Then she set about finding something they could eat. As well as the goat's milk, there was plenty of tea, a sack of potatoes and other winter vegetables available to her, as well as glass jars of pearl barley, flour and yeast. She set about making a nourishing soup and baking some bread. They also had some yeast cake and a few slices of ham and cheese that Mrs Downing had packed for them. Clara sent some of the nourishing soup upstairs in a large cup for Mr McWhirter who sipped it slowly and promptly drifted off to sleep. Returning downstairs, she looked at Patrin.

'Little did I realise when I woke up on Christmas morning, I'd end up here,' she forced a chuckle, though she didn't much feel like doing so.

He looked at her, his green eyes searching hers. 'You're an angel, that you are. You brought that child into the world and you've ended up rescuing him. Though I have to say his father seems regretful now of his actions.'

She nodded as she ladled out a bowl of soup each. Then she looked up at him.

'That did surprise me. I don't know if Lottie would want him back though if he does wish to make amends.'

Patrin shook his head. 'That maybe so, but I've seen it happen amongst gypsy folk. Sometimes the husband wises up after his children are born.'

Clara didn't know what to think and as she placed the hot bowls of steaming soup on the table, she let out a long sigh. *Please Lord, let us all be able to get out of here tomorrow.*

***

Clara had actually managed to get some sleep during the night on the horsehair couch in the living room. Patrin had dozed in the armchair near the fire and the baby was on the other side in the makeshift wooden crib to keep him warm. He had whinged a couple of times during the night and she'd managed to get him back down to sleep again by feeding and changing him, then rocking him while singing a lullaby she remembered her mother had sung to Meg and Edmund when they'd been babies. She'd caught Patrin looking at her with avid interest once or twice when he'd stirred, but he'd not said anything and had been a perfect gentleman throughout. Goodness knew what Mrs Pettigrew would make out of this situation though. Clara, a young lady, alone with two men! She'd have said it wasn't decent, that's what she'd have said. Her mother would be worried about her too, but hopefully Jake had returned on foot to visit the house as he'd promised to see Emily. She'd have realised then where they'd gone to.

She yawned and got herself up, then stirred Patrin who was still asleep by the fire with his jacket draped over himself. It was warm enough now though. Sometimes it felt even warmer indoors after a big fall of snow. She went to the scullery to fetch the kettle to place on the fire. Thankfully, Patrin had filled it from the pump in the yard last night just in case the pipes froze overnight, but Clara was pleased to see that the snowfall had ceased. Patrin awoke as she was brewing up and smiled at her.

'I didn't like to wake you,' she whispered.

'That's all right. If we want to get out of here then we'd best do it today in case any more snow falls. Not sure what to do about the big fella upstairs though,' he said glancing at the ceiling.

'I think we could leave him here as he has enough supplies to fend for himself. Maybe we could warn his neighbour to keep an eye on him in case he relapses, and perhaps the Downings can check on him too when the snow eases off.'

'Sounds like a good idea.' Patrin quirked a brow as he took the hot cup of tea from her outstretched hand.

Clara found a sack of oatmeal, so she set about making some porridge in a pan on the kitchen hob. Then she sent Patrin upstairs with a bowl for Mr McWhirter while they ate theirs at the kitchen table.

'How was the invalid?' she asked.

'Fair to middlin'. Think he'll be all right to stay on his own and we'll do as you suggest and warn his neighbour to check on him.'

'I did tell him to see his wife, but it might be best if we return the baby to her in the first instance and tell her how regretful he is about it all, rather than take him with us. Then it'll be up to her if she wants to give him another chance.'

Patrin lifted his spoon to his mouth to eat his porridge. 'Yes, that's the best idea. We'll just finish this and I'll get Leander out of the barn. Thankfully he had plenty of hay and water overnight so he should be all right taking us back.'

'While you're doing that, I'll prepare Samuel for the journey and pop upstairs to explain our movements to Mr McWhirter.'

Patrin frowned. 'Don't be taking any nonsense from him, mind.'

She smiled. 'I won't and I don't reckon he'll start any either. I think somehow he might have learned his lesson.'

Patrin nodded. 'Some folk 'ave to learn the hard way.'

Within twenty minutes they were on their way back towards the village. Clara planned on stopping off at The Vicarage first to obtain a change of clothing for herself. While she was there she would see if there were some old clothes of the children's there to dress the baby warmly for the rest of the journey, but for time being he was swathed in two warm blankets and secure in her arms. The best present Lottie McWhirter would have this Christmas was her baby boy being returned to her loving arms.

Chapter Ten

Following the Christmas period and all that had ensued throughout, it was exciting for Clara to think of beginning work at the big house. Patrin and Jake helped her to move her belongings on the weekend before the children were due back from their holiday in Scotland. So far she hadn't encountered Lord Stapleton since her interview with him.

After all her bits and pieces had been moved into her quarters, there was just the unpacking of her clothing to sort out which she could do at her leisure. She had brought along a few practical but smart gowns, skirts, and blouses, along with one or two best garments for going to church or for special occasions. Mama had prepared her for all eventualities and had even managed to make her some new cotton nightgowns which were so pretty that it seemed a shame to wear them to bed where no one would see them.

Deciding to wave Patrin and Jake off outside as they left on the cart, she stood at the rear of the property with tears in her eyes – it would seem an imposition for her to have moved herself in via the front door of the property as that was intended for the family and their guests. She did not belong in their world, nor did she belong with the servants downstairs. She was in no man's land. Sighing deeply, she looked at Patrin and Jake seated on the cart with Jake at the reins. On this trip, the cart would be empty instead of laden with her luggage.

'Thank you both for helping me. I hope I can repay you someday,' she said.

Jake smiled. 'No need at all,' he said.

Patrin flashed her a cheeky grin which tore at her heartstrings. 'Maybe you can repay me by enquiring if there are any jobs going here?'

'I will ask, but I can't make any promises.'

He nodded and tipped his flat cap in her direction, before replacing it on his head. 'I was only joking with you, but thinking about it that might not be a bad idea.'

'No, it isn't. I promise I will ask when the time is right,' she said brightly as she forced herself to sound cheerful at their departure.

She waved both of them off until the cart was a speck on the driveway. She turned around to enter the house via the kitchen when she saw Mrs Montgomery peering at her. The woman did not look best pleased. She seemed to have a look on her face as if there was something unseemly beneath her nose.

'The children, Miss Masters,' she said, 'will be back this evening. His lordship is expecting you to teach in the schoolroom from half-past eight in the morning until three o'clock in the afternoon. You will be allowed a half-hour break at half-past twelve where you will be permitted to take your meal in your quarters.'

'Will every day of the week have the same routine?'

'Yes, apart from Sundays. The family attend church three times on a Sunday and you shall be expected to as well, apart from the last Sunday of the month when you are permitted a half-day off.'

She nodded and smiled a smile that Mrs Montgomery did not return. 'Mrs Montgomery,' Clara said tentatively, taking this as an opportunity to enquire about work for Patrin, 'would you happen to know if there are any jobs going here?'

The woman's eyes widened. 'For whom?'

'For a friend of mine who is clever with his hands. He's an excellent gardener and good at fixing things.'

The housekeeper sniffed loudly. 'There might be. Have a word with Mr Postlethwaite, he's the caretaker here.'

'And how will I find him?'

'He's probably in his room where he keeps things needed for repair, it's just offside the kitchen.'

Clara thanked the woman and went on her way. She didn't know what it was about her but Clara just couldn't warm to the housekeeper. She didn't seem like the rest of the staff who appeared warm and friendly, and she cold and hard-hearted.

She found the man just as the Mrs Montgomery had said she would. He was in his room, hammering a nail into a piece of wood. He looked quite elderly as he worked away, with his baldpate shining and his hands gnarled and rough from hard work. His shirt sleeves were rolled up to his elbows and he wore a leather apron. The lack of hair on his head was made up for by bushy sideburns and a white beard. She knocked on the door and he looked up at her and smiled.

'And who might you be, young lady?' he asked, his slate-blue rheumy eyes twinkling as if he was genuinely pleased to see her.

'I'm Clara Masters, the new governess here,' she introduced herself.

For a moment, his eyes looked a little guarded but then he smiled. 'I'm sorry for being taken aback, young lady. No one has told me that another new one was to be taken on here.'

'Oh, I am sorry about that. How many have there been then?'

'Seven at the last count. They don't last long with those Stapleton children.' He lowered his voice. 'They're wilful, you see. No one has managed to tame the young beasts as yet. I thought the last one had as she was here for a while, but she left in tears one day and no one has set eyes on her since.'

'That doesn't sound very good, does it?'

He shook his head. 'No. I'm afraid not. So how can I help you?'

'I have a friend who is a hard worker and he can turn his hand to most anything. I was wondering if you need any help at all?'

'Well, now you come to mention it Mr Drummond, he's the gardener, has been moaning about his back lately. He could do with a bit of help although just part-time, mind you. Tell your friend to come and see me tomorrow.'

She nodded and smiled. 'Thank you, Mr Postlethwaite.'

'Don't thank me, dear. I try my best but they're hard taskmasters and your friend might regret coming to work here.'

'Oh?' she asked. There was no doubt that his words were painting a less than flattering picture of the family. Then he chuckled.

'Don't take any notice of him.' Clara turned around to see Cook behind her. 'He's pulling your leg. Now don't go frightening the girl before she's even begun to work here, Arthur!' Cook scolded playfully.

'No, I was just jesting,' Mr Postlethwaite explained. 'Most are all right here, apart from snobby-nose Mrs Montgomery and those spoilt children.' He muttered something under his breath as he shook his head.

'Come and have a cup of coffee in the kitchen with me,' Cook offered.

Clara chewed on her bottom lip before replying, 'I don't know if I should as the housekeeper said I should keep to myself and stay in my quarters.'

'Stuff and nonsense! She'll have me to deal with if she says anything to you.'

Clara smiled. 'Thank you, I would appreciate that cup of coffee.'

Soon, she and Cook were chatting away like old friends at the well-scrubbed pine table in the steamy kitchen as the maids worked around them peeling potatoes, scrubbing pans and sorting things out for the evening meal. Hearing both the clatter and chatter in the background comforted Clara and reminded her of being in her kitchen back home with her family.

'Those children are back this evening,' Cook said in a surreptitious manner before raising her eyebrows. She enveloped her cup with both hands as if the mere mention of "those children" had turned her fingers to icicles that needed defrosting.

'But surely they can't be as bad as everyone is making out?' Clara couldn't believe that three children could be such a handful. After all, she had young children living at home with her.

'Oh, they can and they are! Why do you think no governess has ever stayed here?' She sucked in a breath between her teeth in a disproving fashion. 'Amelia, she's the eldest one, she's a right little madam. She's the worst of the lot. She had been the apple of her father's eye but I think she plays up more now as he's not taking much notice of her. Danielle, well she's all right I suppose,' she crossed her hands and huffed out a breath. 'Quieter than the other two, very bookish. Like chalk and cheese, the sisters are. James, he's eight and can be as bad as Amelia sometimes. They're right wicked together. But he'll be off to boarding school soon. Though if you ask me,' she looked both left and right as if for fear of being overheard before carrying on in a hushed whisper, 'I don't think a young lad ought to be sent away when he's grieving for his mother.'

Clara nodded, though did not voice an opinion one way or the other. She decided to err on the side of caution for now until she knew she could trust the woman. She didn't want to be part of any tittle-tattle going on at the house as it could cost her job, especially if Mrs Montgomery heard of it. Maybe that's why the woman had warned her to keep away from the rest of the staff. She thanked Cook – whose real name she had discovered was Mrs Cantwell – for the refreshment and was about to walk away from the table when the woman caught her hand.

'Take care, Clara,' she warned. 'Those kids are unworldly creatures.'

A shiver coursed her spine, but she smiled and nodded.

She should have felt delighted as she was about to begin a new job and earn money to help the family, but her mind seemed to cave in on itself as she returned to her quarters. It was then she realised how lonely she would be in this new position. Still, there was no use in resting on her laurels, she needed to send word to Patrin for him to come to the house tomorrow morning to have a chat about some casual work. She wondered for a moment if Billy could take a letter to him for her. She'd pay him of course. There was some lovely notepaper and thick envelopes on the escritoire in her bedroom. She quickly wrote her note, sealed the envelope and put it in her pocket to go in search of him. It wasn't long before she found him polishing the brass in the hallway.

'Hello again, Billy,' she greeted with a smile.

He returned her smile. He was a handsome lad but seemed a little clumsy at times, though she had no doubt he was a willing worker.

'I wonder if you could take this letter with some urgency for me?'

He immediately nodded. 'Yes, miss.'

'It's to be taken to the Dowling's farm about a mile away from here. You know where it is?'

'I do indeed. When the mistress was alive she used to favour the butter and cheese from there.'

'Please deliver it as soon as you have a spare moment. It's a letter for Patrin who is staying there, he's to come here early tomorrow to enquire about a job.'

Billy frowned for a moment, then Clara realised what must be going through his mind.

'You have no fear, he's not after your job! He likes gardening and fixing things. He's an outdoors sort of person.'

Billy brightened up. 'No problem, I'll take it soon.'

She handed him a silver sixpence and he nodded his slicked-back head at her.

'Thank you, miss. It'll be delivered before this evening.' He gazed at her for a long while which made her feel a little uncomfortable, so she thanked him and made her way back to her quarters. The black and white checked marble flooring and the curved walnut bannister in the hallway were quite spectacular and as she gazed up at the magnificent crystal chandelier above her head she could do nothing but gasp.

'Beautiful, ain't it?' She turned to see Mr Postlethwaite stood behind her with his hands behind his back.

'It is indeed. Breathtaking, in fact.'

He tapped the side of his nose with his index finger. 'There's plenty of brass in this household, of course. Earned their money by land owning and opening the wool mill years back.'

'I had no idea,' Clara said, taking it all in.

'Yes, the master's grandfather started it all off. Lord William Stapleton. 'Course, the present Lord Stapleton isn't so bothered with it since his wife passed over. Leaves it all to the agent and the manager. He's daft though. If you ask me, he needs to regain control of the reins.'

Clara felt her cheeks grow hot with embarrassment with such knowledge about the man being imparted to her, but then again his staff were bound to talk amongst themselves. She was aware of erring on the side of caution again and so she changed the subject.

'Word is being sent to my friend Patrin for him to call in the morning, I'm sure he won't let you down.'

Mr Postlethwaite smiled and nodded. 'As long as he's a good worker that's all I care about. Well, I best be off, there's some furniture for me to fix in the library.'

Suddenly there was a flurry of activity with some of the servants rushing to the main door of the house as if in panic. *What's going on here?* she asked herself. She followed after them to see they were all lining up outside the house.

'It's the master's children!' Maggie the kitchen-maid shrieked. 'They've arrived home. One of the servants was looking out of the top tower window and spotted their coach arriving at the gate. We've got to line up to greet them!'

Clara's stomach flipped over. Out of all the staff here, she was the one person who would be in closest contact with the trio. She wondered what she'd make of them and, more importantly perhaps, what they'd make of her. What exactly would "those children" be like?

***

There was a feeling of terror in the air as Clara stood in a line with the rest of the servants. She was stood on the far right end of the line, with Mrs Montgomery in the middle as if she would be the main one welcoming them back home. Surely the children couldn't be as bad as they had been portrayed? She noticed Maggie tremble beside her, but that might have been because of the cold rather than the arrival of the master's children. Well, she herself intended being very open-minded about them. After all, they had recently lost their mother and their father too, in the sense of him seeming distant towards them.

A footman opened the coach door as the driver clambered down and prepared to unload their luggage from the back of the coach. Meanwhile, there was a silence from the staff. Was that in reverence towards the children or apprehension about their return home? She wasn't quite sure. And where was Lord Stapleton? Shouldn't he be around to welcome them back home?

A tall blonde haired girl stepped down from the carriage. She shooed away the footman's offer of a hand of assistance, then she stood on the ground taking in the sweep of staff stood before her. Mrs Montgomery stepped forward, breaking the silence.

'Welcome back home, miss,' she bobbed a curtesy and Clara noticed the other female staff followed suit while the men bowed their heads. Clara did nothing – she was caught out by this and wasn't quite sure how she should act in front of the children. She would be their governess after all.

The girl's icy stare sent a shiver down Clara's spine. It was clear that she was appraising the staff, running her eyes across them all, and then she made eye contact with Clara for the first time.

'Good evening, Miss Amelia,' Clara said curtly.

The girl looked her up and down.

'And who might you be?' she asked in a haughty fashion.

Clara swallowed hard. She did not intend to show any fear towards this child or else she'd have the upper hand over her.

'I'm your new governess, Miss Clara Masters.'

The girl tilted her chin upwards and her china-blue eyes flashed dangerously.

'My governess? What nonsense is this? Papa swore he'd not employ another!'

'Well he has, and I am she,' Clara said firmly, before smiling at the young girl. It was then she noticed that the other two children had arrived to stand behind their sister. Hearing she was to be their new governess, a girl with dark ringlets and dark eyes stepped forward.

'I am Danielle,' she said. Her eyes showed avid interest. *So, this was the bookish, quieter one. Maybe she would welcome having a governess*, Clara thought.

'James,' said the little boy beside her. He had the cutest little elfin-shaped face and looked like a miniature version of his father.

'Hello Danielle, hello James,' Clara greeted. 'I am to be your new governess and I understand we shall be meeting tomorrow morning.'

Amelia rolled her eyes. 'This is absolutely insufferable!' she groaned. 'Another Miss Goody Two Shoes to try to control us. We don't need anyone, we have each other!'

Everyone except your father! The words were on the tip of Clara's tongue, but she kept her thoughts to herself, instead opting to say, 'At any rate, we shall be meeting at half-past eight in the schoolroom tomorrow morning. So please be punctual.'

Amelia turned her back on her and stormed off in the direction of the house. The other two children looked at Clara for a moment as if unsure what to do next. Danielle smiled back at her and made her way after Amelia, but James had tears in his eyes. He simply nodded and followed his sisters up the steps and inside the house.

So those were the Stapleton children, and the eldest was going to prove a handful by the look of it.

''Cor look at you, miss,' Maggie said when the children had departed, 'putting those kids in their place. Not many ever do that, not even Mrs Montgomery. Good on you!'

Clara didn't know what all the fuss was about as she was used to telling her brother and sisters what to do. If she was going to be their governess then she had to command their respect.

The staff began to mutter between themselves and Clara heard Cook say, 'Here we go again, it's back to the madhouse now!'

'Now the peace will be shattered, I was enjoying not having that creepy trio around the place, haunting the corridors!' Billy replied.

Clara thought their comments sounded quite disrespectful. She caught the housekeeper's gaze for a moment and the woman nodded and smiled at her as if in approval. Then she clapped her hands together.

'Chop! Chop! Back inside all of you. There's the evening meal to prepare and the children need settling in and their clothes unpacked.'

Cook shook her head as if she didn't like being reminded that she needed to get on with things as "those children" were now back home once again.

***

A maid Clara had not seen before delivered a tray of steaming oxtail soup and a bread roll to her quarters that evening. The girl dipped her knee in a mark of respect as she laid down the tray on the table. Though Clara wasn't used to such things, she didn't complain. She wasn't exactly a servant here so perhaps she needed to become accustomed to how things were from now on.

'Thank you. What's your name?' she asked softly as she studied the girl who appeared about the same age as Amelia but was waif-like in comparison. Her blonde hair was thick and unruly, having been tied back with a blue bow from which it appeared it might spring loose at any moment. A smattering of freckles covered her small button nose.

'I'm Dilly, miss.' She dipped her knee again. 'I'm to be your private maid, miss, should you ever need anything.'

'Why thank you, Dilly.' Clara glanced at the steaming bowl of soup on the table and her mouth watered. It was apparent that Cook made some delicious concoctions in that kitchen of hers.

The girl made to leave the room and turned for a moment. 'When you've finished your soup, miss, Cook says I'm to bring the roast beef and vegetables next, followed by a rice pudding.'

Clara smiled and nodded. She wondered if she'd ever be able to eat it all but didn't like to complain on her first day at the house.

'I forgot to ask what you'd like to drink with your food, miss?' Dilly continued.

'I have a pitcher of water here, but I'd appreciate a coffee when the dessert arrives, thank you.'

The girl dipped her knee again and Clara noticed how ill-fitting her dress looked on her small frame. Didn't they have a dressmaker at the house? Mama had insisted on packing a sewing kit for her just in case any of her clothing needed interim repair until such time as she could return home. Maybe she could do the girl a favour and take in some of the seams by inserting a couple of darts here and there to ensure a better fit – that way the dress would look more fitted on her form. That girl needed a good feed as well. She decided there and then that any food she had leftover would go straight to her. No one need to know. After all, she was all alone on this floor, and that in itself was a strange feeling indeed.

Chapter Eleven

Patrin arrived at the back door of the house very early the following morning and Clara immediately took him to see Mr Postlethwaite in the storeroom. It was arranged that he begin work there that very day helping Mr Drummond with the weeding and trimming of the elaborate bushes and edges, as well as undertake other general work about the place as required. He was to be taken on for one week as a casual worker, but Mr Postlethwaite said that if Mr Drummond was happy then that would be extended to one month and reviewed again after that. Patrin was over the moon about it all and ran to find Clara in the kitchen where she was speaking with Cook.

'So, you're to be one of us now then, lad?' Cook said. Her face appeared to be ruddier than usual that morning and Clara wondered if she'd been at the gin bottle. Maggie had alluded that she took a tipple in the afternoons when there was a lull at the house between lunch and dinner.

'Aye,' Patrin beamed. 'Thanks to this one here.' He went to grab hold of Clara as if to wrap his arm around her waist but then stepped back, clearly having second thoughts of doing so in front of the staff.

'Good luck to you, lad. There'll be a cuppa and something for you to eat when you're due a break,' Cook said kindly. 'Mr Drummond will inform you when as he comes in here himself.'

'I'm so pleased for you,' Clara said, and she meant it. She liked Patrin a lot and knew that he and his sister could do with the extra money. Now the weather had turned colder, they could hardly go around travelling to fairs and markets to make their money. Flori seemed settled at the farm and would be a great help to the Downings. Patrin would carry on helping there too for their food and board, but by working as a gardener here it would mean a few extra bob in his pocket to spend.

When he'd gone, Clara turned to Cook. 'I'm expected in the schoolroom in a few minutes,' she said with more than a little apprehension in her voice.

'Just keep a firm hold on those kids. The other governesses buckled,' Cook said sagely.

Clara nodded and her stomach flipped over. She'd barely eaten any breakfast, instead using her time wisely to prepare the schoolroom with notebooks, fountain pens, pencils and wooden rulers. She'd also discovered a large globe in one of the cupboards along with some maps. This week it was her intention to expand their minds and speak about a country she'd always longed to visit someday: France. She was interested in Paris, in particular. She thought after discussing the geography of the place, they could talk about the sort of food eaten there. Mama and Papa had gone to Paris on honeymoon and she'd been enthralled to hear them speak about everything from the cuisine in the street cafés to their visit to the Cathedral of Notre Dame and their walks along the River Seine, where they had stopped to observe the street artists at work. To her, Paris seemed such a romantic place. She could speak a little conversational French as she'd been taught it at school but had little chance to use the language. Maybe she would tie it all in with a language lesson for the children too.

She glanced at the wall clock: it was now twenty-five minutes past eight o'clock and as yet there was no sign of the children. She'd give them a few more minutes but if they didn't show up then she was going to have to go and find them herself. She was not going to allow Miss Amelia to have the upper hand. Clara reckoned if she started out firm but fair then those children would know where they stood with her. It was important for them to have rules and boundaries to adhere to. She pottered around arranging and rearranging their notebooks and pens, then she selected a couple of dictionaries from the bookcase. Those would help them if they became stuck on the spellings of any new words or needed to comprehend what they meant. Maybe she'd even give them a spelling test to see how much they already knew.

Huffing out a breath, she glanced at the wall clock again. They were now five minutes late and her hackles were rising. This really was too much to bear. *You'd at least think they'd afford me some respect on my first morning as governess!*

She flounced out on to the landing and glanced up and down the corridor in the hope they were on their way, but there was no sign of them. Then, a fair distance down the corridor, she watched as Mrs Montgomery emerged from a room and locked the door behind herself afterwards. The woman stood for a moment and then rattled the door handle as if checking it were locked before turning her head to face up the corridor. She appeared flustered upon seeing Clara watching her and she quickly replaced the large metal key in the pocket of her dress. *I wonder why that key doesn't hang on the chatelaine around her waist?* Clara thought as she watched the housekeeper approach her. *What is she doing on this floor anyhow?* After all, Clara had been informed she would be the only person to inhabit it apart from when the children took their lessons. Clara walked towards the woman to meet her halfway.

'I … er … didn't see you there, Miss Masters,' she said nervously, her face flushed from the neck up.

Clara smiled, not wishing to make anything out of what she had just witnessed.

'Good morning, Mrs Montgomery. Have you seen the children this morning?'

She cocked her head. 'They were at the breakfast table about half an hour ago. Aren't they in the schoolroom then waiting for lessons from you?'

'No, and I specifically told them when I met them yesterday what time they are to attend. Where is Lord Stapleton, maybe they're with him?'

'He's in London on business today. His coach left early this morning to make headway before all the heavy traffic commenced.'

'I see.' *At least he isn't around to tick me off for not having a firm grip on his offspring*, she thought. 'Any idea where I could look for them?'

Mrs Montgomery frowned and looked at the ceiling, as if in thought.

'There's a treehouse near the lake that they love, but have you tried their bedrooms first?'

'No, I haven't. Thank you. I'll check their rooms in the first instance and if they're not there I shall check the treehouse.'

Mrs Montgomery nodded curtly and Clara chewed on her bottom lip. They were obviously avoiding her, but the question was, why?

***

It was a full hour later before the children were discovered neither in their rooms nor in the treehouse but in the maze area of the grounds, and it was Patrin who found them and brought them to her at the foot of the steps to the house.

'I found these scallywags running amok in the maze this morning!' he declared with a mischievous glint in his eyes.

Amelia had a stern look on her face while Danielle looked as if she had been pulled through a hedge and covered in muck. James, on the other hand, looked quite pristine except that his bottom lip was trembling as if he'd realised he was in trouble a long time back.

'Thank you so much.' She looked at Patrin and nodded for she did not feel much like smiling. 'But how did you discover them?'

'It wasn't hard, believe me. I was clearing up some branches that had fallen from the tree in the high winds last night when I heard lots of screaming and shouting. This lot were just running wild. I could not believe that they were doing such a thing when they should have been having lessons with you this morning.'

'Quite right too,' she said and then stared at the three of them.

Amelia glared at Patrin through squinted eyes as if to say, 'I'll have your job for this,' but Clara realised no wrong had been done towards the children by her or Patrin. The situation they were in was of their own design.

'Return to the house this very minute and I want you washed and changed and sitting at your desks in ten minutes time or your father will be informed of this morning's misdemeanour!' she said in a raised voice as she pointed back up at the house. James began to cry and Danielle looked distressed.

'Now see what you've done!' Amelia shouted at her, but nevertheless she accompanied her brother and sister inside.

'Well done, Miss Masters,' Patrin said, cocking her a cheeky grin. 'Round one to you!'

The rest of the morning the children were quiet … far too quiet for Clara's liking. They did everything she instructed them to do but didn't ask any questions, just answered them. They were speaking when they were spoken to and nothing else. Clara couldn't help but feel that Amelia was planning something, but she said nothing about the situation and dismissed them for luncheon at half-past twelve.

The three of them were highly intelligent, but how could she work here if they didn't properly engage with her during lessons? She had an idea as to how she could pique Danielle's interest, and maybe James's too, but sadly not Amelia's. She had not a clue how to deal with the girl. She was fast physically becoming a woman in every sense of the word, but inwardly still bore some childish traits.

It did not get any better following luncheon either. Amelia bore a sulky expression on her face as if punishing her.

'I shall be seeing each one of you individually in my quarters for a little chat to find out more about you. When I take one of you out of the room, the other two must carry on with the work I've set for you and I shall expect it completed on my return,' Clara said finally.

The three children stared blankly at her but replied, 'Yes, miss.'

Divide and conquer, Clara thought to herself.

Firstly, she took Danielle to her room to prevent Amelia from planning anything behind her back with the girl. She figured that was best. Quite cleverly, she left a book she enjoyed lying around on the table between the two armchairs. That book was *Heidi* by Johanna Spyri. It was a book she'd read herself a few years back when it was first published, and she'd brought it with her from home. Although it no longer had the dust cover on it – that had been worn out from constant thumbing through as it was a favourite with all the family – remaining on the green cover was an etching of a young shepherdess holding a crook, with a heard of goats beside her. It was enough to catch Danielle's attention as she seated herself and Clara could see the girl's eyes constantly drawn to it.

She's positively salivating at the mouth! Clara thought gleefully. Finally, after asking her a few questions about herself and receiving one-word answers in return, she said, 'I see you are interested in my book?'

Danielle was on the point of shaking her head, when instead she replied, 'Yes, Miss. I wondered which one it is?'

'It's *Heidi* by Johanna Spyri. Have you heard of it? It's about a five-year-old Swiss child who goes to live with her grandfather on the mountain.'

Danielle's eyes enlarged. 'Yes, miss.'

'Would you like to borrow it?'

'Oh, could I, please?' Danielle was beaming now.

'Yes, as long as you take good care of it. The book has been in my family for some time and is a firm favourite of ours.'

'I will. Thank you.'

Clara handed the book over to her. 'So, you're an avid reader then, Danielle. What is your favourite book so far?'

The girl looked up at the ceiling as if deep in thought before replying. 'I think I'd have to say *Oliver Twist*, miss. I love anything by Dickens. Every Christmas when Mama was alive we used to put on a play over the season. The staff used to come and watch it too. But now we are no longer able to. Papa doesn't want any merriment in the house but putting on the play would be like Mama was a part of our Christmas.'

Without warning the girl began to weep so Clara draped her arm around her and hugged her close, knowing all too well what losing a parent felt like. She wiped away her own tears with the back of her hand.

'You'd better return to your desk now and carry on with the exercise I set you, but before you do that please send James to see me,' Clara said softly.

Danielle smiled and nodded. Her eyes were still glazed with tears but she returned to the schoolroom with the book tucked safely under her arm.

James was easy to talk to. He wanted to discuss trains and ships and boats and all the countries he'd like to explore when he grew up.

'So, you'd like to go on plenty of adventures then, James?' Clara asked him.

'Yes, it would be whizzo to go to somewhere far away like Africa or India. I could see all those wild animals, but I wouldn't want to shoot any.'

'You like animals then?'

'Yes, I do.' Then quite suddenly his face clouded over. 'But Papa won't allow us to have any pets. Only Mr Granger the gamekeeper has any animals. He's got two hunting dogs … and I forgot, Mr Snelgrove at the lodge has a parrot that someone gave him. But apart from those, there are no other animals except horses in the stable and some livestock here, no pets at all.' James now sounded so sad that she felt like hugging him, but she restrained herself from doing so in case he shouldn't like it.

Those poor children. The dogs weren't exactly pets either as they were working dogs.

'What sort of animal would you have liked as a pet, James?'

His eyes lit up. 'A puppy or a kitten, I suppose. It would be whizzo if you could ask Papa if I could have one. He might listen to you, Miss Masters.'

Clara sighed inwardly. Now what had she started? She was almost sorry she'd mentioned any pets, yet what harm could it do to ask his lordship if his son might have one? He could only say no.

'I'll make no promises, James,' Clara said firmly, 'but the next time I speak with your father I shall mention the matter to him. He might not agree though.'

'Thank you, miss!' James beamed broadly and now she hoped she hadn't excited him too much in case his father refused him a new pet. Having a pet would be a good thing for James right now as the boy was missing his mother, as all three children were. Clara decided she might just as well go the whole hog and mention the play situation too at the same time. Why shouldn't the children be allowed to perform plays as they had when their mother was alive? What did she have to lose by asking? *Your position here!* A little voice reminded her.

Finally, Amelia arrived to see her, but the girl was sullen and Clara could find no common ground with her whatsoever. She could sense from the very beginning by the way the girl's arms were folded tightly across her chest that she was going to find it hard work. Still, she figured it was probably best not to push such things so after a time of getting nowhere she dismissed the girl and sent her back to the schoolroom.

When the day was over and Clara collected the children's workbooks, she was astonished to see how neat Amelia's handwriting was and how her answers were all correct. She was a talented girl and Clara now wondered if she had any other aptitudes too. She decided she'd give the girl a chance to prove herself, and if she could only find that common ground as she had with the other two it would make life a lot easier. Maybe she could ask the staff some questions, but then again if Mrs Montgomery heard her prying she might get the wrong impression.

It had been an eventful first day as governess at Stapleton Manor. As she was getting ready for bed that night, she took her hot chocolate offered to her on a tray by young Dilly and offered her one of the biscuits that sat alongside the cup. The girl's face flushed but she took the biscuit anyhow and slipped it into her pinafore pocket.

'Dilly?'

'Yes, miss?'

'The room on the end of the landing, what's in there?'

The girl blinked several times. 'I don't rightly know, miss. It's always kept locked. To be truthful I've often wondered meself. Anything else I can get for you, miss?'

'No thank you, Dilly. That's all for now. Goodnight.'

Dilly dipped her knee. 'Goodnight, miss.'

Clara guessed Dilly couldn't wait to munch on that biscuit well away from the prying eyes of the other staff. It was odd though that she didn't know what was kept in that room. Maybe only Mrs Montgomery knew for sure and she guessed the woman wasn't about to tell. There was a secret in that room, that was for sure, and Clara intended finding out what it was.

***

The following morning, Clara spoke to Cook on the quiet in the corridor by the kitchen.

'Do you know anything about a room on my landing? It's on the end?' she asked.

Cook shook her head vigorously. 'I tend to keep to my domain down here,' she said, before sniffing loudly as if somehow offended at being asked such a thing. 'Why do you ask, anyhow?'

'It's just that I caught Mrs Montgomery coming out of there yesterday. She seemed to be acting in a very furtive manner and looked a bit taken aback that I'd caught her. She didn't use one of the keys on the chain around her waist either, it was a different, separate one which she slipped into her pocket afterwards.'

'Well, I never,' said Cook and she tutted. 'That is most odd. But if you ask me, that woman is a furtive sort anyhow. Never lets the rest of the staff in on her plans. Maybe she keeps some sort of storage stuff in there. Stuff she don't want the rest of us to lay our mitts upon – supplies and such. I can't blame her I suppose as over the years we've had one or two with light fingers working at this house. 'Course they don't last long if they're up to that sort of thing. So maybe she's keeping some household goods under lock and key until required.'

Clara nodded. 'Maybe you're right. That might make sense.'

Cook pursed her lips in a prudish fashion. 'Any more trouble afterwards yesterday with those kids?'

Clara smiled. 'None whatsoever, though Amelia is very difficult to converse with. Do you find that?'

'Yes, very much so. She was a bit like that before her mother's death but she's gorn right wayward now since the woman died.'

Now was Clara's chance to find out more about the mother the children missed so keenly.

'What was the children's mother like?' she asked gently.

'Lady Arabella? She was a fine sort. A proper lady in every sense of the word and I don't mean due to her title either. All the staff liked her and her children adored her as did his lordship of course – well seemingly on the surface but who knows what went on behind closed doors in their upstairs quarters. But one thing I'm telling you … he ain't been the same since she passed away. All the fun and joy has been sucked out of this place. Before her death, the walls echoed with laughter here. She always made a big thing about Christmas celebrations and tried to include us staff too. There were plays and pantomimes, sing songs with her at the piano, such fun we had playing parlour games and the like.'

'Really?' Clara blinked. She could not imagine the staff joining in with festivities. Then she lowered her voice a notch. 'How did she die then? I've heard it was sudden?'

'Yes, you heard right. She fell from a horse when she was out riding. Bad luck it were as she struck her head on a rock. Devastated, the master was. I can still remember him now carrying her lifeless body back to the house. Of course, a doctor was summoned but it was too late by then. Now the poor horse is stabled but no one is allowed to ride him, though the stable boys allow him to run in the field for exercise every day. I think the horse misses her though, and the children.'

'Have any of the children ridden him since?'

'No. And to be honest with you,' she drew Clara by the arm into an alcove, 'it's Miss Amelia what misses riding that horse. Her mother taught her to ride and promised the horse to her, but she won't look at him now.'

'Is that so?' said Clara smiling inwardly. So it was the horse that might make some common ground between herself and the girl. 'Thank you, Mrs Cantwell. You've been most helpful.'

Cook raised a puzzled brow. ''Ere what have I done? I only told you a few things and don't go repeating what I said mind in front of old Big Ears!' She wagged a playful finger.

'Big Ears?' Clara asked.

'Mrs Montgomery,' Cook sniggered, which caused Clara to giggle.

She forced herself to wipe the smile off her face. She'd never be able to look at the woman in the same way again. Big Ears indeed!

***

The school day with the children went well. They were interested to hear more about Paris and France in general. Clara told them all about the new Eiffel Tower there and showed them a picture of it that she had been given by a local artist who had been there. She couldn't imagine anything so tall.

'I think I'd love to go to France,' said Danielle dreamily. 'I'd love to sit outside one of those street cafes and eat croissants with a big cup of hot chocolate.'

'Me too!' piped up James.

Amelia said nothing, though she did attempt to copy the picture of the tower and a very good likeness it was too.

'You're very talented, Amelia,' Clara said leaning over her desk. 'Have you always liked to draw?'

She nodded.

'Go and fetch your sketch pad!' Danielle shouted.

Amelia looked at her crossly but said nothing in reply.

'You often sketch then, do you?' Clara wanted to now.

'Yes, miss.' Danielle answered for her sister. 'She's good at drawing horses.'

Clara took a chair and seated herself beside Amelia. 'Is that right, Amelia? You like drawing horses?'

She looked up at Clara, her eyes moistened with tears. 'I did, but not any longer!' Then she slammed her exercise book shut and stomped out of the room.

Danielle made to get out of her chair, but Clara held up her vertical palm towards the girl to indicate she was to stay put.

'But miss...' Danielle started.

'It's best she is left to cry it out,' Clara said firmly. 'Have you seen her cry at all since your mother died?'

Danielle shook her head. 'James cries a lot in bed at night, don't you, James?'

James nodded his head. 'I always pray for God to send Mama back home to us,' he said, then he sniffed and she hoped he wasn't about to cry too. Thankfully he smiled and asked, 'Do you think if I keep doing that, he'll send her back home? I'm trying to be a good boy, miss.'

A feeling of great compassion swept over Clara as her heart went out to all three children, particularly Amelia who seemed to be having the hardest time dealing with things. She was at an age where she needed her mother. What would her father know about her developing into a young lady? He was cold and distant, anyhow. Come to think of it, she hadn't even seen the man since the children had returned from Scotland, though she had been aware from the other staff that he had been around but out on business much of the time. What kind of man was he when the children were hurting inside so much?

A half-hour later and Amelia had not returned to the schoolroom so Clara went in search of the girl. She wasn't in her bedroom, but Clara found her sitting outside on a wooden bench near the lake. It was perishing cold and Clara was glad she'd brought the girl's cloak, along with a thick woollen blanket from her bed.

Amelia wasn't aware of Clara's presence as she stared into the distance at the lake and the mountains beyond.

'Is this where you always come when you need to be alone?' Clara asked softly.

The girl stayed motionless, almost as if she was a stone statue.

'Yes, Mama and I would sit here. It was our thinking bench,' Amelia replied without turning to look behind at Clara.

'May I join you then and we can think together?'

'If you must,' the girl sighed.

'Thank you, Amelia. I've brought your cloak and a blanket from your bed.'

As Clara approached, the girl looked up and smiled. She looked so different when she smiled and it gladdened Clara's heart. Maybe this was a breakthrough at last? She draped the thick navy cloak over the girl's shoulders and laid the blanket across her lap, then she seated herself beside her. As she gazed across the lake, she noticed that parts of it had frozen over and the bare branches of the surrounding trees were silver coated with frost.

They sat in silence for a while, but it was not uncomfortable at all. Then she squeezed Amelia's hand and said, 'I think we'd better return to the house now and I'll order four cups of hot chocolate to be sent to the schoolroom.'

The girl looked at her and asked, 'Can we have some currant buns too, Miss?'

'I think we can manage that,' Clara said with a smile.

And so Clara felt as though she had finally made a breakthrough with all three of the Stapleton children.

Chapter Twelve

Sunday 31st January, 1886

Clara had been governess at Stapleton Manor for the best part of a month, but she still hadn't encountered Lord Stapleton since her initial interview. She was aware of his presence as he departed early most mornings for various meetings and returned late at night where she often heard him enter the drawing-room. She guessed he was having a quiet tipple following an arduous day, but for the most part he did not seem to be taking an interest in her presence as governess at the house, nor indeed the presence of his own offspring, and the latter did not sit right with Clara at all.

It was to be her first half-day allowed back home. Mama and the children had found a small cottage to rent in the village of Crownley and in her last letter Mama had described the abode as "small, homely, basic and clean". Clara hadn't known what to make of that. The Vicarage had been an exceptional home to them. Large and airy with a fair-sized secluded garden, any new house would now appear small beside it, she supposed. It broke her heart that she hadn't been there to help when the family had moved out. Jake had taken his cart to help move their furniture and their belongings, and it had taken him a few trips to do so. There hadn't been that much to move as most of the furniture was owned by the Church, but Mama did have a few precious pieces that she'd kept since her marriage to Papa. Those included a beechwood chest of drawers and matching dressing table that had been kept in their bedroom, a couple of good feather mattresses and a beautiful quilt her own mother, who had also been a dressmaker, had skilfully sewn for the newlyweds at the time.

Patrin transported Clara to the cottage that Sunday afternoon with a cart he'd borrowed, with permission, from the Stapleton Manor estate. It was a brisk, sunny day but nowhere near as cold as the day they'd both gone in search of the McWhirter baby up that rugged mountainside. She often wondered how Samuel and his mother were doing. The appreciation in Lottie's eyes the day they'd handed him back over to her was immense. The swell of love was clear for all to see as she'd lifted the child into her arms and taken him to her breast for a much-needed feed. Witnessing the scene before her, Clara's heart had swelled inside. She'd felt a bond with both from the moment of the baby's birth and hoped they'd keep in touch over the years. She wondered for a moment about Mr McWhirter, who had seemed genuinely sorry in the end for causing so much pain and anguish to both his wife and child.

She took a sideways glance at Patrin. He did look particularly handsome today. He was wearing what appeared to be his best-striped shirt rolled up at the sleeves, over which he wore a pair of bracers to keep his trousers firmly in place. The trousers in question were a smart navy pair she was sure she had never seen on him before. She also noticed he had a matching jacket folded in the back of the cart. It was most unusual to see him well dressed as usually he was so casual around the place, but she supposed he had to be really. The life of a gypsy was not an easy one.

'How's your Flori doing?' she asked.

Patrin glanced at her and smiled as his eyes glinted with mischief.

'Now why would you be asking that?'

'I'm interested that's all.'

'Well when I lasted visited the farm, Mrs Downing said she was very pleased to have such a willing helper working for her.'

'That's good then.'

'Yes, it is, but if you ask me she likes having our Flori around as she's a seer.'

'A seer?' Clara asked, unsure what he meant.

'Aye, as in she tells fortunes. Mrs Downing likes that kind of stuff.'

Clara nodded and thought back to the day when Flori had read her fortune. What had she told her at the time? Something about there being a man she feared who she should not be concerned about, but that there was a woman who wished to harm her. That hadn't been very comforting, but Flori had also foreseen danger for Lottie and the baby. On the whole Clara had found her predictions very unsettling, the only nice part had been when she'd conjured up a vision of her father offering a red rose in her crystal ball. That had been a comfort for her at the time. She hoped that some of her predictions for Mrs Downing were better than they had been for her. She didn't think she'd ask for any more readings though as Mama had warned her fortune telling was the Devil's own work and went against the teaching of the Bible.

So, with some trepidation, she asked, 'What has she forecast for Mrs Downing then?'

As the cart clattered along, Patrin paused for a moment before answering.

'That the old bird has a bun in the oven!' He threw back his head and laughed uproariously.

'You mean that Mrs Downing is having a baby?' Clara asked, shocked by the thought.

'Precisely! Can you imagine it at her age?'

Clara couldn't. The Downings had been childless for many a year.

'No, I can't imagine it at all! Mrs Downing must be forty years old if she's a day.'

'And the rest! I think Flori said she's forty-four.'

'Even if she is pregnant, it might be dangerous at her time of life.'

'There is that and all, but Flori is insistent it will be a safe birth and the baby will be the apple of the Downings' eyes.'

Clara folded her arms against her chest. The Downings having a baby indeed, she'd never heard of anything so ridiculous. Any more thoughts of fortune-telling left her mind and she thought of her own home and how they were all coping.

Mama and the children were waiting on the doorstep of the cottage for her when she arrived. It was a charming place with a thatched roof and a colourful front garden, much better than she'd imagined.

'Oh, Mama!' she said as she walked up the path. 'This is a lovely place.'

'Wait until you see inside,' Mama said, smiling as she put her arm around her daughter and kissed her softly on the cheek.

Edmund grabbed hold of Clara's hand to drag her inside while Meg was trying to show off a new outfit on her doll that Mama had made from offcuts of material.

'Where's Emily?' Clara blinked.

'She's inside laying the table for our special tea,' Mama said proudly.

'Yes,' blurted Edmund. 'Mama and Emily have both been baking especially for you, Clara.'

Clara lifted him into her arms and cuddled him. She had missed them all so. She set him back down and they followed Mama inside.

Clara was shocked that there was no passageway. Instead they were straight into what appeared to be the living room. The table had pride of place in the centre of the room laid with a pristine white lace tablecloth, upon which was an array of plates of neat little sandwiches and slices of sponge cake. A large china teapot and the best matching china cups and saucers were nicely arranged beside the food. Clara's eyes were drawn to the merry looking fire in the grate. Papa's chair was one side of the fireside and Mama's rocking chair the other, and on the walls were all the favourite family paintings and portraits. It wasn't quite home from home, but Mama had made the best of it by the look of it. There were even new plum coloured drapes on the window with lace inset curtains to keep out prying eyes.

'My, my,' said Clara, 'you have got it looking nice and cosy here.'

Mama beamed. 'Yes, Emily and I have done our best but this is the only room downstairs I'm afraid. There's no parlour or anything like that, apart from the kitchen but that's even smaller than this room so we won't be able to use it to dine in as we did at The Vicarage.'

Clara smiled and nodded. 'How many bedrooms are there?'

'Just the two, I'm afraid. Emily and I share one now and the children the other. Should you ever need to stay the night you'd have to sleep on the settee downstairs.'

Clara glanced at the small settee on the far side of the room. 'That's perfectly all right for me,' she said.

Emily entered the room carrying a bowl of pickles which she placed down on the table. Then she hugged her sister.

'I heard what Ma just said but I would give up my place in bed with Ma for you to have it if you ever decide to stay,' she said, kissing her sister on the cheek. She sounded like she meant it too. Whatever had happened to spoilt Emily who only thought of herself? She appeared to have matured in thought and deed these days and Clara could only put that down to Jake's influence.

They spent a happy afternoon together, the family firing so many questions at her that her head was spinning like a top, but she didn't mind one jot.

'What are the children like?' Meg wanted to know.

Clara set down her teacup on its saucer. She drew a breath and let it out again.

'Well at first I thought they were going to be a nightmare!' she laughed. 'Apparently, they've been through seven governesses before I arrived, but then I realised they are just grieving as their mother passed away suddenly, just like Papa.'

Meg nodded as she held Miranda close to her chest as if she wasn't quite sure of what was going on.

'But then,' carried on Clara, 'I tried to find things in common with them. For instance, James loves trains and boats and those sorts of things…'

Edmund's eyes widened. 'Does he? I bet I'd like James!'

Clara nodded. 'I'm sure you would.'

'What about the girls?' Megan asked. 'Did you find out what they like?'

'Yes, I did. Danielle loves to read so I loaned her my copy of *Heidi*. Amelia, I have discovered, loves horses.'

Satisfied with the answers given, Mama allowed the children to leave the table so there were only three of them left sitting around it.

'More tea?' Emily asked. They both nodded, so she went off to boil the kettle.

Mama reached out and touched her daughter's hand across the table.

'You would tell me if you didn't like it there though, wouldn't you, Clara?'

She nodded and smiled. 'Of course I would, Mama.' The truth was she wouldn't as she would not wish to concern her mother, but things weren't so bad so far. 'I'm settling in nicely there.'

'What about the lord himself, what's he like?' Emily said, returning to the table and plonking herself beside Clara.

'That's the odd thing. I rarely get to see him as he's out so much.'

'Those poor children,' Mama said, shaking her head.

'I'm going to have to speak to him about them. They need more stimulation. He's forbidden any singing or dancing in the house. They told me when their mother was alive that she allowed them to put on plays and pantomimes at Christmas. I think the poor souls would have had a better time remaining with their aunt and uncle in Scotland than at the big house with a father who is absent or preoccupied most of the time.'

When it was time to leave – after Clara had taken a tour of the cottage and seen the back garden which could have fit into a corner of the one at The Vicarage – she was sent back with a wicker basket of cakes her mother had persuaded her to take with her. She decided she'd share them with young Dilly later. There was a sharp, short rap on the door and she opened it to find Patrin waiting for her on the doorstep, ready to take her back to the house before it got too dark.

Clara's eyes misted over as she said farewell to Mama and the children, but she was relieved to see how settled they all were in their new abode.

'You're quiet?' Patrin said as they sat on top of the cart ready to depart. He draped a woollen blanket her mother had insisted they take with them over their legs.

She nodded at him and brushed away a tear as she waved to everyone, then when they were out of earshot she said, 'It was so lovely to see them all, Patrin. Part of me doesn't want to return to the house.'

'I can well understand that,' he said patting her leg. A pat like that from another man would have seemed improper, but she trusted Patrin – he was like a brother to her. 'Hey, by the way,' he said, changing the subject, 'you'll never guess what?'

'Pardon?' she said, frowning.

'Mrs Downing is having that baby!'

'Never to goodness!' she said. She half felt it was a joke but the look on Patrin's face told her he was telling the truth. It made her wonder if his sister's predictions for her future might come true after all. 'But how will she manage at her age?'

Patrin shook his head. 'I suppose I might have to finish working at the big house and work full time for the Downings,' he said with a little sigh.

'I'd miss you of course, but would that be so bad?'

'It's not that.' His mouth was set in a grim line and she realised there was more to it.

'Then what is it?' she urged.

'We planned on moving on in the spring. It's a gypsy way of life to trade at markets and meet up with other travellers at horse fairs…' His voice trailed off to almost nothing. For Patrin, it would be as if he were denying his heritage to remain in the area. For the first time, she felt a sense of sadness that come spring he might be out of her life.

'I don't suppose the Downings would have any trouble employing someone else around the farm though, if you decide to leave,' she said brightly to keep his spirits up.

'Aye, maybe so, but they trust the both of us, me and Flori. I think Mrs Downing if she'd had children by now, well they'd have been about our ages, I suppose.'

Clara had no answer to that and they sat in companionable silence for the rest of the journey.

***

When they returned to Stapleton Manor, Patrin bid her good evening and went to stable the horse before going to catch a late supper with Cook and the other staff in the kitchen. Clara had to return to her quarters for hers, but nevertheless she didn't mind too much as she had some lovely cakes to share with Dilly.

She was about to take the servants' staircase to the upper floors as she didn't know whether she could use the main stairs or not in her position, when she noticed the back of Lord Stapleton entering the drawing-room. Now might be her chance. She turned around and approached the door and then knocked tentatively.

'Enter!' boomed his voice from within.

Timidly, she opened the door and went inside. Closing it behind her, she turned to face him.

'Excuse me, your lordship,' she said as she approached. She felt as though she should curtesy, but she just wasn't sure so she stood there trying not to tremble.

He nodded when he saw her. She watched as he turned away to pour what looked like either brandy or whisky from a crystal decanter into a glass tumbler which he placed on the small round table beside the leather winged chair near the fireside. Then he turned back to face her.

'Good evening, Miss Masters,' he said, looking as if he was pleased to see her. He smiled broadly and his dark eyes twinkled.

Now she felt bad that she hadn't bid him a good evening first.

'Good evening, sir. I was just wondering if I might speak with you about the children?'

For a moment, she wondered if he might get angry with her, but then he said something she was not expecting.

'Would you like to join me for a drink?'

She shook her head. 'No, thank you, sir. I was on my way to my quarters for my evening meal and wondered … as you seem to be out rather a lot if I might speak with you right now?'

He nodded, the smile had disappeared from his lips and she wondered if she had arrived at a bad time for him. But he seated himself and offered her to take the matching chair opposite him, which she did.

'What is it that has brought you to me instead of to your quarters then?' he asked.

'It's the welfare of your children, your lordship.'

'Are they being difficult for you and you wish to resign?'

'Oh, no, sir. It's not that at all. Quite the opposite. I'd like them to take part in some activities that I know they would benefit from, but you have forbidden them from this house.'

'Such as?'

'Singing and dancing. Danielle said her mother used to help them put on plays and pantomimes?'

Now his eyes took on a guarded look as if she had said the wrong thing. 'Yes.'

'I beg your pardon sir, you're saying that they can now partake of those activities?'

'No. I meant, yes I have forbidden them from singing and dancing out of respect for their mother.'

'B-but sir, it would benefit them so much I feel.'

'Miss Masters, I am not in the slightest bit interested in how you feel. If you think you and the children are getting along well and they are completing their work, that's all that matters as that is what I pay you for.'

Her eyes began to mist with tears and a lump started to form in her throat.

'Then I have no more to say,' she said, standing up as she feared she might break down in front of him. 'Thank you for listening, sir.'

She dismissed herself but as her hand rested on the doorknob he gave her a glimmer of hope by saying, 'Oh, Miss Masters?' She turned around in expectation. 'Please shut the door firmly behind you on the way out.'

Her heart sank, but she nodded and did as she was told. Once outside in the corridor, she began to sob, wiping her tears away with a handkerchief she kept in her skirt pocket. Thankfully all the servants were in the kitchen eating their evening meal. She'd be mortified if they saw her. Then she ran along the corridor to the staircase and climbed the stairs to the confines of her quarters where, after she'd seen Dilly, she'd not see another soul until morning time. The girl was delighted with the cakes and thanked her profusely, then she brought her a bowl of beef stew with a bread roll and a cup of cocoa.

That night, Clara lay awake for a long time mulling things over in her mind. At least Mama and the children were all settled, but the thought of Patrin leaving the area upset her greatly and she didn't know why. And if his lordship would not allow his children to express themselves and feel joyful, why should she bother staying here at all? Maybe she'd just as well move on herself.

***

The following morning Clara was awoken with a terrible racket outside. She noticed that several carriages had pulled up on the driveway and some of the servants were helping to meet and greet a few people, but there was a lot of yelling back and forth as if they'd been taken unawares. Who on earth were the visitors? By the look of the amount of luggage the footmen were now unloading, it appeared they might be staying for some time as there were several trunks and leather cases. Two handsome young men, along with an older, more rotund one, dressed in long black astrakhan coats and top hats were standing around chatting as if appraising the estate. Then finally, a young lady stepped down from a carriage. Clara gasped – even from a distance she could see how beautiful the young woman was. She wore a cornflower blue damask gown with a white fur mantel over her shoulders and matching fur hat. She glanced up towards the window where Clara was peering from, which caused her to take a step back. Had the woman seen her watching? She hoped not. She tried to concentrate her efforts on washing and dressing for the day ahead, realising she'd find out from the other servants soon enough who those people were. If his lordship had been polite the previous evening then he would have informed her of this, but instead he'd been brusque and offhand with her. She realised she was gradually forming a strong dislike of the man.

In the kitchen, Cook was in a stew.

'Them bloomin' people just arrivin' like that. His lordship ain't said nothing about this to me. I bet that Mrs Montgomery knew about it and didn't tell me!'

'Knew about what?' the housekeeper said curtly as she entered the kitchen.

Cook's face reddened.

'About those people comin' here today. No one told me and I ain't got enough provisions in either.'

'Mrs Cantwell,' the housekeeper said sharply, 'I was not informed of this until five minutes ago, so please don't blame me. Now we have to make the best of it. I've just been told by his lordship there are four people in the party, so that shouldn't be too much to attend to. They're staying for two nights only. So, write a list of what you need and send a couple of people out to the village to pick up supplies. I suggest Billy and Maggie. They can take one of the coaches to carry back everything you require.' She glanced at Dilly and another kitchen-maid called Flossie. 'You two, go and light the fires in the bedrooms on the second floor and ensure the bed linen is turned down. It might be a nice touch too if you can put vases of flowers in the bedrooms and a bowl of mixed fruit too. Mr Drummond will have some flowers in the greenhouse. Chop, chop! Set to it!'

Cook gazed at her opened-mouthed. The housekeeper's eyes fell upon Clara.

'And I've no idea what you're doing in here, Miss Masters. This has absolutely nothing to do with you!'

Clara gritted her teeth. Why shouldn't she know what was going on at the house? It might affect her charges after all. But she said nothing, instead she headed towards the schoolroom to prepare it for that morning's lessons. Whoever those people were, they were about to be treated like kings and queens by the sound of it.

Chapter Thirteen

The children were subdued as they filed into the schoolroom that morning, causing Clara to wonder what could be wrong. She decided to leave them be for now and to wait until break time to ask what was concerning them. Finally, Danielle snapped her history book shut and looked straight at Clara.

'Miss, do you know who those people are who have arrived to stay with us?'

Clara felt foolish that she had no answer to give the girl, so instead she asked, 'So, you've no idea who they are either?'

James had his head down and his face had become red.

'What's the matter, James?' Clara asked.

He looked up. 'I don't like it when new people come to stay here. They keep Papa all to themselves.'

He did have a point, she supposed. How callous of Lord Howard Stapleton to entertain and put strangers above his children when they were still flooded with grief for their mother. Surely he should see to their welfare first?

'I'll tell you what I'll do,' she said softly, and for the first time that morning Amelia looked her in the eye. 'I'll try to arrange a time for you to speak with your father to find out what's going on, shall I?'

All three nodded and smiled and Clara let out a breath of relief. The trouble was now she had promised them something she was going to have to go ahead with arranging it, else the children wouldn't trust her word in future, especially as she'd failed at her previous task of asking on their behalf.

At lunchtime Clara found Mrs Montgomery hovering on the landing as if she had just emerged from the secret room again. She cleared her throat before speaking to the woman.

'Mrs Montgomery?'

The woman peered at her over her round spectacles. 'Yes?'

'The children seem quite unsettled this morning as they haven't seen much of their father of late and I think having the visitors at the house is causing that.'

The woman's eyes widened and Clara could feel her whole demeanour change before she said in a raised voice, 'And what do you expect me to do about that?'

'You misunderstand me. I meant to say, do you think it would be appropriate to arrange a time when the children might speak with their father?'

Mrs Montgomery raised her chin as if somehow affronted by Clara's suggestion. Then she lowered her voice to barely a whisper as she drew closer to Clara.

'One does not make suggestions of any kind to his lordship, do you understand me?' Clara nodded reluctantly. 'If he wants to see his offspring then he will ask either you or myself to bring them to him.'

Clara stepped back from the woman who had invaded her personal space. A shiver ran down her spine. What kind of a home was this where a child wasn't permitted to speak to their own father?

Mrs Montgomery let out a sound like a harrumph and then said, 'His lordship has a lot arranged at the moment. He's given me an itinerary and it involves dining with his guests and various members of the community, along with the arrangement of a shooting party and a ball for the final night.

A ball? At a time like this? she thought angrily. Yet the man wouldn't allow his children to sing or dance in the house. It didn't make any sense to her. Maybe she should put in her resignation right now, but then she'd be letting the children down and they were beginning to put their trust in her. No, she was going to have to speak again with his lordship. This time she hoped he'd listen.

***

Instead of Dilly turning up to serve her lunch in her quarters, it was Cook herself who brought a tray with a plate of minced beef and mashed potato along with some homemade ginger beer. She looked stressed and a little flummoxed. For a moment, Clara wondered if the woman had been at the gin bottle, but then she puffed, 'Do you mind if I take the weight orf me feet for a moment, Clara?'

'Not at all. What's the matter? Why are you serving up lunch today and not Dilly?'

Cook plonked herself down in Clara's armchair while Clara sat at the table to eat her meal. 'Do you mind if a eat while you speak to me?' she asked.

'Naw, go right ahead. It's like this. With regards to those unexpected visitors, I'm just not prepared. No one warned me.' She warmed her hands by the fireside and it was almost as though her train of thought had trailed off for a moment.

'Yes, I heard you mention that earlier.'

'Sorry, I forgot you were there when old Big Ears was present. I bet she loves all this.'

Clara ate a forkful of the mince and potato; it had gone cold but she wasn't about to add to Cook's stress by asking her to warm it up for her.

Clara laid down her knife and fork at the side of her plate and paused thoughtfully for a moment. 'I'm not so sure about that. She seemed a little stressed earlier and practically shouted at me.'

'Did she now?' Cook said through half-closed eyes, then she folded her hands across her lap. 'Well between you and me,' she tapped the side of her nose with her index finger, 'I reckon the master has designs on that young lady what's staying 'ere.'

Clara's eyes widened with interest. 'Surely not?'

'She was a regular visitor here a long while back, a cousin of his wife's. The children wouldn't remember her as there was some sort of falling out between Lady Arabella and Miss Susannah a long time ago. She flounced out of here one day and we never seen hide nor hair of her again … until today!'

Clara wrinkled her nose. 'But that doesn't mean there's something going on between her and his lordship, surely?'

Cook puffed out her cheeks. 'There was gossip here back in the day that they were discovered together *in flagrante*, as it were.'

Clara almost choked on the lump of potato she was in the middle of swallowing, noting that whoever had mashed those potatoes hadn't made a good job of it. She lifted the glass of ginger beer beside her plate and took a long sip, but that made her cough vigorously. Cook quickly rose from her chair and poured her a glass of water instead. Clara reached for it gratefully.

'All right now?' Cook asked with a look of concern on her face.

'Yes, thank you.'

'Aye, well maybe I shouldn't have told you that when you were eating.'

'It's quite all right. I bet that caused quite a stir at the time?' Clara said with a hoarse voice before taking several sips of water to soothe her throat.

Cook sat herself back down. 'Aye, it did.'

For someone who should have been busying herself with all she had to do, it was evident the woman wanted to stop for a natter.

'Aren't you needed in the kitchen?' Clara asked.

'No, they can manage without me. I'm waiting for a couple of the staff to return from the village with extra provisions. I can't make anything for the nobs until then, so I've sent a maid to serve them coffee and cake to keep them ticking over.'

'Good thinking.' Clara pushed her plate to one side, no longer having an appetite for the poorly served meal. 'So, who actually caught his lordship with Susannah?'

'Well,' Cook said with a twinkle in her eyes, obviously enjoying the attention she was receiving from relaying this piece of juicy gossip, 'the previous housekeeper 'ere reckoned it was Lady Arabella herself what discovered them. Trouble was as she was so loose-lipped about it all, I reckon that's why she got the push from here. Then Mrs Montgomery stepped into her shoes. Before that the woman was head parlour maid so she went up in the world in one fell swoop! Her ladyship didn't want reminding about the dreadful incident, and it was at that time that Miss Susannah parted company with her, so I reckon there's something in it.'

'Hmmm,' said Clara thoughtfully, 'it sounds like you might be right.'

***

For the rest of the day, Clara couldn't banish the thought of the lord's shenanigans from her mind. She was going to have to tread carefully in her thoughts and deeds though as she didn't want to upset the children if they got to hear of any gossip. Back then, they would have been too young to understand what was going on, but now Amelia would understand. Maybe Danielle would too.

She told Patrin about it later and warned him not to mention it. They were speaking in one of the greenhouses at the far end of the garden, having first checked that no one else was around to hear them.

'The dirty dog!' Patrin said with a raised eyebrow. 'Those poor children if he plans on moving that woman into the house to replace their mother.'

'This is my fear.' She chewed on her bottom lip. 'They've been through so much already; it would devastate them.'

'Though,' said Patrin, 'we mustn't jump to conclusions as it appears to be staff gossip what happened at the house. It might just be a coincidence the woman arriving here as a guest.'

'You might be right, Patrin, though his lordship has been barely present of late. He returns home sometimes in the early hours of the morning and immediately takes himself off to the drawing-room to pour himself a glass of brandy. Maybe he's been with her this past couple of weeks.'

'How do you know that?'

'I got up in the middle of the night once and went to get a glass of milk from the kitchen as I couldn't sleep. The drawing-room door was half open and his lordship was sitting there with his back to me, drinking out of one of his best crystal glasses. The decanter on the table beside him was half-empty.'

'If I were you if you want to keep your job, just keep your head down and say nothing. A still tongue in a wise head and all that,' Patrin warned kindly.

She knew what Patrin had to say made sense, but Clara wasn't the sort who could sit by and say nothing while those children were suffering in silence.

***

Clara tried to find Lord Stapleton that evening but she was informed that he was dining with Miss Susannah and her family. From the bellows of laughter coming from inside the dining room, she guessed the wine was free-flowing and she tutted in disgust to think how those children had gone to bed yet again without a kind word from their father while he was enjoying witty repartee and copious amounts of alcohol downstairs.

The following morning was no better either as he'd left early to assemble the hunting party to go partridge shooting. There were other men outside with their shotguns and horses who she didn't recognise. It was a little late in the season for it, but there was other game available for them to fire at if there weren't any partridge about. She didn't understand what they saw in the sport, but then again she'd been more than happy to purchase a partridge from the poulterer's shop in the village on occasion.

The men stood around chatting, some smoking cigars. No doubt it was a jovial get together for them. Then she saw her. Susannah. She was in the midst of it all, though not dressed for the occasion, and was making her way back to the house with extreme purpose with every footstep taken. Oh no, Clara didn't want to be spotted by her, but it was already too late as she mounted the steps.

'Hello,' Susannah greeted as she entered the hallway. 'Are you the new governess I've been told about?' She extended a long, well-manicured hand which Clara took, unsure what to do next. This woman wasn't of the same class, yet she was treating her like she was.

Her face had lit up like a beacon as if she was pleased to meet a kindred spirit.

'Hello,' said Clara. Wondering how to continue, she said the first thing that came into her mind. 'Would you like some coffee in the drawing-room?'

Susannah's crystal blue eyes sparkled. 'Yes, thank you. Providing you'll join me as I feel lost in this house now my father and brothers have left it to go off on that dreaded shoot looking for partridges in pear trees!' She giggled at her own witty comment.

Clara smiled. She had an hour to fill before she was needed in the schoolroom, so she escorted Susannah to the drawing-room and pulled on the elaborate bellpull beside the bookcase. Soon Dilly rushed to their attendance. The girl curtseyed.

'Could you arrange for a pot of coffee for two and some tea cake to be sent here please, Dilly?' She asked.

'Yes, miss.' She dipped her knee again and went off to fetch their order.

'She seems like a nice young girl,' Susannah said to her surprise. Usually, people didn't mention the servants unless they needed reprimanding.

'Yes, Dilly is. She's my attendant in my quarters upstairs.'

'I see. And how do you like life at the house? I hear the children are rather a handful?'

Clara smiled. 'That's understandable though with the recent death of their mother.' She watched to see if there was any sort of reaction from the woman and saw a faint blush appeared on her cheeks.

Susannah nodded at her but didn't comment, then quickly changed the subject.

'I hear the cook here is marvellous.'

'Yes, she's an excellent cook,' Clara confirmed.

'She made us a fantastic feast last night,' Susannah continued.

'Is it correct that Lord Stapleton is going to hold a ball here before you return home?' Clara asked suddenly.

For a moment the young woman looked flummoxed and Clara worried that she had spoken out of turn. Maybe the ball was intended as a surprise for her.

'Oh, no. He did ask me what I thought, but I suggested he postpone it for a few months as it has not yet been a full year since Arabella's death. In any case, it would be nice if it were a summer ball and not a winter one. That way, all the doors and windows can be opened and people can go outside on the terraces. A winter ball is so stuffy.' She waved a hand in front of her face which caused Clara to smile.

Stuffy indeed!

They made polite conversation for a few minutes, Clara finding it impossible to dislike the woman even though she felt she should. Finally, Dilly turned up with the tray of coffee and tea cake and left them to it as both women chatted quite easily with one another.

'Next time we dine, I shall ask Howard if you might join us!'

Oh no! What had she got herself into? She'd feel so awkward being at the same table as the lord and his guests. After all, she was little more than a high-class member of staff at the house, even if she wasn't exactly a servant. Somehow she found herself nodding and hoped the woman would soon forget about it. But just before Clara dismissed herself to make her way to the schoolroom, Susannah added, 'Yes, I'd like it very much if you could join us for dinner this evening, Clara. The conversation the men have is so very boring, I find myself almost nodding off to sleep.' She stifled a mock yawn with the palm of her hand.

Clara smiled and nodded before excusing herself and leaving the room. The only good thing about joining them all for dinner would be the fact that she might get another opportunity to speak with the lord. She'd have to choose her time carefully though and this time maybe not be as direct.

As she made her way along the corridor she almost collided with Billy who appeared to be in a rush as he walked at an extreme pace with his head down.

'Where's the fire, Billy?' she asked.

Breathlessly, he replied, 'I've just been asked by his lordship to saddle up another horse.'

Clara frowned. Did that mean that yet another person was joining the shooting party?

'Who for?' she asked.

'I'm not sure, but I've got to get the person suitable riding gear as well. Sorry I can't stop, ain't got the time,' he said over his shoulder as he flew off towards the back door of the property to get to the stables.

Curious, Clara thought. She took the servants' stairs to her quarters and then peered down onto the driveway below where a pack of hunting hounds were now also assembled, many wagging their tails with the excitement of it all. In amongst them stood Patrin. Surely he wasn't going hunting with his lordship and associates? But then again, wouldn't he know more about hunting than anyone as he'd had to live off his wits? Deciding she'd better not keep her charges waiting any longer than necessary, she made her way to the schoolroom.

***

The first thing Clara was greeted with when she entered the room was a question from James.

'Did you ask Papa about speaking to us, Miss Masters?' he asked hopefully, looking up from his desk with eyes wide with curiosity.

She smiled. 'Not yet, James. But I think I'll have the opportunity to do so this evening.'

Amelia narrowed her gaze. 'Why? What's happening this evening?'

Danielle nudged her sister. 'That's most rude of you, Amelia. You should address our new governess as Miss Masters and say please and thank you.'

Clara let out a long breath. 'I think I'm going to be invited to dinner downstairs.'

Danielle gasped. 'But why, Miss Masters?'

'Because Miss Susannah invited me, though I don't know for sure yet until she makes her feelings known to your father.'

'But why did she invite you to dinner at our house?' James wanted to know.

'I think it's because of all the male talk around the table. It seems she'd like another lady to talk to.'

Danielle smiled. 'You'd have plenty of things to talk about, miss. You know such a lot for a lady.'

Amelia rolled her eyes, folded her arms beneath her chest and huffed out a loud breath as if she could bear the conversation no longer. Clara guessed that deep down she felt a little jealous that two other ladies would get some attention from her father and not herself. After all, hadn't she been his blue-eyed girl previously? That's what Cook had told Clara at any rate. Amelia's reaction made her more determined than ever to speak to the man.

'Now then,' Clara began, 'today we're going to speak about the cocoa bean. Where it comes from and how it's transported over to our country and what can be made from it.'

James's eyes widened in wonderment. 'I love cocoa!' he said gleefully.

'Well, if you all complete today's lesson and pass the test I set for you afterwards, then you shall all receive a special treat!'

'Really, miss?' James asked, his eyes now shining like two beacons in the night.

'Yes, James.'

In her desk Clara had hidden three small bars of milk chocolate which she'd sent Dilly to purchase from the confectioner's shop in the village a couple of days beforehand. She'd also given the girl some extra money so she could choose something for herself. Dilly had chosen her absolute favourite, a poke of peppermint creams. To see the girl's delightfully broad smile upon her return had been worth every penny as she'd handed over the bars of milk chocolate to Clara and thanked her profusely for her special treat.

Amelia scowled and shook her head. 'Father forbids us to have any treats, so you'd better check with him first before giving us something you shouldn't.'

'Stuff and nonsense!' said Clara, clapping her hands. 'If I want to give you all a little treat as part of the lesson, then I can. Your father will have to deal with me if he says otherwise!'

To Clara's surprise, a smile began to form on Amelia's face. Before long she was giggling with her siblings until everyone, including Clara, was chuckling wholeheartedly. The children had probably never heard their father spoken of in such an underhanded manner before as if he were simply a nuisance for the governess to deal with. Maybe that's how she should treat him from now on. *Until you get your marching orders*, a little voice warned. Well maybe she did need to take care, but in this case she decided the children deserved a treat.

The lesson went well and the children soaked up all the information she had to tell them about the cocoa bean and its origins. They passed the test with flying colours so she promised them their treat when they returned from lunch. It seemed quiet in the house with the men being away and she wondered how Patrin was getting along at the hunt. Had he impressed his lordship so much he'd decided to take him along?

Dilly arrived with Clara's meal on a tray, right on time. Cook had prepared a small bowl of beef stew for her with dumplings. It was a hearty feast indeed but was too much for her at luncheon time though so she transferred some into a cup and handed it to the girl with a spoon. Dilly glanced at her nervously, not knowing what to do as usually Clara only gave her bits of leftovers to take away with her.

'Eat it here with me at the table before it gets cold,' Clara ordered and then smiled.

The girl didn't need telling twice. She sat in the chair opposite Clara and gobbled up the stew so fast Clara could've have sworn she hadn't eaten in weeks.

'Dilly, when did you eat last?' Clara asked with some concern.

Dilly's face grew red as she shook her head. Then, to Clara's horror, tears appeared in the girl's eyes and she began to sob, 'Oh, miss!'

Clara rose from the table, no longer caring about her own meal, and knelt as she hugged the girl in the chair whose body was now fiercely trembling. Finally, when she'd calmed down, Clara asked her, 'When was it?'

'Yesterday morning, miss. I ain't even touched those peppermint creams you allowed me to buy for meself as she's locked them in her cupboard,' she wailed.

'But that's preposterous! No wonder you are so thin. Why didn't you get to eat?'

'M-Mrs Montgomery said I should go without until supper today, miss. And I doubt I'll get me sweets back.'

'But why on earth is she punishing you like that?' Clara could hardly believe her ears.

'B-because when I went to light the fires in the bedrooms upstairs for the new guests, one of the fires started spitting and then a piece of hot coal spat out on the rug, miss. It bloomin' burnt it an' all.'

'But that was hardly your fault? That was simply an accident,' Clara said softly.

Dilly sniffed loudly and Clara handed the girl a handkerchief. It was obvious how upset the girl was over the incident, but to allow her to go all day and night without any food inside her was appalling in Clara's book.

'Look, you finish my stew and the bread roll too. I can pick up something else from Cook in a few minutes and I'll be asking her to feed you up too.'

Dilly nodded gratefully as Clara pushed her bowl of stew and the plate containing the bread roll across the table towards the young girl, who began to attack it with gusto. When the girl had finished, Clara dismissed her with a few kind words and went in search of Mrs Montgomery, who she found sorting out the linen situation in the store cupboard downstairs.

'Mrs Montgomery, please may I have a word with you?' Clara watched as the woman laid down some neatly folded sheets on the shelf and turned to face her.

She sighed loudly. 'Oh, very well. I'm up to my neck in it as you can see so please make it snappy.'

'It won't take long. I am concerned about young Dilly and the way you punished her so she should go without her meals for a full day. You even locked away those sweets I paid for her to enjoy.'

Mrs Montgomery's right eye began to twitch. It was obvious to Clara she didn't like the fact she had been caught out. Then she lifted her chin. 'And did the girl tell you she had taken a bowl of sugar from the kitchen to sprinkle on the fire to get it alight?' Mrs Montgomery said.

'No, she did not, but I have heard of people doing that before now to stubborn fires.'

'That maybe so, but she did not seek permission from either myself nor Mrs Cantwell to take that sugar bowl, and she's ruined a perfectly good rug in the bargain.' Mrs Montgomery held up the palm of her hand for a moment as if to strike Clara, but then it became plain she was doing it almost as if in defence of her actions.

'No matter if the girl did wrong or not, starving her is not the answer. She looked so weak and tired when she called with my midday meal to my room that I allowed her to sit down and eat with me.'

The woman's eyes were gleaming now as she spat out the words, 'You. Did. What?'

'I fed her and allowed her to sit down.'

This was all too much for the woman as she brushed past Clara and began to walk angrily away from her. Oh dear, had she made things worse for the child by speaking her mind?

'Mrs Montgomery, stop right this minute!' Clara ordered.

The woman carried on walking so Clara followed after her.

'If you touch that child then I shall be forced to tell his lordship and the other staff that you are using a room on my landing for illicit purposes!' Clara shouted.

The housekeeper stopped abruptly in her tracks and turned around to face Clara. It was evident she had got through to her and she swallowed hard as now Clara stood inches away. This time it was she who was invading the woman's private space and not the other way around.

'I-I don't know what you mean,' she said.

Clara put her hands to her hips and threw her head back as she carried on.

'I've noticed you have a separate key for that room that doesn't hang on the chatelaine around your waist with the others. None of the staff have access to that room, so tell me right now what that room is used for or I shall report you for mistreating young Dilly!'

To Clara's astonishment the woman began to cry huge shuddering sobs, so much so that Clara found herself putting her arm around the housekeeper.

'There, there, it can't be that bad, can it?' Clara soothed, confused at the turn the conversation had taken.

'It is and it was,' Mrs Montgomery said. 'Come with me and I'll show you what is in that room. It will be a relief to show it to someone.'

Chapter Fourteen

Clara gasped as the housekeeper unlocked the door, throwing it wide open so she could clearly see what was inside. Mrs Montgomery stood back and allowed her to enter, and Clara could not believe her eyes at the sight before her.

In the far corner of the small room was a baby's white wicker crib, complete with beautiful Broderie Anglaise bedding. Beside that was a rocking chair, a wooden box of toys and a small white wardrobe which matched the crib. In the opposite corner stood a dappled wooden rocking horse.

'But what? How?' Clara could barely speak.

'I come in here from time to time you see.' The housekeeper followed Clara into the room and carefully closed the door behind them so they would not be overheard.

'But why?'

'I usually sit in the rocking chair and reminisce.'

'Reminisce about what?' Clara was puzzled. Was the woman speaking of one of his lordship's children?

'I once had a young baby that was hidden away in this room,' Mrs Montgomery admitted.

Clara gasped for a second time as she tried to process what the woman was telling her.

'You see, when I was a young woman I started out as a maid at this house and worked my way up to head parlour maid. I fell in love with the butler here at the time. He was married and very charming. He paid me a lot of attention, which I was unused to. I felt he was the only friend I had in this big lonely place.'

For a moment Clara thought the woman was going to cry again, but instead she choked back a sob and then took a deep breath to compose herself, before carrying on with the story.

'I am ashamed to say so, but the inevitable happened and I found out I was going to have his baby. We needed to keep it a secret. Only I had the key to this room and told Lord and Lady Stapleton that the room was used for storage. When the baby was born, I hid her in here during the day and popped back and forth to see her.'

'But who delivered the child?'

'The butler knew of a lady in the village who often helped women with their confinements. She had to be paid for her services, which he did.'

'It was the very least he could do,' Clara said, shaking her head in disgust at the thought of the man.

'But the woman was too fond of the gin bottle.' She paused for a moment. 'He sent her to me and we both stayed in this room throughout, apart from the delivery itself. She was of little help as she kept falling asleep, that inebriated she was, but at least she'd sobered up in time for the birth. The butler informed the rest of the staff I was ill and shouldn't be disturbed and that he would deliver my meals, so no one bothered to look out for me. None of them liked me anyhow, so that was of no surprise to me.'

Clara shook her head as she looked deep into the woman's eyes. She recalled what had happened to Mrs McWhirter when she gave birth and felt a great deal of compassion for Mrs Montgomery. At least Lottie had had someone who had cared beside her.

'No one staying here ever suspected a thing?'

She shook her head. 'It was well enough away from the rest of the house as the schoolroom was on another floor then and the rooms up here were for guests. The master's children were young back then, so it wouldn't be unusual to hear one of them crying in the nursery on the floor below.'

'But what happened then? I have a feeling this is going to be a sad story.'

Mrs Montgomery nodded sombrely with tears in her eyes. 'The butler's wife found out about the affair as she caught us together with our baby when we'd ventured out for a walk one day. She put two and two together and threatened to tell the master. I had to get rid of the child as quickly as possible and deny everything. I left the baby on the steps of the local church, I'm ashamed to say.'

'Do you know what happened to her?'

'No, but I don't believe she would have lasted the night in that cold weather, not unless someone had found her within the hour.'

Clara patted the woman on her shoulder. 'Did you ever go to the village to find out if anyone knew anything about an infant being left on the church doorstep?'

'Yes, of course I did when I came to my senses,' she sniffed. 'That was the following morning. I kept returning to ask but no one knew a thing and treated me as if I had lost my senses. Obviously, I didn't say that it was my child that had been left there, for fear of retribution. People aren't going to understand something like that, but I look back on it and think I must have had a severe nervous breakdown. I wasn't in my right mind at the time or I'd never have done something like that in the first place.'

Clara nodded, then bit her lower lip. 'And you probably panicked too,' she soothed. 'Although I have great sympathy for your plight, how would all of that cause you to treat poor Dilly with great disdain?'

'I'm not proud of it,' Mrs Montgomery choked back a sob, 'but don't you see?'

'No, I'm afraid I don't,' said Clara.

'Dilly is about the age my own child would be right now if she were still alive, and she is also a girl. I suppose I feel aggrieved that the girl is alive while my girl may not be. I often have nightmares that she was dragged off from that church step by a pack of wild dogs and savaged while they sated their blood lust,' she said bitterly.

'But you must not let bitterness consume you,' Clara said sharply. 'Dilly comes from a poor family and she's had to work to help them since she was a young child.' Clara thought of Meg, who was not far off the same age as the girl but had been born into a more privileged lifestyle. 'My words might sound harsh in light of what you've been through, but it doesn't excuse you from ill-treating a young girl like that.'

Mrs Montgomery slumped down in the rocking chair and put her head in her hands to weep. Yes, Clara had sympathy for the loss of her child but not for her treatment of Dilly. She walked towards the door and, reaching for the knob, she turned to study the sight in front of her. 'I shan't tell anyone of this, nor about this room which appears to provide you with some sort of comfort, but only on the proviso that from now on you treat Dilly with the dignity, respect and compassion that little one deserves.'

Mrs Montgomery looked up at her through glassy eyes and nodded.

'Thank you,' was all she managed to whisper before Clara left the room, closing the door firmly shut behind her.

When Clara had finished lessons with the children for the day, she was making her way to see Cook about Dilly and the sugar incident when she was accosted by Susannah. The young woman had a gleam in her eyes.

'I've squared it all up with his lordship, you are to attend dinner tonight with us,' she said with great excitement.

With all that had transpired, Clara had forgotten all about the girl's suggestion. Thinking it would be something though to lighten her mood, she nodded.

'Yes, thank you. I should like to attend but don't think I have anything suitable to wear.'

'That's all right. I have plenty of gowns and we look to be about the same size after all. Come along to my room in about an hour and I'll have you all kitted out.'

Clara smiled, feeling as though she had made a new friend at the house.

'Thank you,' she said. 'I'll call by later.'

Susannah smiled salaciously as if they were both doing something a little wicked. Clara thought of how the woman had managed to get around Lord Stapleton. She seemed to have that sort of knack, and if there had been something going on between the pair before his wife's death then maybe Susannah's powers of persuasion had had something to do with it.

***

Clara caught Cook snoozing by the fireside in the kitchen with her feet up on a footstool. She appeared to be mumbling something under her breath and Clara wondered if the woman had been at the gin; some of the servants alluded to the fact she liked a nip now and again, though wasn't what one would class as dependent on it like that midwife of Mrs Montgomery's, thank goodness. Then she noticed the teacup by her side and realised the woman was so tired due to the extra work from the new guests that she'd simply fallen asleep.

Cook stirred for a moment and then sat bolt upright with a look of alarm on her face.

'Oh, me giddy aunt!' she said, 'I was 'aving a right old dream then, something about Billy running in to tell me that a couple more coaches of guests had just pulled up outside.'

Clara chuckled. 'I'm sorry if I disturbed you,' she said softly, taking the seat opposite the woman. 'I hear that a bowl of sugar went missing from your kitchen today?'

'Yes, and if I catch the varmint I'll pulverise them I will!' she held up a fierce-looking fist.

Clara let out a long breath. 'It was young Dilly,' she said. 'But it's not what you think. She was having trouble lighting the fires in the guest bedrooms so she took the bowl to sprinkle some sugar on top to encourage them to ignite. I think she was under pressure from Mrs Montgomery to get the fires going to air out the rooms.'

Cook nodded. 'I see,' she said. 'Well as long as the rest of the sugar is returned to me then I'll say no more about it.' She placed her hands over the arms of her chair and put her feet on the floor as if to haul herself out of her seat. 'But I'll be warning that young 'un that next time that she must ask me first!'

'Thank you, Mrs Cantwell. She'll appreciate your forgiveness and will learn a valuable lesson that she needs to ask permission first. No need to get up on my account.'

'I weren't, I have other things to attend to.' Cook stood and muttered something under her breath about putting a roast in the oven for dinner.

'I'll be dining with his lordship and his guests this evening,' Clara informed her.

Cook quirked a silver eyebrow. 'And how come? Not that you ain't as good as what they are, but that don't happen often with someone in their employ here. In fact, I've never known a member of staff dine with that lot before now.'

Clara lowered her voice and leaned in towards Cook in a conspiratorial manner. 'Well, between me and you, Miss Susannah has asked his lordship if I might join them as she'd like another female at the table, and he's agreed.'

Cook pursed her lips. 'Don't sound much like his lordship to me, but you never know, grief does funny things to folk. Just take care with that Miss Susannah one, mind.'

Clara stepped back feeling as if the wind had been taken out of her sails. She had been looking forward to an evening of fine dining and convivial chat. 'Why do you say that, Mrs Cantwell?'

'I just don't think she's to be trusted, that's all. I know I ain't got any proof about her and the master, and it's more than likely to be just staff gossip here, but she seemed to get under Lady Arabella's skin at times. It was more than she could bear to have the woman around and she upset her on more than one occasion.'

Clara nodded. Forewarned was forearmed, after all, but maybe the gossip about Susannah supposedly being caught in flagrante with his lordship had clouded Cook's better judgement. Clara just couldn't believe that was possibly true. 'I'll take care. In any case, she'll be gone soon. I just need to get through this supper tonight and maybe I'll not see much more of her.'

Cook smiled broadly. 'Right, I better get on then. No need for me to send your supper up tonight then and I'll prepare dinner for one more in the dining room,' she said with a wink.

'Thank you.' Clara nodded and then left the kitchen for her quarters. She was wondering how she'd wear her hair for the occasion and if she should put it up or not when she ran into Billy in the corridor who appeared in all of a fluster again.

'What's going on?' she asked.

'It's that hunting party again. They've just arrived back. They've done well by the look of it and the lord is asking for me to fetch the port wine outside with some silver goblets to celebrate the hunting victory.'

Clara shook her head. She didn't much hold with blood sports. 'I suppose they often go fox hunting too?'

'Yes, I can understand why the lord does as a couple of foxes have got into the hen houses on more than one occasion. One morning all that were left were feathers everywhere and pools of blood. It was a bleedin' massacre!'

She could well comprehend how that might feel, but still she preferred to leave foxes alone. After all, this was nature. 'I better let you go then, Billy,' she said.

He grinned at her and she could see he was appraising her with his eyes, which made her feel slightly uncomfortable. He was probably a few years younger than her, but still a man nevertheless. Maybe she ought not be so chatty with him in future in case he got the wrong impression and had designs on her.

***

'I have just the right dress for you,' Susannah said later, drawing a teal green damask silk gown from her wardrobe and laying it on the bed. It had puffed sleeves and an overlay of black Belgian lace inset into the bodice and around the neckline.

'I've never seen anything so beautiful in all my life!' Clara gasped, running her hands over the garment.

'It will suit you down to the ground. I also have here the perfect choker to go with it. It's black velvet with a large cameo at the throat.'

'You're so kind, Susannah,' Clara said breathlessly. She overlooked Cook's earlier warning – she had obviously misunderstood the girl.

'Go ahead and try it on,' Susannah urged. 'Use that screen in the corner.'

For the first time, Clara noticed the elaborate oriental decorated screen in the corner of the room. She smiled and took the gown with her. It felt so soft and smooth in her hands. She'd never be able to afford anything like this, but her mother had made several gowns of this quality for the wealthier villagers who could afford to pay for both material and a high-quality dressmaking service. Clara could only dream of owning such a gown, but to wear one like a proper lady for just one evening would do for now.

She slipped it on over her corset and it slid effortlessly down over her form; it seemed to be made for her. She glanced down and noticed that the low-cut bodice showed off her decolletage nicely, making her feel all together more of a woman. Shyly, she emerged from the screen.

'There! I told you so!' Susannah jumped up and down in excitement. 'It looks perfect on you.' She walked towards Clara and produced the choker from behind her back. 'Now to affix this for you.' Clara stood still whilst Susannah affixed the choker around her neck. 'Go and look in the full-length mirror!' she ordered, gesturing to the long oval walnut-encased mirror on a stand.

Tentatively, Clara made her way there and gasped. Could that really be her reflection in the mirror gazing back at her approvingly? She looked so stylish and such a lady too.

'Well say something,' Susannah urged.

'I just can't believe it's me!' Clara said excitedly.

'I'm going to ask my maid to style your hair in the latest Paris fashion mode too,' Susannah said. Clara had noticed the woman had brought an attendant along with her, and whoever the girl was she made a good job of Susannah's hair.

'Thank you,' Clara said, feeling robbed of her breath. She couldn't believe this was happening to her. It was just like the fairy tale of Cinderella, but instead of going to a ball she was off for dinner with nobility.

'Now to complete the outfit,' Susannah said, 'I have a long pair of black velvet gloves you may borrow. They'll match the black velvet of the choker.'

Clara smiled. 'You have a good eye for fashion.'

'Mama and Papa sent me to a finishing school in Paris, and it was there I developed quite an eye for it. Those continental sorts know how to dress. I also visited several fashion houses.'

'I just don't know how to thank you enough,' Clara said, unable to help being impressed and excited about dining with the group.

'No need for that. It's payment enough just to see your eyes sparkle with the delight of it all. Just one more thing.' She picked up an elaborate glass bottle from the dressing table behind them, removed the stopper, dabbed a little on a handkerchief and handed it to Clara. 'It's an exquisite perfume from the famous House of Guerlain. It's the masterpiece in the Guerlain crown. It was created recently by Aimé Guerlain, the son of the House founder Pierre-François-Pascal Guerlain. I was fortunate to meet the creator during my trip to Paris. It's said to be a scent that stirs the emotions and is a truly magical perfume.'

Clara sniffed the lace handkerchief. 'It's such a delicate fragrance,' she said. Usually, she didn't use perfume, but she thought she'd make an exception tonight.

Susannah's maid, Lucinda, arrived to coif Clara's hair. She brushed it upwards, sweeping the tresses into a coil and securing it with pins, leaving soft tendrils to frame her face.

Susannah clasped her hands together as she admired her maid's handiwork before saying brightly, 'We're meeting in the dining room at a quarter past six so you've got a good half-hour if you wish to return to your quarters.'

'Yes, I'll do that.' Clara looked at the maid and thanked her. She felt she ought to pay her for her service, but Susannah had already warned her not to do that.

'Thank you so much, Susannah. I'll see you in the dining room later.'

Walking on air back to her room, Clara felt as though she was in a dream. Was it possible she had gone up in the world in one fell swoop? If her sister Emily could only see her right now, she'd be green with envy!

***

Feeling like a queen, Clara made her way to the dining room with her heart thudding beneath her bodice. But when she arrived and opened the door, she was stunned to discover the party was already in the middle of the first course which appeared to be some sort of soup.

Feeling flummoxed, she looked around in bewilderment. Spoons clinked on dishes and everyone had their heads down eating. How had they started without her? It didn't make any sense at all. If anything, she was a few minutes early, and there was no sign of his lordship as yet. One of Susannah's brothers set down his spoon and looked up as she stood at the entrance of the room.

'And who have we here? A newcomer by the seem of it!' he bellowed.

Didn't he know she would be joining them? Maggie, the kitchen-maid, was there in attendance along with one of the older maids. Noticing Clara's distress, she quickly approached.

'I'll escort you to your seat,' she said. 'Cook told me to set an extra place at the table.'

Clara smiled at her and thanked her for her kindness before whispering, 'What time did they begin?'

'At six o'clock,' Maggie said politely, seemingly astonished that Clara didn't know what time the dinner was set for. That just wasn't the case: Susannah had told her it would be a quarter past the hour. As if reading her mind, Susannah looked up at her.

'Please forgive me, Clara,' she said in a sweet tone, 'I muddled up the time.'

Clara said nothing, just shrugged her shoulders and took her place beside Susannah at the table whilst Maggie dished up a bowl of soup for her and placed it in front of her.

'It's game soup, miss,' she said.

'Thank you, Maggie.'

The others around the table stared at her as if she had done something wrong, then she realised that they weren't accustomed to thanking servants. There was a long pause as everyone seemed to hold their spoons still for a moment, until Susannah's father, Clement, cleared his throat.

'It's nice to meet you, Miss Masters. My daughter has told me so much about you.'

Clara's cheeks flamed. She didn't want to be caught like a young deer looking up at the barrel of a gun. How should she respond? She wasn't quite sure, but she knew she would have to as it would be churlish not to. 'Thank you,' she replied almost coquettishly.

'I say, Raymond,' one of Susannah's brothers said to the other, breaking the uncomfortable silence that had ensued, 'that was a spiffing hunt earlier, wasn't it?'

Raymond smiled as his head nodded vigorously. 'That gypsy was great though, knowing how to track animals, and he was a crack shot with a rifle.'

'Please, Cedric, and you too, Raymond,' Susannah addressed her brothers, 'do we have to speak about such things at the table? It is so tiresome.'

They both grinned and carried on eating.

'What's happened to his lordship?' Clara whispered to Susannah.

'He was called away on urgent business but says he'll be back in time for port and cigars in the drawing-room. We might as well have a little tipple ourselves,' she giggled. 'A glass or two of sherry won't harm either of us.'

Clara wasn't keen on alcohol but figured she would have to go along with things or else she might be singled out and thought to be a bad sport.

The rest of the dinner went quite well and Clara began to relax. As they were sipping their coffee at the end of the delicious meal, the butler arrived to tell them that Lord Stapleton was ready to entertain them in the drawing-room. Clara walked amicably with Susannah along the corridor behind the men.

'His lordship has had a long day then?'

Susannah smiled. 'Yes, but I suspect he dined before he got here. Howard isn't one to miss out on a meal!' she exclaimed with a giggle before picking up her pace and leaving Clara to trail her.

She certainly sounds as if she knows the lord quite informally indeed, Clara thought as she approached the drawing-room. *Maybe the staff gossip was true after all.*

Clara was the last to enter the drawing-room and the butler closed the door behind her. Lord Stapleton was stood in front of a roaring fire as a maid was pouring liquid from a decanter into wide bulb-shaped glasses. Seeing one of those glasses reminded her of Papa as he often had a nip of brandy at Christmas or New Year, though alcohol had not been a way of life for him.

The lord was greeting his guests in a jovial manner and offering the men cigars from an elaborate looking wooden case. His eyes were drawn to Susannah and he met her with a smile which made him look devilishly handsome. He took both her hands in his and held them to his lips for a moment. Then looking into her eyes said, 'I trust you've had a good day?'

'Yes, the best, thank you,' Susannah replied sweetly.

He nodded at her before his eyes were drawn to Clara who was stood in hesitation some way behind her. The look Lord Stapleton was giving her made her feel so uncomfortable that she squirmed inside. Was it because he might not have been informed that she would be in attendance or was it something else? That warm smile he'd had for Susannah had lit up his eyes but now they were cold, the colour of hard flint. He opened his mouth and stared at Clara.

'And why on earth are you wearing my wife's dress, Miss Masters?' he said, his voice rising until he was almost bellowing.

Clara's mouth fell open and she was mortified as she heard one of the young men groan. And was that a gasp from Susannah there? What kind of cruel trick was this? She'd been given the impression that it was Susannah's gown she wore. She looked at the woman for confirmation that maybe it was by some coincidence that she had the same dress as the one Lady Arabella had once worn, but what Clara noticed wasn't shock on the woman's face but a look of smug satisfaction. A smirk appeared on Susannah's lips, unseen by the lord who had moved in front of her to approach Clara.

'I-I don't understand,' Clara said, trembling. Now all eyes were upon her. She was just about to explain that Susannah had given her the dress when the woman glared hard at her with a look as if to say, 'You tell him and I'll make even more trouble for you.'

In her anguish, Clara dropped the scented handkerchief she'd been carrying and fled out of the room, not even pausing as she heard the lord's voice emanating from behind her.

'This is an absolute disgrace, young lady! Pack your things and I want you out of here immediately!' he shouted before the drawing-room door closed with a thud of finality.

Bitter tears flowed as she pounded up the stairs and ran across the landing towards her quarters, holding up the skirts of the beautiful gown as she fled for fear of tripping over in her haste. She was wearing a dead woman's dress and couldn't wait to remove it. She hardly remembered arriving back at her quarters or the removal of the gown as she lay on her bed sobbing into her pillow.

He wanted her gone right away, so she didn't have time to wallow in in her grief. Nor would she have an opportunity to say farewell to the staff or those poor children. Just minutes ago she had felt hopeful about getting the lord in a good mood to speak to him about the children, but now that had all gone up in a puff of smoke. A magician's illusion, a conjuring trick of fate, a sleight of hand. She had been deceived, and that deception was by Susannah herself. What had made the woman play such a cruel trick on her? Surely there was a valid explanation? But then again, she hadn't spoken out in Clara's defence in front of his lordship. She imagined the woman running along after her to apologise and explain what had occurred. Clara was convinced she'd hear a knock on the door at any moment, but as she waited with a thumping heartbeat, none came.

Sadly, she wiped away her tears, washed her face and began to pack her trunk and carpet bags. She'd ask Patrin whether he could take her back home now and bring the rest of her belongings over sometime tomorrow. How would she manage to explain to her family what had occurred? And now she would need to search for a new job elsewhere. How could she explain to a new employer that she had no reference from her last?

Still sobbing, she left her room along the corridor. It seemed to echo the sounds of her cries, but thankfully there was no one around to hear them. She walked down the staff staircase where she encountered nobody at all as most were busy either cleaning up in the kitchen or seeing to the lord's guests, and then she fled out through the back door to see Patrin. She knew he'd be at the lodge house as that's where he was being put up while he worked at the big house.

A wild wind whipped up as she hammered breathlessly on the wooden door with her bare knuckles, hitting so hard that she scuffed her skin in the process of bringing the lodgekeeper to the door.

He looked tired as he rubbed his eyes. 'What's going on 'ere?' he asked.

'Is Patrin here, please, Mr Snelgrove?' Clara said, hoping not to have to explain why she wanted to see him.

Thankfully Mr Snelgrove wasn't that inquisitive, instead he limped away, leaving her stood at the open door. She pulled the collar of her jacket up around her neck, wishing she'd dressed more for inclement weather. It was not a minute or two before Patrin arrived at the door, his hair messed up as if he'd been asleep. She felt a tremendous pang of guilt for disturbing him as he'd been out for hours leading the hunting party.

'Clara? What's wrong?' he asked, concern in his eyes.

'It's his lordship, he's asked me to leave. Given me my marching orders…' She began to sob again, so much so that she couldn't get the rest of her words out. He took her in his arms so that she rested her head against his shoulder and felt the comfort of his warm body.

'Do you want to come inside and explain?' he asked gently, her pain mirrored in his eyes.

She looked up at him through glassy eyes and shook her head.

'No, please can you take me home as soon as possible? Can you hook your horse up to the cart and come back to the house to get my trunk and other things and take me back home?'

'Yes,' he said softly. 'I'll just grab my jacket and cap and we can talk on the way out of here. It will be like old times again.' He smiled at her, but she couldn't even force a smile back at him. There was a lump in her throat that was refusing to go away.

They went to her quarters in silence. She showed him what needed to go with her for now and he promised he'd deliver the bigger items to her the following day. As they left via the lodge gate on the cart, she took one final last look at the big house and blinked her tears away.

Chapter Fifteen

On the journey back home, Clara opened up to Patrin about the events that had led up to her dismissal forthwith.

He listened intently to begin with, and then said, 'I can't believe that happened to you, Clara. You didn't deserve any of it and more fool his lordship for believing that little minx. It's my guess that she saw you as some sort of a threat to her. It's obvious that she has the man wrapped around her little finger and sees herself as the next lady of the manor, as it were.'

Clara nodded slowly. That explanation hadn't occurred to her until Patrin voiced his thoughts. 'But why would she see me as some sort of threat, Patrin? I don't have designs on his lordship.' She swallowed the lump that was still in her throat and sobbed quietly. Although talking about it so soon was bringing waves of grief, it felt good to have the opinion of Patrin with whom she could be completely open.

'But don't you see?'

'No, I honestly don't.'

'You're young and of a marriageable age. You're attractive and you've got something she hasn't?'

'Pardon?' Clara sniffed.

'You're a threat to her because you have a good relationship with the lord's children. They've grown to like you and she won't like that. How does she act around them? Do they show any interest in her?'

Clara thought for a moment before saying, 'She tends to stay away from them. Only once have I been in her company when she has spoken to them and even then it was very polite and reserved.'

'Well, there you go then,' Patrin said definitively.

Clara huffed out a puff of resignation. So that's what it all boiled down to: a simple case of jealousy had lost her the position as governess at that house. How cruel of the woman to go into her deceased cousin's bedroom and select a dress for Clara to wear, knowing full well what sort of reaction it would provoke in the lord.

'I'm better off out of there then!' she said, now feeling anger towards Susannah and Lord Stapleton. 'If what I've heard is true, those pair deserve one another.'

Patrin let out a long whistle.

'Whoah now, I've heard those rumours about the canoodling between the pair, and not just what you confided in me the other day either. Billy told me about it as well just yesterday, but I don't think it's true. He wasn't even working there at the time. The only one I know of who was there at that particular time was Mrs Montgomery. She'd know if there was any substance to it.' He paused for a moment. 'In fact, I could sense today just before we went out on that hunt that the lord didn't want Susannah around.' Patrin shook his head. 'He dismissed her and sent her back inside the house!'

'What a liar she is! She told me she didn't want to join the men on the hunt,' Clara exclaimed.

'Liar or not, I do believe the lord is an honest man. He shouldn't have dismissed you without speaking to you in private first, but I'm guessing it was too much to bear to see you in his wife's gown. You do bear a striking resemblance to her, so maybe that was another factor in all of this.'

Clara frowned. 'How do you know what Lady Stapleton looked like, Patrin?'

'I was asked to repair a piece of furniture in his bed chamber and there's a portrait of her hanging there.'

Clara felt her face grow hot. 'Oh, I've never been in that room to see it.'

'And nor would I expect you to go in there, either,' he chuckled. 'Look, there's something I was going to tell you and then changed my mind in light of all of this, but I'd better come clean.'

'What is it you want to say to me?'

He hesitated for a moment before saying, 'When I went on that hunt with the lord and his guests today, he was pleased with me and asked me to become gamekeeper at the Stapleton Estate.'

'Oh! And would you like that?'

'I'm not too sure,' Patrin rubbed his chin in contemplation. 'If I took the position it would mean settling down and not moving on as I'd planned, and now hearing your news I'd feel like I was betraying you.'

For the first time since her dismissal, Clara smiled wholeheartedly as she rubbed his arm with affection. 'If it's what you want then you must accept the position, and if you do then you can keep an eye on the children for me. Would you do that?'

He nodded. 'I will indeed, but first I'm going to discuss it with Flori before I accept, though I think she might welcome it as she's well settled at the Downing's farm.'

'So, Flori's all right then? Settled for now?' Clara asked, turning to him in the darkness.

'Aye, she is and all, but she's not a proper gypsy see,' he said, lowering his voice. 'She was given to me mother and father as a baby.'

'So, she doesn't have the wanderlust that you do?'

'No, indeed she doesn't!' he chuckled. 'She'd rather stay put, thank you very much!'

Clara was about to ask about Flori's parentage and then thought better of it. There would be time for that later, she hoped, now that Patrin wasn't going to be moving on.

***

It was late when they arrived at the family cottage in Crownley, but Mama was still up as Clara noticed the oil lamp burning on the windowsill. No doubt she was working on a garment for someone while the children were asleep upstairs. Maybe Lillibeth Pettigrew's wedding gown? Clara knew that Mama had almost completed it but intended sewing seed pearls into the bodice to finish it off.

'I'll unload your belongings for you and then I'll be off,' Patrin said solemnly. 'I'll need to be up bright and early in the morning to complete my work so I can have time to bring your other things over to the cottage for you.'

Clara felt another pang of guilt, this time for putting him to so much trouble.

'You'll probably need to square all that up with Mrs Montgomery first,' Clara warned. No doubt the housekeeper would have a fit if she saw Patrin tramping upstairs to Clara's old quarters without seeking permission first, particularly in light of that secret room at the end of the corridor.

'Yes, I'll do that,' Patrin agreed as he helped her down.

Mama was on her feet and rushing towards her daughter as soon as Clara and Patrin entered the cottage carrying her belongings. She hugged Clara tightly to her chest, allowing her to weep for she realised she would not have arrived home without warning at this ungodly hour for nothing.

'I have to leave now, Mrs Masters, but I'll bring the rest of Clara's things here sometime tomorrow for her,' Patrin said softly.

Mama nodded, patting her eldest child on the back as though she were a young infant. When Patrin had departed it was some time before Clara could speak about what had occurred at the big house, so Mama brewed up a cup of tea for them both and they spent a good hour going over things, with constant reassurance from Mama that all would work out for the best. Then she climbed the stairs to fetch some warm blankets and a pillow for Clara to sleep on the settee. Clara thought she'd have trouble getting off to sleep, but due to her exhaustion she drifted off right away and was not awoken until the following morning when Meg and Edmund came bounding down the stairs, terribly excited to find their big sister asleep on the settee.

***

Over the following days, Clara became accustomed to being back with her family, even if the home was now a different one. It was cosy enough and the family liked living there but there was no getting away from the fact that she felt more confined here. Mama didn't have all that much room for her dressmaking business either and usually worked upstairs on a wooden table in the bedroom she shared with Emily. When everyone was asleep she would use the downstairs living room, but now Clara was back home she couldn't work late into the night as often. Seeing the predicament, Clara came up with the idea to help her mother's business.

'You could take on more work if I help you, Mama,' she'd said excitedly one day when the children were at school and Emily had gone out on an errand.

Mama looked thoughtful for a moment. 'Indeed you could, Clara. You're a good seamstress yourself because I taught you … even if you can be a little clumsy at times. You need more faith in yourself,' she angled her head to one side and smiled. 'But you are destined for bigger and better things, I believe.'

'Well just let me help you then. I can deliver the garments for you, help you measure up, sew the less intricate work. That way I would feel I was paying for my keep. The money I was paid from Stapleton Manor has all but run out now, so please let me do this one thing to help you.'

'Oh Clara, you are such a good girl. Very well then, just help me out until you find something more suited to your abilities. Why don't you see if anyone else is looking for a governess?'

Clara chewed on her bottom lip. 'That's all very well but I would never get a letter of recommendation from my last employer, would I? And even if I didn't need one from there, the new employer would be bound to ask why I hadn't lasted there for very long.'

'I do see that you have a point. Please pray about this, my darling. God answers prayers.'

Mama spoke such words of comfort and Clara decided that when she went to bed that night and the house was as quiet as a little mouse, she would pray about her situation.

***

A couple of weeks later, Patrin turned up at the house unexpectedly and asked Clara to take a walk with him. The weather was warming up a little although it was only the end of February. They strolled through the village to the duck pond and watched a little boy and his father sail a wooden boat on the water. There was no ice on the pond now; everything was thawing out nicely and the only remaining snow was a smattering on the hilltops. It had been a particularly harsh winter, but Clara reminded herself that they had all survived it, even the McWhirter baby. She often thought about Lottie and baby Samuel. Auntie had written a letter to Mama telling them that Jethro McWhirter had turned up at her cottage unexpectedly one day professing to be a changed man and Lottie and the baby had returned home with him. Clara could only hope that was the case and that he'd never take to the drink again.

'Oh to be a child again!' Patrin said with a broad smile on his face as he broke into her thoughts.

'Oh, indeed. They don't have the same sort of worries as us adults, do they?' she said, trying to force any worries she had about the McWhirter family from her mind.

He shook his head. 'And you, Clara, are you still worrying about things as they stand for you?'

'I am, yes. I worry about keeping a roof over the family's head if Mama's business dries up. She's not getting any younger and I think she's developing arthritis in her fingers. She doesn't tell me, but I watch the pain on her face sometimes when she's stitching away. Other times I catch her flexing her fingers as if they've seized up.'

He nodded. 'Well, one thing I wanted to tell you is that Susannah hasn't been to the house for a week or two.'

Clara quirked an interested eyebrow. 'Oh, really?' she asked, angling her head to take in what he was about to say to her.

'Yes, something has gone on regarding the children. I don't know what it is but Cook said she heard raised voices coming from the drawing-room one morning as if his lordship was ticking Susannah off. She heard him mention their names.'

'How are the children doing? I am concerned about their welfare.'

'To be honest with you,' Patrin said as he rubbed his chin, 'they've not been the same since you left. They walk around looking quite sorry for themselves. There was a plan to bring in another governess but Cook told me that didn't work out.'

Clara huffed out a breath. 'Maybe his lordship dismissed her too for something she didn't do.'

'No, it wasn't like that at all. Apparently, she was due to start work and he changed his mind last-minute for some unknown reason. I have had an idea though, and that's one of the reasons I came today'

Clara looked up at him and nodded her approval to continue.

'I know how much you are missing those children and how much they are missing you. Early afternoon they now tend to go to the lake and play in the treehouse there. I think they like being away from the house, to be honest with you. Now I was thinking as his lordship is usually away on business during the day and the staff are often resting for a period, it would be a good time for me to summon the children together and bring them to the lodge gate for them to speak to you. How would you feel about that?'

At that suggestion, Clara's eyes brimmed with tears and she nodded as she blinked them away. 'Yes, I would like that very much indeed. Thank you. But which day would it need to be?'

'I think this coming Monday would be a good day. If you could arrive at the gate say for two o'clock? I promise I'll do my best to bring them there to you. But you'll have to be careful no one sees you. Don't worry about old Snelgrove, he knows about my plan and won't say anything to anyone.'

'Nothing and no one will keep me away,' Clara said, smiling now.

'Then I shall see to it that the children come to see you there. Now there is nothing we can do about it today, so I suggest we go and visit Old Ma Perkin's Tea Room for a sticky bun and a pot of tea, what do you say?'

She nodded and he took her arm to escort her to the tearoom which was a quaint little shop on the corner of Hillside Row with white lace curtains covering the bottom halves of the bay windows. A little bell tinkled as they stepped inside and Ma Perkins greeted them warmly.

'It's a long while since I last set eyes on you, Patrin,' she said, smiling broadly.

He removed his flat cap and nodded. 'Aye, I know. I'm working at the big house these days.'

'Stapleton Manor?' She raised her silver brow as if surprised by this nugget of information.

'Yes, I've been helping the head gardener there on a casual basis, but now I've been offered a permanent role there.'

'The old gardener gone sick then?'

He shook his head. ''Tis nothing like that at all. His lordship has asked me to take over as gamekeeper.' His face flushed red and it was at that moment that Clara realised he had decided.

Before Patrin had a chance to explain to Ma Perkins, Clara said to the woman, 'Is it all right if we take a window seat?'

Momentarily distracted, the woman smiled and showed them to the table which was in a prime position for watching the people passing by outside. When she was a young child and Papa was still alive, if they had gone to a tearoom or a restaurant she'd preferred to sit at a window table and would often point out the things she could see.

When they were seated and Ma Perkins had taken their order, Clara turned to Patrick.

'So, I take it you've made a decision about the gamekeeper position then?'

He nodded, his eyes looking a little guarded.

'I've turned it down,' he admitted.

Clara felt her heart slump and quite suddenly she felt breathless. Patrin would be moving on again. 'So, this means you'll be leaving the Foxbridge area?'

'I'm afraid so, but it won't be for good. I'll be back by the summer. My restless gypsy blood tells me it's time to move on for the foreseeable future.'

'Then take me with you,' Clara blurted out without thought, so much so that she surprised even herself.

Patrin leant across the table and lifted her chin with his thumb and forefinger so that he was peering into her eyes.

'I couldn't do that. It would never work. You're a lady, you're not cut out for such things. You deserve a better life.'

She drew a lace handkerchief from her dress pocket and dabbed at her eyes, knowing deep down he was right about it all. Patrin was a man whose spirit was so free it could take him anywhere the wind blew. He'd never settle down in one place long enough to find out whether he could put down roots. The gypsy way of life was in his blood.

'I suppose you're right,' she sniffed.

He smiled at her and said softly, 'I know I am. Now, Flori, it's different for her as her parentage isn't my own.'

'Yes, you mentioned that. What were the circumstances of her birth?' Clara asked, grateful to have something other than Patrin's impending absence to think about.

'Apparently, she was found on a bitterly cold night, not quite a newborn but a couple of months old. An old lady in the village asked if my parents would like to keep her. She was the one who'd found her you see, and she didn't want to give the child up to the authorities. My Ma said she was waiting for someone to come forward and claim her, but no one ever did.'

'Why do you think she was reluctant to give her up?'

He shrugged before saying, 'Maybe she was afraid the baby would be placed in the workhouse or something.'

'I see,' Clara said, then something suddenly occurred to her. 'How long ago do you estimate that happened?'

'Well Flori is almost a young woman now, so maybe thirteen years? I wasn't very old myself when out of the blue I had an infant sister. There was no time for me to prepare for her coming like there would have been if Ma had been pregnant. One moment I was the only child, then the next there was this young baby girl who took most of Ma's attention,' he chuckled to himself. 'A right little beauty she were and all. I think I fell in love with her the moment I first laid eyes on her. I was never really jealous of her, just wanted to protect the little mite.'

Clara's heartbeat began to pound as her mind made frantic connections. She looked at Patrin wide-eyed before asking, 'Would you happen to know if your Flori was found abandoned on a church step? Not St. Bartholomew's, but maybe some other church?'

'To be honest with you, all I remember when Ma and Pa went to collect Flori was that she was the dearest little thing, but I can't recall where she was found.'

Clara hesitated for a moment as her mind pulled all the strings together. Before she had a chance to think anything through properly, she said hurriedly, 'There's something I have to tell you. I think I know who abandoned Flori … and why.'

Chapter Sixteen

Patrin blinked several times.

'But how would you know a thing like that?' he asked slowly.

'I think, going by the age of your Flori and the circumstances in which she was found, her mother might be Mrs Montgomery,' Clara explained, keeping her voice low.

Patrin swallowed hard. 'Not Mrs Montgomery the housekeeper, surely?'

'The one and the same.' Clara let out a long breath as she prepared to tell Patrin the story. 'I'd discovered she was using a room on my landing that no one else appeared to have access to. Indeed, she even used a key that wasn't on the chain around her waist with all the other household keys. Naturally, I became suspicious. The woman acted flustered when I caught her in the act, so one day I confronted her about her use of the room and she broke down in tears. That shocked me as she's such a strong person, or at least acts that way in front of us all.'

'Old Big Ears crying!' Patrin mocked.

'Please Patrin,' Clara urged, 'she was like a different person when she showed me what was inside that room. It was a child's nursery! You must swear not to mention what about I am about to tell you to any of the other staff.'

His face took on a look of concern. He nodded. 'I can keep a secret. You can trust me,' he said solemnly.

'Apparently, Mrs Montgomery was involved in a romance with the butler at the property back then. She became pregnant.'

Patrin's mouth popped open and then he closed it again. 'Wouldn't he marry her?'

'It wasn't as simple as that as he was already married to a lady who worked at the house.'

'Oh, I can see why that may prove difficult then,' he said with a wry smile.

'Quite. She did what she could to hide the pregnancy well. When she had given birth she kept her baby hidden in that room. The floor was only used for guests back then. No one suspected anything as Amelia and Danielle were only young and often heard crying, but when the butler's wife found out about the baby and the affair she threatened to tell Lord and Lady Stapleton. Mrs Montgomery admitted to me she wasn't in her right mind at the time and she thought it best to leave the baby at the church. She regretted her decision and went back but the baby was gone. She's grieved for a long time for that little girl and used to go into that room and sit in the rocking chair as a form of comfort. The butler and his wife left Stapleton Manor not long afterwards, so maybe she didn't need to have abandoned the baby at all.' Clara sat back, glad to have finally got the secret off of her chest.

'Well if all of this is true then we need to speak to the woman before we say a word to Flori, I reckon. I don't want her heart breaking in case her mother, if she is her mother, doesn't want to know her.'

'Oh, believe me, she will want to know her,' Clara confirmed, remembering the heartache she saw in Mrs Montgomery's eyes.

Patrin nodded. 'Then I shall have a word with Flori tonight and ask her if she would like to meet the woman to discuss the circumstances and to find out whether she could be her mother, though I can't say as I see any likeness there myself.'

Clara nodded gratefully. She had to admit she couldn't see a resemblance either, but still it needed to be checked upon. She'd never live with herself if they were mother and daughter and never had a chance to be reacquainted.

'Thank you, Patrin, being with you today has been a tonic for my soul. I've been so low after what happened,' she said.

'Now don't you be worrying at all. You shall get to see those children on Monday by hook or by crook!' he laughed.

***

At five minutes before the appointed hour, Clara stood with bated breath just outside the lodge house. If someone were to pass in a carriage right now then the whole meeting would be put at risk, so she spotted a bush she could hide behind should one come her way. Fortunately for her, no one arrived or left the big house. By five minutes past the hour, she was beginning to think something in Patrin's plan had gone wrong but then she spotted them, four specks in the distance. He was bringing the children to her. Oh, joy!

It seemed a long while until they had walked the length of the drive to the lodge. Clara's heartbeat seemed to increase with each step they took. She felt like entering the property and running to greet them, but she couldn't risk getting caught by someone and thrown off the property in disgrace yet again.

Soon they were drawing near and the beaming smiles on their faces when they saw her said that they were as pleased to see her as she was to see them. She watched as Patrin unlocked the side gate.

'Miss Masters!' Danielle shouted in excitement. The girl ran towards her old governess with her arms outstretched. Clara leaned down to give the girl a hug and then James was hugging her too. She glanced up at Amelia who looked unsure of what to do. Clara knew she was not used to signs of great affection, but when she beckoned her with her hand, the young girl too went running towards them. They stood in a group hug as Patrin looked on seeming most amused.

'Well, in all the time I've been at this house I've never seen you look so pleased to see someone as I now witness you are with Miss Masters!' he said.

The children giggled but it was James who broke the silence. 'But why did you leave us like that?' he asked in a breaking voice, looking up at her with glassy eyes.

A searing pain like an arrow pierced Clara's heart and she knelt so she was on eye level with the boy, wiping away a lone tear that was coursing down his cheek. She looked first at him and then the two girls.

'Will you believe me if I tell you none of this was of my doing? I didn't wish to leave you nor the house.'

The girls nodded but looked slightly confused. Finally after a long silence Amelia said, 'So whose doing was it?'

Clara deliberated whether she ought to tell them the circumstances but then thought better of it. She smiled. 'Let's just say a mistake has been made regarding something I was supposed to have done in malice that was done in innocence on my part.'

James shrugged his shoulders. Clara noticed the girls were whispering and then Danielle said, 'I know it was something to do with Miss Susannah. We're not keen on her, Papa sent her back home.'

'Yes, I had heard about that. I'll say no more for now. Maybe the truth will come out someday, but today I'm here to see how you are. You three are all I care about at this moment. I've been thinking about this and I don't want you to keep any secrets from your father. You may tell him that I called to see you all. I won't call again because I'm not allowed to be here, but would you ask him if we might write to you? If he refuses, then please leave it at that.' She delved into her skirt pocket and produced a folded piece of paper. 'My new address is on this sheet of paper. Please pass it on to your father. I don't know what reaction he might have but do not be disappointed should he refuse, will you? Just remember I shall always think fondly of you all.'

Now the three children were sobbing but Clara knew she had done the right thing. Patrin placated them as she turned to leave with her own tears streaming down her face too. Life could be so cruel at times, and it was clear that those children needed someone to show them some affection. If there was just one wish she could make it would be that she be allowed to remain in contact with the children and see them every now and then. Was that really too much to ask?

***

The following day, Patrin arrived at the cottage to inform Clara the children were alright after she'd left them. They'd returned to the lake afterwards and he'd whittled a sailing boat for them out a piece of wood which James in particular had gleefully sailed on the water. Amelia had put Clara's note in her pocket but he said he couldn't be sure whether she'd pass it on to her father or not.

Clara nodded. 'I don't want to get the children into trouble with their father. Maybe she won't even pass it on to him, but I had to at least try. You see that, don't you?'

Patrin nodded. 'Of course I do. For the time being you must stop worrying about the children. There's nothing that can be done, it's all out of your control.'

He was right, of course.

'Have you spoken to Flori as yet?' Clara asked, taking her mind off of the three souls.

'That's the other thing I was going to tell you. She's fine about meeting Mrs Montgomery but she says she doesn't think she could be her mother as Ma and Da never said anything about her being found on a church step. She knows all about the elderly lady who took in her, mind.'

'Ah well, at least it might give comfort to both just to speak to one another as they have something in common…' Clara's voice drifted off into almost nothingness, feeling a little deflated as she'd hoped she had found the baby Mrs Montgomery had abandoned so many years ago.

'You may be right, but I won't hold my breath that this meeting will be the answer to their prayers.'

'There's just one thing that I don't understand though, Patrin?'

He raised a brow.

'If Flori doesn't have gypsy blood flowing through her veins, how is she so good at fortune-telling?'

'I don't know to be honest. She might have the gift anyhow, I suppose. You don't have to be a gypsy to be a seer and forecast what's to come in the future.'

'I suppose not. She told me a few things that seem to be coming true,' Clara admitted. She had been thinking on this ever since her return to the cottage, Flori's words swirling in her mind.

'Such as?'

'She had mentioned that there was a young woman who might cause me harm. That must have been Susannah. I didn't heed her warning as I didn't connect it with anyone at the big house.'

He nodded. 'Well she has done you harm in a way, but I still blame his lordship. He didn't give you a chance to explain a thing to him before turning you out.'

Clara sighed. 'He's so used to dismissing governesses that I suppose it's become a way of life for him,' she said in a scornful manner, but deep inside she felt a sharp pang of regret. Whatever scheming Susannah had dished out to cause trouble for her, there was no getting away from the fact it all boiled down to Lord Howard Stapleton doubting Clara's intentions in the first place. He hadn't even given her a voice to appeal, never mind a fair hearing.

'So, when is Flori going to meet Mrs Montgomery then?' Clara asked, careful not to refer to the housekeeper as the girl's mother after Flori's reservations.

'I'm going to take her to the big house tomorrow. I've told Mrs Montgomery there's a young lady who would like to speak to her and she's agreed to it.'

'You didn't say what it was about then?'

'Er, no. I think she thinks the young woman is after a position at the house. I don't want her to get her hopes up too soon.'

'That's probably the best idea,' Clara agreed.

'You know, Flori told me something quite amazing though,' Patrin divulged. ' Ma had told her that the old woman had found her wrapped in a crocheted blanket that was edged with a fancy silver thread. It was most unusual. Over time it had yellowed with age but it's still distinctive. There can't be that many of them around.'

Clara raised her brow in surprise. 'Does Flori still have it?'

'Yes, she does. She said the old lady wanted to keep it, probably to sell on to make some money for herself, but Ma wasn't daft and persuaded her to hand it over.'

'That's something to go by then,' Clara said, brightening up a little. 'If Mrs Montgomery wrapped her child in a shawl like that then surely she will remember.'

Chapter Seventeen

Clara busied herself over the following few days helping her mother with her dressmaking, fiddling around with pins and hems and taking in darts here and there. The main pièce de résistance was the bridal dress for Mrs Pettigrew's daughter – Clara thought it was a masterpiece. Lillibeth was due to come to the cottage for a final fitting before the big day. But as well as *the* dress, there were other dressmaking orders waiting to be finished off and delivered around the village. Mama had been so busy of late that they'd had fewer callers, so it was quite out of the blue when there was a knock at the cottage door one day at a quarter past three in the afternoon.

'Are you expecting Lillibeth for a fitting today, Mama?' Clara asked.

Mama vigorously shook her head. 'No, I'm not. Perhaps it's someone with a request for me to do some work for them, but as you can see we're up to our eyes in it at the moment.'

Clara nodded, understanding all too well how overworked and tired her mother was of late. Muttering to herself, she went off to answer the door and intended to turn whoever it was away for time being, but she was in for a shock for there, outside, was a gleaming black coach. Stood beside it was Lord Stapleton himself, smartly attired in a black frock coat with a silver-grey cravat.

He's come to tell me off for giving my address to the children! was Clara's immediate thought, but then he smiled at her.

'I've come to apologise if I may,' he said, removing his shiny top hat.

She hitched a breath, feeling her heart beat like a drum. 'Apologise, Lord Stapleton? Whatever for?' She was mocking him and she guessed he realised it.

'For sending you away as I did.' He began to walk towards her, pausing inches away. 'You had been doing a good job as governess to my children and had even managed to get through to Amelia from what Danielle has told me, but I was very harsh towards you,' he admitted.

'You were?' She raised her brow, enjoying her tone of sarcasm. 'How, pray?'

He cleared his throat. 'Because I made an immediate judgement based on what I thought to be the case and what I felt about Miss Chamberlain.'

Clara frowned for a moment, wondering who Miss Chamberlain was. Then she realised he was speaking about Susannah. She let out a breath of resignation. 'You did?'

He shook his head. 'I know I've wronged you, but I've since discovered that she led you to believe my wife's dress belonged to her. I know you did not put that dress on as a deliberate act to provoke me. It's just—'

'It's just what?' Clara could hear the pain in his voice and realised how hard it must be for him to arrive at her door to apologise. The great Lord Stapleton himself, acting ever so humble in front of her.

'It's just that you looked so much like Arabella in that dress and in the way your hair was styled that your image staggered me somewhat.'

'So, my hairstyle that evening was the same as your late wife's?' Clara asked, incredulous that Susannah had gone to so much trouble to make her look like Lady Arabella.

'Exactly like hers. The maid who styled your hair is the one who used to style my wife's, and Susannah knew that.'

'How calculating of her,' Clara said through gritted teeth. Oh, she'd felt angry in the days after she had been dismissed, but hearing this from the lord's lips himself was astonishing.

'Precisely. When I'd found out the full extent of her behaviour and how she planned to orchestrate your dismissal to try to secure myself and my fortune, I banished her from the house. I've been so blind. The children never took to her at all and that should have told me something as they are very good judges of character.' He smiled broadly at her and she found herself returning the smile.

'You're not wrong there.'

'So, please would you return to us? I found out from James that you'd been to visit them as you were so concerned, and then last night the girls asked if they might write to you. I told them we could do better than that and that I was going to apologise and bring you back home with me.'

Clara felt her cheeks grow hot. It was almost as though he were claiming her for himself. She didn't know if she liked it or not, but still she'd be a fool to turn the man down when she not only needed the money for her family but wanted to return to the children out of a sense of love and duty. Looking him squarely in the eyes and with her head held high, she said, 'I'll return, but on a number of conditions.'

'Name them,' he said.

'Firstly, that you allow fun and laughter for those children. I'd like to play the piano to them and allow them to sing and dance. Number two, I'd like you to allow Amelia to visit the horse in the stables whenever she likes, as long it's not during class time. Number three, you allow James to have a pet. He's been asking for a puppy or a kitten for some time. Number four, you purchase the complete set of Dickens works for Danielle as he's her favourite author.' She paused for a moment as if thinking things through. 'And number five, you allow me one week before returning so I can help my mother to finish off her current dressmaking orders.' She held her breath in expectation.

'Granted as you wish!' he declared. 'I have been wrong to stop the children enjoying themselves, and I can see that now. I have spent too much time away from the family home. All of that is about to change from this very moment,' he promised.

She let out a long breath of relief and wondered what had caused his change of heart. *Maybe there would be time to ask him later*, she thought. But for time being, she welcomed this new side to the lord.

'Thank you,' was all she managed to say. He nodded and replaced his top hat on his head before retreating towards the coach, swinging his gold-tipped cane and whistling a song she did not recognise. She guessed he was off to attend to business somewhere or other, but right now she was just happy to know all would be well from here on in.

***

Clara hadn't heard anything from Patrin and she was beginning to wonder what had happened between Flori and Mrs Montgomery. Had they discovered that they were mother and daughter after all or was it simply a case of wishful thinking and the woman knew nothing whatsoever about the beautiful shawl Flori had been wrapped in when she was discovered? She decided to stop fretting about things she could not control and so she busied herself helping Mama with the upcoming orders.

Eventually, Lillibeth Pettigrew and her mother arrived at the cottage for a final fitting of the wedding gown. From the way she appraised the cottage, Clara got the distinct impression that Mrs Pettigrew was looking down upon them for their financial circumstances changing so drastically. Previously, she might have considered them the same class as herself but as they gathered in the small bedroom and Lillibeth stood gazing at her reflection in the long oval mirror, Mrs Pettigrew's eyes were everywhere. Mama kept the cottage spotless so she'd have no cause to complain there, but Clara could tell by the gleam in the woman's eyes that she now considered herself to be a superior class of person and would probably waste no time telling her cronies as much.

'So, you're now working as a servant at Stapleton Manor, are you?' the woman said, addressing Clara as if to pull her down a peg or two. *Maybe she's never forgiven me for that incident at the post office.*

'Oh, she's not a servant,' Mama said proudly. 'She's a governess to Lord Stapleton's children. In fact, he called around in his coach to see her just the other day.'

Mrs Pettigrew sniffed loudly. 'I see,' she said, then changing the subject she gazed at her daughter. 'Does the dress feel comfortable, Lillibeth? Speak up now for goodness sake as we're not coming back *here* again,' she said tersely. Clara was in no mood for the woman's delusions of grandeur, but her daughter was affable enough and seemed to love the dress Mama had created.

Lillibeth turned around to face them all. 'Yes, it's simply beautiful and far better than I'd ever imagined it would be. Thank you, Mrs Masters.' She lowered her head to kiss Mama on the cheek, causing Mrs Pettigrew to recoil in horror. She wasn't a woman for great shows of affection and now the Masters had gone down in the world, she would surely hate to think of her daughter kissing one of them.

When Lillibeth had changed out of her gown, Clara carefully folded it and wrapped it in tissue paper, a covering of brown paper and finally tied it neatly with string. Then she and Mama watched as Mrs Pettigrew and Lillibeth walked up the path towards their awaiting coach.

'She won't be back again by the seem of it,' Clara said as she draped an arm around her mother. They watched the coach depart with Lillibeth waving from the window while her mother stared ahead.

'I don't much care if she never darkens my doorstep again, but you're wrong about that. She will return as now she loves the fact she can lord it over me and gossip with all her cronies. It's a sad fact of life I'm afraid.'

'What is, Mama?'

'That the worse sort of class are those that previously didn't have much but have risen above the ranks, as it were.'

Clara frowned, not understanding what her mother meant by that. 'Pardon?'

Mama sighed. 'Well, Mrs Pettigrew came from very humble beginnings. She was from a large family where there were lots of hand-me-downs and her father fought to put food on the table for them all.'

'What happened to change her circumstances?'

'She married well. She worked at the flour mill at Crownley and caught the eye of the youngest son who fell for her. He even fell out with his family over her, but he was a man of means. He wanted to marry her against his father's wishes. He left the mill over it and took up baking instead.'

Clara let out a long breath of disbelief. 'Who would have thought it?'

***

When Clara returned to Stapleton Manor, the first thing she did was go in search of Cook. The woman had her hands in a bowl of flour and appeared to be scolding Maggie about something or other.

'Hurry up, gal!' she shouted. 'I've got all this baking to do and all you're doing is staring into space! Go and get those buns out of the oven.'

Clara smiled. It was nice to see that some things never changed. Maggie sighed behind Cook's back and looking heavenward, moved off to attend to the buns in the oven. Suddenly, Cook turned as if she was aware that someone was watching her.

'Oh, my giddy aunt!' she said smiling as she walked towards Clara with her hands covered in flour. She wiped them on her pinafore. 'So, you're back for good, gal?'

Clara nodded. 'I am indeed.'

'Nasty business that were. The lord told us what went on with that Susannah one and he also told all the staff he wrongly dismissed you.'

'He did?' Clara arched an eyebrow, realising it couldn't have been easy for the man to summon his staff to tell them that. He'd certainly gone up in her estimation.

'Yes, he was most regretful about it all he was, bless him. Look, I'll just wash me hands and we'll have a cuppa. I need to let that pastry rest in the pantry anyhow.'

Clara nodded gratefully. It would be lovely to catch up with Cook and hear the latest news of the goings-on at Stapleton Manor.

They both settled themselves down in front of the fire while Cook sent Maggie to brew up for them.

'I'm worried about that girl,' she said, scratching her chin.

'What do you mean?'

'Her head is elsewhere lately. It's like there's something she doesn't want the rest of us privy to. She often seems to be staring into space like she's daydreaming about something or other. It's all very well, but when I need her to work I don't want to have to keep cracking the whip.'

Come to think of it she had noticed Maggie and Billy whispering to one another in the corridor earlier as she passed. Oh no! If the pair were sweet on one another then maybe one of them would be dismissed from the house, staff relations were frowned upon unless a couple was already married. She decided, for now, she would not mention what she'd seen to Cook but instead would warn Maggie. After all, look what happened to Mrs Montgomery back in the day. She decided she wouldn't risk telling the girl the housekeeper's sorry tale, instead she'd invent some faceless creature who got despoiled when working at another house when she fell in love with someone there. All Clara could do was warn the girl. It was up to her how she behaved after that. And from what she'd seen of young Billy lately, his ardour would be difficult to cool down.

'I suppose it's because she's young and full of hopes and dreams like we all were at that age,' Clara said knowledgeably.

'Young? When I was her age I'd been married for a couple of years and I already had a baby to tend to! I didn't have time to bloomin' idle about the place daydreaming all day long.'

'Maybe not,' Clara said lowering her voice as Maggie drew near to present them each with a cup of tea. She waited until the girl was out of earshot before adding, 'but cut the girl some slack for time being and I'll have a word with her. Would that be all right?'

Cook scowled, but then her features relaxed and she smiled again. 'Has anyone ever told you what a calming influence you have here?'

Clara had never thought of that before but she was secretly pleased that it seemed she had that effect on most people around the house.

They sat in an amicable silence together, Clara's mind running through the things she needed to do before she recommenced teaching the children. Jake had brought her and her belongings back to the house as she hadn't seen Patrin for a few days to ask him to do it instead.

She took a sip from her cup and set it down in the saucer on the small table by her side. 'Have you seen Patrin lately?'

'Haven't you heard?' Cook replied, looking quite surprised.

'Heard what?'

'He's left already. There was some sort of palaver the other evening and Mrs Montgomery left at the same time.'

Clara chewed on her bottom lip. 'Did they say where they were going?'

Cook shook her head and pursed her lips. 'No, they did not. It was most rude of Mrs Montgomery to go off like that without as much as a bye as you leave. The woman's gone and left us all in the lurch without a housekeeper now!'

Clara arched an eyebrow. 'Don't worry, Mrs Cantwell. I'll have a word with his lordship about it.'

'Well please see as you do, we can't carry on like this,' Cook said, gesturing to the kitchen.

Maybe Mrs Montgomery leaving in haste like that had something to do with Flori, Clara thought to herself as Cook harrumphed and returned to sipping her tea. She could hardly tell the staff of her suspicions though, but it was strange as she was sure Patrin had said he'd be bringing his sister to the house.

Clara forced a smile as she bid Cook goodbye, although she was now concerned about all three: Patrin, Flori, and Mrs Montgomery. Whatever could have gone on to make them all disappear without word so quickly? Still, she had other more pressing matters on her mind now, namely getting settled in once again and taking care of the children. The thought of those young ones brought a real smile to her lips as she walked along the corridor. Maybe his lordship wasn't so bad after all.

Chapter Eighteen

James was out of his desk chair and running towards Clara as soon as he saw her enter the classroom the next morning, Danielle and Amelia following suit. She hugged them all for a couple of minutes as they all wiped away their tears of happiness, but then it was strictly back to schoolwork for them.

Sniffing and wiping her tears with a clean cotton handkerchief, Clara smiled.

'Please take your seats now as we have a lot to catch up on today. Your first lesson will be Geography. James, please fetch the globe and Danielle the textbooks from my desk, will you?'

Both children nodded eagerly and Clara's eyes fell on Amelia.

'Are you all right?' she whispered to the girl.

Amelia slowly nodded but was quiet for the remainder of the morning. When the children were headed off for luncheon downstairs, Clara kept the girl back to speak to her for a moment.

'What's wrong?' she asked.

Amelia's china-blue eyes could not disguise the sadness within. 'It's Papa,' she said, 'he still hasn't allowed me to ride Gideon. I miss him so much.'

'Don't you worry about that. Your father made a firm commitment when he came to ask me to return here. One of the conditions I made was that you are allowed to visit the horse at the stables.'

Amelia nodded and smiled.

'In fact,' carried on Clara, 'I think we shall make it part of your lessons this afternoon to visit the stables.'

Amelia looked confused. 'How is that? What is there to learn?'

'Just leave that and your father to me,' Clara said firmly.

***

While the children were eating their midday meal, Clara went in search of their father whom she found in the drawing-room stood near the fireplace as if deep in thought.

'Excuse me, Lord Stapleton, but I think it's time Amelia was reunited with Gideon,' she said firmly, making eye contact with the man.

He looked thoughtful for a moment and then said, 'I'd prefer it if she weren't.'

'But whyever not?'

He held up a vertical palm. 'Because I can't risk it.'

'Risk what? I don't understand why you would keep your daughter away from the horse that she loves so much.'

'I … I don't wish to discuss this any further. You have been back here for less than one day and already you are making waves, young lady!' His eyes gleamed with something she thought might be pain, but she wasn't sure.

Clara wrung her hands in anguish as she looked at him for an explanation. She had promised Amelia she could see the horse and now he was turning down the request after agreeing to it on her mother's doorstep just the other week.

'But why? Please tell me your objection to my request and then I might understand. I thought you were a man of your word, my lord.'

He bit his bottom lip. 'Very well.' She thought she detected a catch in his voice. 'It's because my wife died due to a fall from that particular horse. I don't want that to happen to any of my children, I just couldn't bear it.'

She nodded. 'I understand now but please just let Amelia see Gideon at least? Allow the girl to spend some time with him, groom him and feed him. It will do wonders for her and help lift her spirit,' she said softly to appease him.

'I'll have to think about that,' he said gruffly.

'Well don't think on it too long as I'm taking the children to the stables and to see the other animals on your land after they've eaten their midday meal,' she said firmly.

Lord Stapleton looked taken aback for a moment as his mouth gaped open in surprise, then a small smile played upon his lips. 'You are determined when you want something, aren't you, Miss Masters?'

She smiled back at him. 'Yes, I am. That's something you'll learn about me, your lordship. I promise I'll just take them to see the animals and I won't allow Amelia to ride the horse as yet, just pet and groom him. The riding may come at a later point.'

He quirked a brow and nodded at her. 'Thank you for considering my feelings,' he said. 'And I am glad that you've returned to us after the shabby way I treated you. Will you please forgive me?'

'I think I can forgive you under the circumstances. That must have been quite a shock for you seeing me in your wife's gown. I honestly had not a clue and had been given the impression it was Susannah's.'

'I understand that now. Don't worry about that woman. She won't be darkening my door again.' He looked pensive for a moment as he rubbed his chin. 'Would you consider dining with me tonight?'

She smiled as she trembled inside. Her, dine alone with the lord?

'I'm not sure I ought to, given my position here at the house and protocol.'

'Stuff protocol!' he said heartily. 'I owe you another meal as that evening you dined here was disturbed. Think about it, will you?'

'I will if you'll consider allowing your daughter to ride her horse someday soon?'

'You drive a hard bargain, Miss Masters!' He said with a twinkle in his eyes.

Clara left the room with a smile on her face. The children were going to be so pleased.

***

As Clara and the children entered the stables, the smell of fresh hay mixed with shovelled manure permeated Clara's nostrils, causing her to gag slightly. She'd never had a horse of her own, but she knew how much Amelia had yearned for Gideon. The stable boy led them to the stall and Clara had never seen the girl so animated before, the sheer joy when she was faced with her horse brought tears to Clara's eyes.

'I've missed you so much, boy,' Amelia wept openly, then she opened her palm to offer the horse a sugar lump which he chewed. Amelia turned around to look at Clara. 'I'm sorry Miss Masters, I know sugar isn't good for his teeth, but I wanted to give him a treat. I'll bring an apple or something else next time.'

Clara smiled broadly at the girl and, nodding her approval, she turned to the stable boy who was only a little taller than Amelia.

'Would it be all right if you led Gideon out to the paddock? Miss Stapleton won't be riding today, just becoming reacquainted with her horse.'

The lad nodded vigorously and Clara noticed from the look he gave Amelia that it seemed he'd missed her as much as Gideon had, though of course his lordship would disapprove of such a union. *Still, it's innocent enough at their ages,* Clara thought.

They spent the next half-hour with Amelia walking Gideon around the paddock as Danielle and James were willing companions. They were excited as they were looking forward to feeding the ducks and goats on the land and Clara had promised them a picnic at the treehouse afterwards. They were well togged up for it as the weather was still a little chilly, but it was nice for them all to get out in the fresh air for a change, especially as they had a promise from Cook that she'd give them big steaming cups of hot chocolate and freshly baked currant buns when they returned.

**

The kitchen was in uproar later that afternoon.

'Yer never guess what, Clara!' Maggie said with great excitement in her eyes. The fading sun cast a shadow across the kitchen counters as Dilly set a tray of cakes on the cooling rack.

'I'll be the one to tell her!' Cook said sharply. *Where had she come from*, Clara wondered. She appeared to have entered via the back door, standing there with her normal ruddy face looking a faint shade of blue. 'Just wait until I warm me trotters by the fire,' she said. 'It's flamin' perishing outside, mind the French!'

Clara giggled.

'Maggie, go and make us some tea will you, there's a good girl – do something useful for once. Yer make a nice cuppa, I'll say that for you, gal!' Maggie nodded and smiled but Clara could tell Cook had taken the wind out of her sails as she was dying to let whatever news she had, slip out. 'Come and sit by the fire with me,' Cook said as she plonked herself down in her favourite armchair while Clara took the seat opposite to her. Whatever the news was, there was no mistaking the fact that Cook intended to get in there first.

She groaned loudly. 'That's better, I can feel the life coming back into me body,' she said. 'Now where was I?'

'You had something to tell me?' Clara arched an inquisitive brow.

'Oh yes. Well yer never guess what happened just not an hour since?'

'I've absolutely no idea,' she said in an amused fashion as she shook her head.

'Only that Mrs Montgomery has returned here with that gypsy lad, Patrin, claiming to have found her long lost daughter! I mean, I had heard rumours that maybe she had given a baby away years ago, but she admitted to me that she'd abandoned the child at a church door on a cold winter night as she was out of her mind at the time.'

'Yes, I know,' Clara said, looking intently into Cook's eyes.

'You knew and you never said anything?' Cook sounded most affronted.

'How could I tell you? She told me in confidence. Anyhow, so Flori, Patrin's sister, is Mrs Montgomery's child?'

'No,' Cook shook her head. 'Apparently it was thought the child was but the woman who had taken in Patrin's sister had also taken in another baby around the same time. That's why there was some confusion. You heard about the blanket with the silver thread?'

Clara nodded. 'But I still don't understand?'

'Flori had kept in touch with the old woman, Mrs Boddington, over the years, more so since her adoptive parents died. She and Patrin took Mrs Montgomery to visit the woman just this morning. It turns out that the other little girl is definitely Mrs Montgomery's child and arrangements are being made for them to be reunited. Mrs Montgomery had left a little ragdoll she had made by hand with her child the night she abandoned her, which the young woman still has! So there's no doubt she's the right baby. Though it seems strange to me that Mrs Boddington looked after abandoned babies like that. Maybe she was looking to sell them on or something.'

Clara realised that Cook might well have been right as she had heard of that sort of thing going on. But whatever the case may be, Mrs Boddington had experienced a change of heart. *Or maybe she had received recompense from the new parents of both infants* a little voice told Clara. At least she'd provided both babies with a roof over their heads. They might've ended up as wards of the parish otherwise, or even worse.

'Well, I never!' said Clara gasping. 'This is wonderful news. But what about Patrin? Is he back for good?'

Cook shook her head. 'No, he left almost as soon as he'd dropped the woman back here.'

A pang of sadness hit Clara full force. He hadn't left her a note to say he was leaving, even though he had warned her this day might come.

'Aw, don't take on so, Clara,' Cook said, noticing tears in Clara's eyes. 'The young man is a free spirit. He enjoys the gypsy way of life.'

Clara knew that Cook was right, but it still didn't stop the tears escaping from her eyes and coursing down both cheeks. The feeling she might never see him again fair nearly broke her heart.

***

Clara had composed herself by the time she was due to dine with Lord Stapleton, realising she just had to accept the fact that Patrin had moved on and it was his way of life. She let out a long sigh as she gazed at herself in the full-length mirror in her bedroom. Her cheeks which had been gaunt and pinched when she'd left the house had now filled out a little and were rosy, and her eyes sparkled once again. The dress she chose to wear was one her mother had skilfully made for her from a roll of cerise damask silk. Although she didn't feel quite as exquisite in this one as she had unwittingly in Lady Arabella's dress, at least she knew she still looked smart and ladylike. Maybe that's how she ought to appear to the lord: business-like instead of alluring.

As she entered the dining room with her heart beating out of her chest, she saw the lord stood there. His head whipped around as she entered the room. A broad smile spread across his face and he stepped forward to take both of her hands in his much larger ones.

'I'm so pleased that you're joining me tonight, Clara,' he enthused.

Could this be the same lord who not a month since had ordered her out of his house? It took a little getting used to.

She smiled back at him before saying, 'You know me, Lord Stapleton, I don't like to let anyone down, I'm trustworthy and honest,' she couldn't help saying, not to emphasise a point but more that he should have realised from the beginning that she would not be capable of game playing or deceitful behaviour. There was only one person capable of that and that person was Susannah.

He nodded and then led her to the table to seat her. He took the chair opposite.

'Cook has prepared something special on my request,' he said with a twinkle in his eyes.

Clara wondered what it could be? Maybe pheasant in red wine and juniper berry sauce or something a little less fussy, like beef wellington? But instead, she was surprised to find a silver salver with a lid placed on the table, that Maggie opened with a flourish to reveal a long salmon decorated with slices of cucumber to look like scales. The fish was garnished with swirls of duchesse potato and sprigs of parsley. It did look lovely, too nice to eat in fact. She looked up at him and giggled.

'We'd better not eat too much as this is just the first course,' he said. 'It's been my favourite since I was a young boy.'

She had to admit she couldn't imagine his lordship as a young lad.

'It does look very appetising,' she said, shaking out her napkin to place on her lap.

'Caught from the river that passes through the Stapleton Estate,' he proudly announced.

There was no denying the food was delicious, accompanied by the butler pouring white wine into fine cut crystal goblets. There was a different wine with each course and, not being used to drinking much alcohol, Clara's head was feeling quite light and she seemed to find most things the lord said amusing. By the time they arrived at the final course – a chocolate bombe with fresh cream – she thought she'd better slow down and asked Maggie if she could fetch her a pitcher of water and a fresh glass.

'I'm so sorry, Miss Masters,' the lord's face took on a sign of concern. 'I thought you'd enjoy the wine.'

'Oh, I am,' she said enthusiastically. 'It's just that I'm unused to drinking alcohol. Papa was the vicar of St Bartholomew's, so we didn't tend to have much in the house.'

He smiled. 'I'm sorry, I was forgetting. Please forgive my manners. Most of my guests here are well used to the stuff, especially Susannah.'

She set down her spoon and looked at him thoughtfully. 'What happened to her in the end? Was she always so spiteful?'

He shook his head. 'In all honesty, no, she wasn't. She used to be such a nice young lady, but I now realise she wanted to take the place of her cousin in this house.'

Clara frowned. 'You mean as your wife?'

'Precisely. To be honest with you, the way things were going it might have happened over time, but when I found out how she was so devious as to hurt you like that, I realised that no doubt she saw you as a rival for my affections and would stop at nothing to remove all opposition from her way.'

Clara arched an eyebrow. 'Really?'

'Yes, really.'

'But we have never thought of one another in that sense. You are my employer and I am your employee.'

Hesitation flashed across his face before he smiled. 'Precisely. But in Susannah's eyes, anyone who possessed an ounce of beauty was a rival for my affection. Sad, but true.' His eyes darkened for a moment. 'It wasn't just that though. The children did not take to her at all. Not like they took to you, Miss Masters. Look, may I call you Clara when we are alone together?'

She smiled and nodded. 'Yes, I'd like that.'

'Then you may call me Howard when no one else is around,' he said with a twinkle in his eye.

Her heart somersaulted and a warmth spread through her. *Maybe it's the wine*, she thought. *Perhaps it's not*, a little voice said in reply.

Chapter Nineteen

Soon dining together in the evenings was commonplace for Clara and Howard, and fast became the times of the day that Clara enjoyed most. She felt she could fully relax and speak to him about almost anything, and the whole situation reminded her of Flori's prophecy: *"There is a man you fear but he is not out to harm you. However, the young woman will…"* The man Flori had spoken of must surely be the lord himself, as there had been no doubt she had feared him when she first commenced duties at the house. That fear had only intensified when he had ordered her out of the house and off his property, which had caused her utter humiliation. And if Howard were the man, then the young woman who wanted to cause her harm was surely Susannah. A shiver passed over her as she thought about the trouble that young woman had caused for her. But now, Clara realised, there was nothing to fear from the lord.

'You look troubled, m'dear,' he said later that evening as they dined.

'Is it that obvious?'

He nodded and his grey-blue eyes took on a look of concern. He lowered his voice as he softly said, 'I'm afraid it is. We have come to know one another so well these past few weeks. Pray tell, what is it?' He blotted his mouth with the cotton napkin before him and set it down beside his half-eaten plate of food as if to listen intently to her response.

Clara let out a long breath. 'It's Patrin, Howard. He left here in such a hurry and now I have no idea where he is.'

The lord looked thoughtful for a moment. 'Ah, so that's who has been troubling you. I should have guessed.'

'I … it's not like you may suppose,' she said rather hurriedly, a faint bloom appearing on both cheeks.

'And how may I suppose?' he said as a smile danced across his lips. His lips were full-bodied and seemed to match his strong, deeply chiselled chin. Sometimes his features reminded her of one of the Greek gods she had once seen at a museum in London – statuesque and immobile.

'Patrin had become like a brother and watched out for me. It hurts that he left without even saying goodbye to me.' She paused for a moment to collect her thoughts as she fiddled about with her napkin as if it might somehow reveal the answer to her. Then she looked up.

'How did he leave here? In the same manner? Without any sort of farewell, in a clandestine sort of way?'

Howard looked deep into her eyes. 'Not at all. He gave me one week's notice and told me he was keen to be on the road and would be meeting up with relatives in a town which is about forty miles or so from here. He'd pick up more work there. I told him I'd been more than satisfied with his work here and any time he wished to return to ask to speak to me.'

She nodded as her heart ached. The thought that Patrin could be so frank with his employer but not with her – someone he'd once been so close to – cut deep inside.

Howard looked at her thoughtfully for a moment. 'You had feelings for him?'

She looked up at him and dabbed at her eyes with her cotton napkin. Thinking back to the first time she had laid eyes on Patrin in the woods to now, she said, 'Yes, but not in the way that you might imagine. In the short space of time that I knew Patrin, we had been through so much together. Remember when I couldn't attend the interview for the position of governess here so I turned up a day later?'

He nodded as a small smile played upon his lips. 'How could I forget? You helped to deliver a baby. That doesn't happen every day. You ought to be proud of yourself, Clara.'

'Maybe. Well afterwards the husband, who had been physically violent with his wife, snatched the child. It was Patrin who accompanied me to search for the baby in all that bad snowfall we had. He took his horse and cart and we went together and rescued the infant from the family's cottage at the top of a steep mountain in a terrible blizzard. If I'd not had help, who knows. I could have died of exposure if I'd gone alone and on foot. His horse is a shire horse, so very strong and capable.'

'Just like his owner.' The lord folded his hands on the table in front of him as he continued to look at Clara with great interest. 'But I have a feeling you are about to tell me more?'

She nodded. 'It wasn't just that though, he was helpful in other ways too, particularly when…' She looked up at him.

'Particularly when I threw you out of here?' he said as if reading her mind.

'Yes. Particularly then. He helped me move my belongings from Stapleton Manor and kept coming over to the family cottage to check on me even though he was quite busy himself. I shall never forget his kindness.'

'And neither should you,' Howard said softly. 'I know I did you a great disservice and I want to make that up to you, Clara. But what can I do? Anything?'

'Do you mean it?'

He nodded and closed his eyes briefly before opening them again. 'I do. Just name it. Anything.'

'Then the best thing you can do for me is something for the children. I am told this house once rang with laughter. There was lots of music and dance, and the children were allowed to put on plays even. Open it all up again! They have shared your grief and despair for months and it's just not fair on them. After all, it even said in your advert when seeking a governess for them that you wished for someone who showed an interest in dancing, singing and piano playing, so why am I not allowed to teach your children those things? I've already asked you once, but nothing's been done about it.'

He nodded slowly. 'You know something,' he said, swallowing hard, 'I think you're right. That was in the original advert, but I did not place it myself – Mrs Montgomery did.'

Clara's chin jutted out in defiance. 'Well, if you wish to keep this place like a mausoleum then you might just as well have buried your children along with your wife!' She stared at her half-eaten meal before her as tears pricked the back of her eyes. She could hardly believe the cruel words she had just spoken, unable to stop them tumbling from her mouth. She feared she had gone too far and had angered him.

'Look at me, Clara,' he said softly, and she returned his gaze to see he too had tears in his eyes. 'You are quite right, and no one has dared to speak to me like that before. No one. No one has had the gumption to, only you.'

He was on his feet and she found him standing beside her. He took her shaking hand in his and helped her to stand. They were inches away from one another when he took her in his arms. Then he was hugging her and they were both crying together: she for her father and he for his wife. Then he lifted her chin to look into her eyes and what she saw in his own set her heart alight as he brought his lips down to meet with hers.

***

As they held their passionate embrace it was as if time stood still. Clara was so thankful that the servants had already departed from the room, but of course if they hadn't then neither would have spoken to one another in such a manner and that kiss would not have taken place.

'I am sorry,' he said suddenly, breaking into her thoughts. 'I should not have done that. It was very ungentlemanly of me. I am your employer after all.'

She looked up at him and smiled. 'I have to admit that I liked it, but you did take me somewhat by surprise!'

He nodded. 'I know. I think I surprised myself. The truth is, Clara, I think I began to fall in love with you from the moment you breezed in to meet me, though I had not realised it at the time.'

'Love?' She swallowed hard, not expecting him to say those words to her. She had never had any sort of romantic liaison before, apart from admiring Patrin from afar in those woods a couple of years ago.

'Yes. Love,' he said taking her hands. 'Oh, my Clara, what is there to stop us from being together?'

Clara could think of a million things: the children, for one. They might be quite hurt about it all, and the servants would be disapproving. She supposed there might even be some jealousy towards her here at the house as she would be seen to have risen above her station. And then there was her own family. Oh, what would her mother think of this coupling? The more she considered it, the more pitfalls there seemed to be.

'But what about the children?' she asked finally.

Howard looked perplexed as his brow furrowed with confusion. 'The children? But what of them?'

'What of them indeed! They are the most important people in all of this and I should not want to hurt them.'

A smile played upon his lips. 'But the children love you, Clara. If you were to become my wife—'

'Then I would no longer be their governess but their stepmother!' she interrupted. 'Our relationship would not be the same at all. They would hate me then as I would have replaced their beloved Mama, don't you see?'

He shook his head as if that was not obvious to him at all, and then those tears which were threatening to spill earlier began to fall down her cheeks.

'I'm sorry,' she sniffed. She turned and fled the room, reminded of the day he had banished her from Stapleton Manor. But now the circumstances were entirely different. Now he wanted her forever in his life, and that she simply could not deal with.

***

Over the following few days, Clara avoided the lord and remained either within the confines of her quarters, in the schoolroom or out in the grounds visiting Amelia's horse. If the children realised something was wrong, they weren't saying so, so she assumed she was making a good job of disguising her sadness at the situation. Yes, she had decided she'd like nothing more than to be courted by Lord Howard Stapleton, but for everyone's sake that would not be wise. The lord no longer sent for her to join him in the dining room in the evenings and she kept well away from the kitchen staff too to avoid letting slip what happened, as surely they would ask questions as to why she was no longer his affable companion in the evenings.

Lord Howard Stapleton threw himself into his business world, rising early to go to London for meetings or sometimes staying late at the mill, checking with the foreman that all was going well. It seemed to Clara that it was the only way he could keep his mind from wandering onto the very thing that was occupying it – their liaison.

Clara no longer felt like singing and dancing with the children, even though she'd been given the go-ahead. Her heart was now not only grieving for the loss of her father and the absence of Patrin, but for the blossoming love she was feeling for Howard Stapleton. It seemed to be increasing each day, yet having spurned his advances there was nothing she could do about it. She should not have been left alone with the man without an escort of some kind, but it was deemed proper because the servants were usually hovering around during their meals, except for the night he had professed his love to her. That was most strange indeed. *Had he purposely dismissed them as he'd intended proposing to me?* she thought. Now she might never know his true intentions.

'Miss Masters?'

Clara turned after being jolted back to the present. James was tugging on the sleeve of her dress.

'What is it, James?' she asked, forcing a smile.

'I don't know where Australia is. I can't find it on the globe.'

Clara rose out of her chair and accompanied James back to his desk to look at the globe.

'There see, it's on the other side of the world to Great Britain on the globe,' she said as she spun it and then pointed to the country with her finger.

'Does that mean the people there are living upside down?' he quipped as he angled his head to one side with curiosity.

'No,' she giggled. It was the first time she'd found something amusing in almost a week. 'The people living in Australia are stood the right way up, but their seasons are the opposite to ours. When it's cold here in winter, it's hot and sunny in Australia,' she patiently explained.

Danielle was busy studying her book about the country, but Amelia shot her a strange glance.

'Anything the matter, Amelia?' Clara asked.

'Maybe I ought to ask you the same thing, miss?' Amelia pursed her lips.

Clara was taken aback. 'What do you mean?'

As if thinking better of it, Amelia muttered, 'Nothing, miss. Please forget I mentioned anything.'

Now the seed had been planted, it was apparent to Clara that the girl had picked up that something was wrong. *I wear my heart on my sleeve for the whole world to see,* Clara thought to herself.

Clara said no more on the matter. She helped the children with their school work and then sent them off for luncheon downstairs, breathing a sigh of relief as the schoolroom door banged shut behind the three of them. She began to collect in their exercise books so she might mark them, becoming startled as she heard the click-clack of a lady's shoes in the corridor outside. Peeping out of the glass window in the door, she glimpsed Mrs Montgomery headed her way. Oh no, that's all she needed to be told off about something or other. The woman rapped on the door and when Clara allowed her access, she smiled at her. She'd never seen her smile as broadly before.

'I've come to thank you for all you've done to help reunite me with my daughter, Miss Masters,' she said in a cheerful tone.

Clara found herself inviting the woman back to her quarters for a cup of coffee, and for the first time the pair got on like a house on fire. Why had she been so silly as to dismiss the woman in the first place? She'd simply been grieving for her lost child, and Clara knew all about grief and loss herself.

As they sat either side of the hearth staring into the flames of the fire, Mrs Montgomery said, 'What's wrong? You haven't been yourself for a couple of weeks.'

To Clara's horror, she found herself blurting out her secret about herself and the lord to the woman. She figured if anyone could keep a secret it was Mrs Montgomery as she'd kept her own for long enough. When she had finished speaking, the housekeeper handed her a clean handkerchief to blot her tears away.

'Well, would that be so bad for you and his lordship to marry, Clara?' Mrs Montgomery asked.

Clara sniffed and dabbed away at her eyes. 'Pardon?'

'You seem well suited to me and you would undoubtedly make an ideal mother for those children. You also come from a good background.'

'But what do I know about nobility?'

'About as much as Lady Arabella did, I suppose.'

'You mean she wasn't born into it either?' Clara raised her brows.

'Heavens no! Her father was a London lawyer. Well respected, yes, but noble, no.'

That put a whole new perspective on things for Clara. Why had she assumed that she needed to be of noble birth to marry the man, and why should the fact she was the children's governess hold her back? She already had an advantage that they had grown to like and trust her when they had never taken to Susannah at all. What if that awful woman – or someone like her – had become their mother?

Clara gulped. 'I'm afraid I have made a terrible mistake in rebuffing Lord Stapleton. He has only shown me kindness since I have returned.'

'Then you must tell him that, Clara. That is what you must do.'

Clara continued to stare into the flames of the fire, feeling for the first time that things were beginning to make sense at last.

Chapter Twenty

Clara waited in expectation for Lord Stapleton to return home that evening. While she bided her time, she found herself pacing up and down in her quarters like a lion in its cage, practising what she was going to say to the man. She must have paced between the living room and her bedchamber twenty times in all.

'Lord Stapleton.' She shook her head. 'Howard, I am so sorry to have doubted having a relationship with you ... No, that's no good. I don't know if I can say the words.' She took a seat at her escritoire and, dipping her pen in the inkwell, began to write just how she was feeling inside, the words coming from her heart. She blotted the paper and neatly folding it, slotted it into an envelope which she addressed to Lord Howard Stapleton Esq. She slipped the envelope into her dress pocket and decided to leave it on his bureau in the drawing-room. He would surely see it this evening when he came home as he often took a drink of brandy there before dinner.

She was on her way down the staircase when she heard a commotion in the hallway. Billy and some of the other servants seemed in a fluster and Mrs Montgomery was issuing out orders. 'Help him into the drawing-room!' she shouted.

Help who? Then Clara's eyes were drawn to the coach driver and footman who between them appeared to be assisting Lord Stapleton, flanking him either side and supporting him beneath his arms as if he were inebriated. Surely not?

'Be careful how you go, Jeffers,' she was saying to the coachman, 'we don't know if his lordship has broken something. I'll summon Dilly to fetch Doctor Alderman right away. He'll know what to do.'

It was beginning to sound serious and Clara's stomach flipped over with the anxiety of it all. She stood with her hand on the bannister of the staircase to steady herself. Mrs Montgomery glanced up at her and then hurried up the stairs towards her.

'Go back to your quarters, dear. This will be too upsetting for you,' she urged, putting a firm hand on Clara's shoulder.

Clara shook her head. 'No, please let me go to him.'

The housekeeper looked her in the eyes. 'That wouldn't be wise right now.' She lowered her voice for fear of being overheard. 'The best thing you can do is keep away for time being. The doctor has been summoned. If you should go to him right now the staff will guess your feelings towards him and you wouldn't want that now, would you?'

Clara shook her head as she realised the woman was speaking sense, then something occurred to her. 'What happened?'

Mrs Montgomery sniffed loudly. 'It appears that the coach veered out of control. Mr Jeffers says another coach and horses almost collided with his lordship's coach.'

Clara's heart began to race. 'I might be wrong here, but I believe Mr Jeffers was driving his lordship's coach a few months ago when he almost ran our cart off the road. It was horrible. It's my belief that maybe the man was intoxicated at the time.'

The housekeeper stiffened momentarily, causing Clara to wonder if she'd said the wrong thing to her. But then the woman said, 'You may have a point there as Billy has said much the same thing. His lordship should have fired the man a long time ago. Though it is not the time nor the place to discuss such matters. Return to your quarters and I'll keep you abreast of what's going on after the doctor calls here.'

Clara nodded before she turned and made her way shakily back up the stairs.

***

It was another hour or so before Mrs Montgomery knocked on Clara's door with the news that the lord was going to be all right. Doctor Alderman had said it was a simple case of concussion and just to watch that he didn't vomit or lapse into a state of unconsciousness. For that, someone would need to be by his bedside for the next day or so.

Clara blew out a breath of relief. 'Thank goodness for that,' she said, swallowing hard.

'There is one other thing,' the housekeeper said solemnly. 'The doctor noticed the odour of alcohol on Mr Jeffers' breath and has suggested we eject him from this house forthwith. Billy and the footman tried to get him to leave a few minutes since, but he won't. I've tried myself but to no avail. He's making such a fuss defending himself, shouting at the top of his voice and I don't wish to disturb his lordship only to cause him further distress.'

Clara's chin jutted out with determination. 'Then I must try myself,' she said, realising it was something she could do to make amends to Howard. If she hadn't snubbed his advances then maybe he wouldn't have been out on business as much as, after all, he had been settling down to a pattern of dining with her most evenings. She followed Mrs Montgomery down the stairs where an altercation between Mr Jeffers and Billy was in full swing, with the footman also removing his tunic and rolling up his shirt sleeves as if to prepare himself to wade in for a fight.

'Stop this at once!' Clara shouted from the foot of the stairs, causing all three heads to whip around in her direction. In her haste, she pushed past Mrs Montgomery. Then she stood in front of the men and she wagged her finger at Mr Jeffers.

'You almost caused a bad accident on the road for us a few months ago which I suspected was due to you consuming alcohol. I didn't have any proof then but from what the other staff have told me, I do now. Mr Jeffers, you sir are a liar!'

The man's eyes widened, clearly shocked that he was being shouted at and by a woman, no less. His mouth opened and it snapped shut again.

'I have not been drinking. Not the shhhhlightest drop has passhed my lipsssh,' he slurred, then hiccupped loudly.

Clara moved closer to him to check that it was indeed alcohol, rather than a concussion, that was causing his slurring. Immediately she could smell the pungent fumes, leaving her in no doubt.

'I suggest that you remove yourself from this property forthwith before his lordship fully recovers and throws you off his property himself.'

Mr Jeffers began to scuffle with Billy and the footman just as the front door burst open, a familiar voice declaring, 'It looks as if I have returned here just at the right time!'

***

All heads turned in Patrin's direction and he simply smiled.

'I would normally use the servant's entrance but the front door was ajar and I heard the commotion,' he explained. 'From what I can see and what I just overheard, Mr Jeffers needs ejecting from the property?'

When Clara had got over her surprise to see Patrin once again, she nodded.

'Yes, the man's intoxicated and he's caused a coach accident which has left his lordship concussed.'

'That's good enough for me,' said Patrin as he grabbed hold of the man, putting him in a headlock so that his bowler hat fell on the black and white floor. The man was unable to struggle as Patrin easily applied his strength to move the him out of the door. He returned ten minutes later after having ejected him from the grounds of Stapleton Manor with a stern warning of what he would do to him if he ever set foot on the property again.

Meanwhile, Clara made her way to the drawing-room to see to Howard. He was being attended to by Dilly when she arrived, who was holding a damp washcloth to his head as he lay reclining on the sofa. Clara gazed down at him and felt a swell of love for the man in her heart. Before this, she had been confused about her feelings for Patrin, but she was becoming ever surer that it was Howard she held the romantic sort of love for. There was no doubt that she was pleased to see Patrin once again, but it was Howard who needed her now.

'Thank you, Dilly,' she said. 'I'll take over now. If you could just fetch a couple of his lordship's pillows from his bed chamber and a warm blanket as well.'

Dilly stood. Then she nodded and dipped her knee in Clara's direction.

'And if you could then bring me a glass of milk and a cake or something as I have missed out on my evening meal. And a glass of water for his lordship,' Clara asked, realising she would need to take care of herself too if she were to sit up with Howard all night.

'Yes, miss.'

Howard began to stir and then groaned. 'Where am I?' he asked as he tried to pull himself into a sitting position as Dilly left the room.

Clara gently pushed him back down. 'You're in the drawing-room. I'm afraid you had an accident in the coach earlier. That's quite a bump on your head you have there.'

'I did?' His eyes darted around the room as if he was trying to make sense of everything.

'Try to stay where you are for now. Dilly has gone to fetch some pillows for you. You have been examined by the doctor.'

'I was? I have no memory of that.' He went to shake his head but Clara stilled him.

'Try to remain where you are or else that cold washcloth will end up on the floor,' she playfully scolded him, causing him to smile at her.

'I'm sorry. I'm not the best person to have as a patient, but I couldn't wish for a better nurse,' he said, taking her hand and planting a kiss upon it.

'Well, I intend to stay up with you to watch you all night long,' she said softly. 'There is one other thing to tell you … well, two actually.'

'Oh? Good or bad?'

'Both.'

'You'd better give me the bad news first.'

'Very well. The accident was caused by Mr Jeffers because he'd been drinking alcohol.'

'Really?'

'But surely you must have suspected something during the time the man has worked here? Remember that time your coach collided with the cart where I was a passenger? I suspected it then,' Clara explained.

'No, I hadn't realised. I am so sorry. I've been so wrapped up in my grief that if someone had told me the moon was made of green cheese, I'd have believed them.' He laughed and then touched his head and winced. 'And the good news?'

'Patrin has returned and ejected Mr Jeffers from the property.'

The lord looked thoughtful for a moment as he rubbed his chin as if in contemplation. 'Someone is happy then?' he said looking up at her doubtfully.

'Yes, but don't you worry about that. It is you I have strong feelings for, not Patrin.' It was then she realised what she had uttered out loud and she wondered whether she should have said those words or not.

'Oh, my dear,' he said softly as he sat himself up. It was clear he wanted to embrace her, but she made him lie down again.

'Please do not exert yourself,' she said, smiling. 'Our time will come. I am sorry I ran off when you revealed your feelings towards me that night, it was such a shock'

'I'm sorry about that.'

She shook her head. 'No, I meant it was more of a surprise.'

'If you want to know the truth, it was a surprise for me too,' he said as Dilly entered the room with two pillows and a folded blanket which she handed to Clara, oblivious to the tender moment she had interrupted.

Chapter Twenty-One

April, 1886

Until a new coach driver could be found, it was decided that Patrin would take over Mr Jeffers' duties, though he was not required in that capacity until his lordship regained his full health. Meanwhile, Clara was on hand when she wasn't teaching the children to help nurse him and keep his spirits up. Mrs Montgomery and a couple of the maids filled in for Clara when she wasn't available. The children were delighted to have their father so close at hand and they were told that they could call to see him in his quarters at any time. The only time they were refused entry was when the lord was asleep or when they needed to be at their desks. Clara thought it was wonderful to see the man rebuild his relationship with his children.

James had been keen to show his father the new toy boat that Patrin had whittled for him from a stray piece of driftwood. The boy was thoroughly delighted when his father asked him if he'd still like to have a puppy or kitten, with James choosing a puppy. Patrin promised his lordship that he'd bring one over from the Downing's farm the following day as their sheepdog, Bess, had given birth to a litter a few weeks back and they were seeking good homes for them. Danielle loved to read her father stories from her favourite books in the afternoons after her schooling, and Amelia regaled tales of Gideon from the stables. So all in all, it became a cosy family scene at Stapleton Manor and it warmed Clara's heart to witness it.

While Patrin awaited being summoned as a temporary coach driver, he continued to work in the grounds of the house as he had before and sometimes helped the new gamekeeper. Clara found him in the woods one afternoon, and glad of it she was too as she wanted to speak to him alone. There often seemed to be someone else around at the big house.

'I'm glad I caught you, Patrin,' she said as she watched him hammering a wooden fence post into the ground with a mallet.

He looked up and smiled at her and then stopped what he was doing. His tweed jacket was strung over a tree branch. Clearly the manual work he was doing made him warm, even though it was a chilly day. He brought his hand to his face to push back the peak of his cap so that he could see her properly.

'What brings you out here?' he smiled.

She hesitated, knowing she was going to have to tell him before he worked things out for himself. 'It's me and...'

He raised his brow in a quizzical fashion. 'You and who?'

'His lordship and myself.' She swallowed hard, not wishing to stumble upon her words. Clasping her hands and deliberating as she chewed on her bottom lip. 'We have grown close to one another of late and he would like to marry me.'

To her astonishment, Patrin turned his back on her as if he hadn't heard her say those words and began to hammer away at the post with even greater intensity.

'Patrin!' she raised her voice. 'Did you hear what I had to say to you?'

He dropped his mallet on the ground and turned towards her, avoiding eye contact. 'Aye, I heard,' he said in a short, clipped manner. 'What do you expect me to say?'

She stood there open-mouthed, hardly believing her ears. It wasn't that she expected a huge congratulations from him, more that he'd be pleased that she'd shared the news with him first. She hadn't even told her mother as yet. Only Mrs Montgomery had an inkling of what was going on and if it hadn't been for her wise advice, then none of it would happen anyhow.

'I-I thought you might be pleased for me. For us.'

He tossed his head and turned to face her properly before saying, 'My dear Clara, you are free to do as you see fit, but you are not a member of the aristocracy. Lord Stapleton is of a different class, a different ilk if you like.'

'And so are you!' She raised her voice at him, scaring herself as the wind picked up and made the leaves on the trees rustle around them, almost as if people were whispering.

'Aye, I'm a gypsy and make no mistake. Maybe you don't belong in my world either, not that I wouldn't want you in it mind. You need your inside emotions brought out by some man, that's for sure. You've lived a very tame life, Clara. Been told what to do for long enough.' He stepped forward, filling the space between them so she could smell his skin. Suddenly she was in his arms and his face was inches from her own, his lips hovering over hers. Then she heard a loud cracking sound as if someone had stepped on a twig, jolting her to her senses. She pushed Patrin away to release herself from his embrace, then she slapped him hard against his face. He recoiled backwards. Touching his jaw, he stood open-mouthed as he stared disbelievingly at her.

'How dare you make advances towards me!' she said, feeling most affronted. Yet, she couldn't deny that until the moment the twig snapped she might well have succumbed, carried along by the wave of passion that had welled up inside of her.

'You pack a powerful punch for one so gentle, my dear,' he said, rubbing his jaw. Then he turned back to his task in hand, lifting the mallet to bang once again at the wooden fence post as if nothing had happened at all.

She heard a rustle and saw a fox emerging from the bushes behind her. So that's what had made the snapping noise that had startled her. Thank goodness it had arrived at that moment and made her believe they were being watched, because if it hadn't then who knew what might have happened.

***

The following day the lord was on his feet once again and excitedly making plans. He wanted the children informed first about their upcoming engagement, but this all seemed to be going a little too fast for Clara. She was sure she loved him – despite what had almost happened with Patrin casting a small shadow of doubt in her mind – but felt there needed to be a period of courtship before the engagement. The thought that maybe Howard was just looking for a replacement mother for his children did flit through her head briefly, but as fast as she thought it she dismissed it.

She realised that her mother would have to be informed soon as gossip had a way of getting out of big houses. She would hate it if Mrs Pettigrew was the one to inform her; she seemed to know everyone as her husband was such a popular baker, often supplying the kitchen with bread and cakes if there was a special function on at the house. The staff would be informed soon enough of the engagement. Howard had said he'd like to throw the doors open for a big spring party as the last year had been a sad one, but now the light had come back on in his life after meeting and falling in love with her.

Patrin's words and actions had taken Clara aback. She had seen something in his eyes that she'd never seen before, and she wasn't quite certain whether it was love or lust. Maybe it was both. Whatever it was though, he posed an element of danger for her and she was best off keeping out of his way from now on.

***

On the Saturday afternoon of that week, when there was no school work for the children, they were summoned together in the drawing-room where their father stood beside Clara to tell them the news that they had fallen in love and that eventually she would become his wife.

Danielle and James seemed excited by the prospect, but Amelia just scowled. That was to be expected, Clara supposed. The girl had been hard to win over in the first place and being that little bit older she had much more understanding of the situation. But even so, she eventually forced a smile and said, 'I suppose you'll do.' She tossed back her curls. 'I had thought Papa was going to marry that dreadful Susannah!' Then the ice was broken as they all laughed in unison.

So now there was only Clara's family to inform before the staff would be told of the situation. The children were warned to keep it to themselves for time being, which they agreed to do. When the children had left the drawing-room to go to the treehouse to play, Howard looked at her thoughtfully.

'It's good to see you so happy, my dear,' he said with a smile. 'I'm putting that down partly to our engagement and partly because Patrin has returned here. I don't know how I ever managed without the man.'

Clara wished with all heart that he had not returned, but how could she possibly tell her husband-to-be what had transpired in the woods the other day? If he found out about how the man had been on the verge of kissing her, he would banish him from Stapleton Manor for good. No, it was best that no one knew for time being, not even Cook or Mrs Montgomery. She didn't want to burden either of them with her concerns. She forced a smile before saying, 'Precisely! I have never been happier.'

The truth was, she would have been happier if Patrin had not tried to kiss her, because now he had caused some confusion for her. Before that had happened, she hadn't been sure what her feelings for the man were. *But surely you have always felt something for him*, she thought. *Otherwise you would never have picked up that gold necklace, nor brought it with you to Stapleton Manor.* Why hadn't she given it as a gift to Emily or Meg instead?

'Now then,' Howard continued, 'when do you think we ought to tell your family the good news?'

She hesitated for a moment. 'How about Sunday afternoon?' she suggested.

'That sounds delightful,' he said, drawing near to her. She was aware of his masculinity although both knew that to act on any desires would be unacceptable until they were legally wed. 'I'll arrange for Mrs Montgomery to take care of the children while we visit your family.'

Clara nodded. 'Yes, I think we should go alone to break the news and maybe invite the children to meet my family soon thereafter,' she said, thinking to herself that it would be good for Meg and Edmund to meet the Stapleton children as they were similar ages. Of course they were of different backgrounds, but Clara's family was respectable and had, in previous years, more money than most in the village of Foxbridge. The only thorn in Clara's side who might ruin her future happiness was Patrin and his feelings towards her.

***

After Clara and her betrothed went to visit her family that Sunday afternoon and received their somewhat surprised but happy blessing, life began to settle down at the house. The staff weren't as surprised about the upcoming engagement as Clara thought they might have been as Cook explained to her that walls had ears in the big house and a couple of the staff had taken word back to the kitchen to say they thought the Lord had designs on her, even before she realised it herself. But all in all, everyone was pleased ... except for the one person whose blessing she wanted the most.

It was a week after announcing their upcoming engagement that Clara encountered Patrin again. This time he was far from being lustful for her, rather he was quite the opposite. She could see in his eyes that something had changed: they were cold towards her. When he had to speak to her his words sounded guarded, almost as though he were erring on the side of caution. She wished it were not so, but if she were to give him the slightest morsel of encouragement that could make him warm towards her once again. As a woman she knew full well what that could lead to, especially as she was not convinced that she would have pushed Patrin away had the fox not made itself heard.

***

It was a full month later when she discovered from Howard that Patrin would be taking some time off to work at the spring fair in Crownley. The spring fair attracted a lot of folk from neighbouring villages and beyond and it was to be held on the same ground where she first encountered him: the green common. *Was that only just last Christmas?* She could hardly believe it was so as it seemed so long ago now.

The upshot of it all, the lord explained to her, was that Patrin was going to set up his boxing booth again offering to take anyone on. The draw for excited young men was that they could win a purse of money which was rumoured to be five sovereigns, though where Patrin had obtained that sort of money from she wasn't sure for he could not have saved all that in the short time he worked for his lordship. Lord Stapleton recounted the tale of Patrin's intentions, *'I do not intend to lose! No one around these parts is capable of winning it! I am still the champion! The Gypsy King!'*

'So he sounded quite arrogant and boastful when he told you this?' she said in astonishment.

He chuckled. 'I suppose he has to be like that to prove his manhood, my dear.'

She shook her head. 'I hope all goes well for him.'

'You hope?' said Howard crossing his arms as he stood near the fireplace in the drawing-room. 'My dear Clara, you shall be there as a spectator sitting in the front seat alongside me to see that it happens.'

She cringed and closed her eyes. 'Oh, I couldn't possibly watch something like that.' The truth was, she could watch a boxing match, but not one that involved Patrin. Her heart hurt at the mere thought of him becoming injured.

'Very well. You don't have to come along, I just thought it would be a lovely afternoon out for us, that's all.'

'Can I say I'll think about it then? What else is going on at the fair this year?'

'All sorts of attractions, I'm told. Wandering minstrels, a sword eater, even a man who can swallow fire! Oh, and there'll be clowns there too. The children will love all of that. You can bring Meg and Edmund too.'

She found herself relenting as he spoke so enthusiastically. Indeed, he now seemed a far cry from the man she'd first encountered at the fair at Christmas. That man had been rambunctious in the way he'd shouted at that poor elderly fellow and tried to beat him across the shoulder blades with his walking cane. The poor beggar had only asked for money, but still, she reminded herself, Lord Howard Stapleton had been blinded by grief at the time. Since then she had not seen any sign of aggravation in his nature, apart from the time he'd banished her from his home, and even that she quite understood.

Chapter Twenty-Two

From her bedroom window, Clara could see Patrin running towards the woods. It was evident he was in training for his boxing booth sessions at the weekend. These days, he rarely came into the house except for the odd occasion when Cook called him in for a meal, but even then Clara guessed he was eating at unusual times to avoid bumping into her. She surmised that he must rise at the crack of dawn to eat before she had even risen from her bed, and maybe he ate very late at night when she was asleep too. Why and how did things end up this way? She felt sorrowful for their fall out, but what could she possibly have done about it? To relent to his passionate ardour would only have spelt out trouble for her. She couldn't be a gypsy wife – he had already warned her of that. So in her book he was being most unfair. He was only after some sort of romp with her that would leave her feeling cheap, demoralised and ashamed of herself. She could even end up in the family way from one foolish fling, like Mrs Montgomery did, with no father for her baby. It was only just occurring to Clara that maybe the housekeeper might never have been a Mrs at all, but a Miss who used the married title to give herself an air of respectability. After all, it was most unusual for a woman to be sat upon the shelf at her age. Still, the woman was now reunited with her child, Lorna, and she was most pleased for her.

As Clara gazed around her bedroom at the beautifully flocked ornamental wallpaper and matching chintz curtains, she thought it a strange feeling that soon she would be the mistress of all she surveyed. *Imagine me, the wife of a lord!* She began to hum softly to herself as she ran her hand over the soft coverlet that adorned her bed, wondering what she could wear to the spring fair at the weekend. She was taken up sharply as she heard a knock on the door. She patted down her hair and smoothed down the skirts of her dress.

'Please, enter!' she said loudly.

It was Dilly who stood by the door. These days the girl seemed to have come out of her shell and didn't keep her head lowered when she spoke. Cook reckoned it was Clara's influence – and leftovers – that had achieved this change, and since being reunited with her daughter, Mrs Montgomery had got off the girl's back too.

'Please, miss,' Dilly began, 'I was told to give you this.' She looked up and down the corridor outside in a surreptitious manner as if afraid of being seen by someone.

Seeing nothing at all in the girl's hands, Clara frowned in puzzlement.

'What is it you have for me, Dilly?' she asked.

The girl dipped her hand into her pinafore pocket to hand Clara a brown envelope.

'Patrin told me to give you this.'

Hearing his name made Clara's cheeks burn and her heart began to pound. Dilly was standing as if waiting for Clara to take the letter from her outstretched hand, read it and issue a reply. But instead Clara took it and said, 'Thank you, Dilly. That will be all, you may leave.'

Dilly dipped her knee, turned, and left the room.

When the girl had gone, Clara closed the door behind her and went to her escritoire to find her silver letter opener. She laid the envelope on the desk and slit it open, removing the white folded sheet of paper from inside. Inhaling deeply, she read:

My dearest Clara,

I am so sorry I upset you so much the other day. If you had any doubt about my feelings towards you in the past, you now know for certain what they are and that I honestly love you. However, as you are betrothed to someone whom you love, it is unfair of me to stake any claim whatsoever on you. The truth is I have loved you since that first time I saw you watching me in the woods. I think it's best now that I leave after the spring fair. I'll never forget you. I no longer expect you to think of me in the same way but please know this, I shall love you until my dying day.

Your loving servant,

Patrin

Salty tears streamed down her cheeks. *It hadn't just been a romp he had been after all those weeks ago.* Reading his words brought into sharp focus the feelings that had been circling her heart since the day in the forest. She had the urge to run to the woods after him, but how could she do so? She would upset so many people: Howard, his children, her own family and even the staff at Stapleton Manor. The wheel was already in motion. She loved Howard and could have a good life here, wanting for nothing ever again, but if she left with Patrin to follow the heart that she had been denying, then she might have a hard life and never see her family again. The wanderlust in Patrin would mean he would never settle down.

Is it possible to love two men at the same time but in altogether different ways?

Sadly, she took the letter and envelope over to the hearth and allowed them to fall into the flames of the fire. The flames glowed brightly, blackening the paper and destroying the very words that would surely hurt his lordship if he were ever to discover them. Although she'd have loved to have kept it and held the letter to her heart, she wisely realised it would be foolish to hang on to something that could do so much damage. Thank goodness Patrin had passed that letter to Dilly and not any of the other staff as questions could have been asked, particularly if it were intercepted by Cook or Mrs Montgomery. *Had someone seen him hand the letter to the girl?* She'd have to ask Dilly later what the circumstances of her receiving the letter were. If the girl asked, which she probably wouldn't do, she'd explain by telling a little white lie that it was a message that needed to be passed on to Patrin's sister, Flori.

It saddened Clara that she was wracked with deceit when just a short while ago her heart had been so light and carefree.

***

Preparations were being made for the engagement ball at Stapleton Manor. A firm of caterers had been booked as the many dignitaries and associates that had been invited were too much for Cook to cope with alone. A team of decorators was brought in to freshen up the paintwork in the ballroom, and several new paintings now hung there. The crystal chandeliers were taken down and cleaned in preparation and the expensive furniture waxed, polished, and moved around by the staff until Mrs Montgomery was quite satisfied with their placements.

'I've never seen such a palaver in all me life!' Cook moaned as she took her usual seat by the fireside in the kitchen. Clara sat opposite.

'I'm sorry, Mrs Cantwell. I didn't think the arrangements would have caused this much fuss and extra work for the staff, but it's what How— I mean his lordship wants.'

Cook sniffed loudly. She was never one for mincing her words. She sat forward in her rocking chair and stared at Clara which made her feel most uncomfortable. 'I'll tell you this much,' she said, wagging a finger in Clara's face before withdrawing it as if realising she shouldn't speak to the future lady of the house in such a manner.

'Just what is it you would like to say to me, Mrs Cantwell? I appreciate your honesty. Most of the staff have become quite sycophantic of late as if they're afraid to say anything to me unless it's praise or the extolling of his lordship's virtues. But you I know I can trust to tell the truth.'

Cook smiled and then her face changed to one of grave concern and she linked her fingers together almost as if in prayer.

'I am worried about you, Clara. People are talking about it not being a year since Lady Arabella has died and now his lordship wants to turn this house from a mausoleum into some sort of fairground circus!' She visibly relaxed having cast the weight of the words, and their meaning, off of her shoulders.

Clara's voice trembled. 'To be truthful, maybe it's my fault as I encouraged him to let there be music and singing in the house. I wanted the children to be able to enjoy themselves.'

Cook pursed her lips. 'This isn't about the children. Let them sing and dance and be young. It's just his lordship has gone from one extreme to the other and I'm concerned for you.' She lowered her voice to barely a whisper. 'I could lose my job for telling you this, but when Lady Arabella was alive, he wasn't a nice man at all.'

Clara startled in her seat, her spine becoming as stiff as a rod of iron. It was as if someone had thrown a bucket of ice-cold water over her as she waited to hear what Cook had to say next. 'In w-what sort of way?' she stammered.

'Some of the staff said they thought he was knocking his wife around. I saw some of the evidence with my own eyes. One morning she came down for breakfast and I noticed a purple bruise by the side of her eye and some on her wrists as if she had been restrained by someone. No amount of powder could cover that. It took some days for the bruises to fade and the swelling to subside. After breakfast that day, she remained in her room so that no one could see the evidence.'

Clara swallowed hard. 'Might something else have caused that though?'

Cook harrumphed. 'Well she tried to make out she had walked into something, but the marks on both wrists looked like someone's fingers had got at them and applied a great deal of pressure.' She shook her head vigorously.

Clara tried to make sense of it all, feeling quite uncomfortable with the way Cook was going on. Surely Howard couldn't be that cruel to his wife, could he? But then again, she had once seen him strike that old man with his cane. 'I'm sure Howard wouldn't have harmed a hair on Lady Arabella's head,' Clara said sharply.

Cook narrowed her eyelids. 'Are you that sure, Clara love?'

Clara nodded and swallowed hard. Then she rose from her chair to leave the warm kitchen so that Cook wouldn't see how upset she was by the woman's accusations. Clara would just have to have a word with Mrs Montgomery about it all. The woman had been at the house much longer than Cook and, unlike Cook, she had often been in close quarters with Lady Arabella.

***

Mrs Montgomery was most affronted when Clara found her in the linen cupboard taking an inventory.

'I'm not saying Mrs Cantwell is a liar,' the woman said, 'but she doesn't have the full facts.' She laid down her ledger and fountain pen on the shelf and closed the door behind them so not as to be overheard.

'What are the full facts then?' Clara wanted to know.

The housekeeper lowered her voice. 'It's like this you see, Lady Arabella had a mental illness after her last child.'

'James?'

'Oh no, there was another baby a few years after he was born. He passed away eighteen months ago. He was born full-term but lived only for a couple of weeks. Before that, the lady had been full of life, but after Benjamin died she became a shadow of her former self. She kept thinking she could hear his cries and even wandered out into the grounds at night in her nightdress in the perishing cold. Haunted, that woman was. His lordship was concerned so he brought his physician in who wanted her admitted to a lunatic asylum, but the lord refused and kept her locked away in her quarters. I was the only servant permitted to see the state she was in, so Cook nor any of the other staff had a clue about her condition except that once the gardener caught her barely clothed walking near the lake. It's my feeling she might well have intended to drown herself.'

'How awful,' Clara gasped, trying to take it all in. Why hadn't Howard told her any of this? 'But the marks on the lady's wrists, the bruising Cook mentioned to me?'

The housekeeper nodded. 'Sometimes the lady needed restraining for her own welfare as she was a danger to herself. The doctor called a couple of times a week to sedate her with some kind of injection. Don't know what it was but it used to knock her out for hours at a time, although she needed holding down to be sedated. She could be quite violent if opposed and his lordship was covered in bruises and scratches himself. Horrible it was.'

Clara thought it sounded shocking, but then again she supposed the doctor knew his own business and if the lady had been admitted to a secure asylum she might have even been confined to a padded cell and restrained for hours at a time in a straitjacket. *No, it was out of love and kindness that Howard had arranged for the doctor to sedate his wife,* she told herself.

'And then,' Mrs Montgomery continued, 'one day Lady Arabella went riding on her own. She'd managed to escape from the house. That was the day she died after falling from the horse. It was a sad day, and until you arrived at the house the sadness persisted. You have done wonders for his lordship and the children too,' Mrs Montgomery said approvingly. 'I should have a word with Mrs Cantwell and set her straight maybe.'

Clara nodded. 'Maybe. I'd hate the staff to assume the lord is someone who manhandled and mistreated his wife when he did no such thing. I knew a man who was like that once.'

'Did you?' the housekeeper arched her brow.

'Yes, but thankfully he's now a reformed character since his wife gave birth.'

Mrs Montgomery nodded. 'In my opinion, there are not many men who change, but maybe in that man's case he grew up a bit when his child was born.'

Clara hoped for Lottie McWhirter's sake and that of her child that she was right. Mama had informed her on her last visit home that Jethro McWhirter was now involved with The Temperance Movement to help him abstain from the evils of alcohol, so that sounded promising.

Feeling a little better now she decided to check what she could wear on Saturday to the fair.

Chapter Twenty-Three

The sun shone brightly on the morning of the fair and it did, indeed, feel like spring had finally emerged after a long and never-ending winter. Clara marvelled as the yellow heads of a host of daffodils danced in the sunlight and bowed in the breeze in the flower beds surrounding the ornamental fountain outside Stapleton Manor. The children were excited about attending the fair too as the Punch and Judy show would be there once again, along with some fairground rides they were longing to try. It was arranged that Mrs Montgomery should take charge of them while Clara and Lord Stapleton watch the boxing matches taking place inside the tent. The children had even managed to persuade the housekeeper to try a few sideshow attractions with them at the fairground. The woman seemed a different person these days since being reunited with her daughter and it was warming to see this reflected in how she treated those around her. Mama had decided not to attend the boxing matches. Although she was particularly fond of Patrin, she said she couldn't hold with any violence but she was more than happy for Meg and Edmund to attend the fair with Emily and Jake as long as they kept them well away from the boxing tent.

When Clara and Lord Stapleton arrived at the fair the place was already packed with people excitedly looking around at the various attractions. Squeals of delight and howls of laughter were carried along by the breeze and gentlemen and ladies of all classes were smartly dressed everywhere she turned. There were men in their straw boaters and ladies in Sunday best bonnets and pretty dresses, all surrounded by children clutching toys won from hoopla stalls, pin the donkey or the lucky dip tub: teddy bears and rag dolls, sailing boats and colourful spinning tops were the order of the afternoon.

Then Clara spotted the boxing tent with its candy-striped roof awning. To the side of it were Patrin's horse and his caravan. She took a steadying breath and then looked up at the man beside her. Howard looked most handsome this afternoon in his smart blazer and straw boater hat. He had also grown a thin twirled moustache which she felt suited him well. Oh, she did feel proud to be on his arm.

She turned, her attention attracted towards a stall that sold sewn garments like tea cosies and tray cloths, their colourful pastel ginghams and florals drawing her eyes. She wondered if her mother might like to run such a stall in the future. Clara had uncoupled herself from Howard's arm to inspect the stall more closely and, in the jostling of the crowd, could no longer see him. A young boy and girl ran past her, almost toppling her over. From behind, two strong arms steadied her. Assuming it was Howard at her side, she was about to smile but as she glanced up it felt as though her heart had ceased beating.

Patrin!

He smiled at her, looking unsure for the first time. 'You did get my letter?' he asked.

He was wearing his dressing gown and she guessed beneath it he wore a pair of boxing breeches and his chest would be bare, just like that first time she'd seen him strip washing himself in the woods and again the day Flori had told her fortune.

'Yes,' she said breathlessly. 'But for obvious reasons, I did not keep it.'

He nodded. 'I quite understand. You do realise that after this evening, I shall not be returning to Stapleton Manor so as to give you the chance to make a go of things with his lordship?'

She forced a smile when all she felt like was crying. 'Thank you.'

'That's how much I love you, Clara. I love you enough to let you go because I want you to be happy. Your happiness comes before my own.'

Hearing him say as much fair nearly broke her heart. He lightly touched her shoulder and gazed into her eyes.

'We both know it. I believe in my heart that you and I are soulmates. Maybe we're not destined to be together right now, but someday.' Then he turned, leaving her standing there with her eyes glistening as he walked towards the tent.

'Ah, there you are!' Howard said as he walked cheerfully towards her. 'I wondered where you'd got to. I just got talking to an old acquaintance at the beer tent.' Noticing her distress, he asked, 'Whatever's the matter?'

What could she possibly tell him that wouldn't break his heart? He was a good man, she was sure of that, but come this evening Patrin would have moved on and things would eventually become easier for her to bear.

'Oh, it's nothing,' she said, sniffing back a sob. 'I've just been speaking to a lady who told me she knew my father.'

He nodded and linked arms with her once more. 'I do understand,' he said, then he patted her hand. 'Now, we better make our way to the tent. I've managed – well, Patrin managed – to secure front row seats for us.'

Oh no, she was hoping that they'd be able to sit at the back so she hadn't been in any rush to get there, instead leaving the horde to go in first. As they drew near the tent's entrance, a man was collecting money and issuing tickets. Two men were trying to argue with him and as he sought to deal with them, Clara could feel the tension beginning to mount until finally they came to some sort of agreement, paying the man and stepping inside.

When it was their turn to be admitted, the man smiled and doffed his hat to her.

'Special guests at the front!' he said jovially, pointing in the direction of where they were to sit. Inside, most had already taken their seats to see the spectacle. There were many bobbing heads and chatter so that a loud thrum filled the place. Theirs were the last seats to be taken in the centre of the front row.

Patrin entered the ring. The bowler-hatted man beside him was jacketless in his shirt and fancy waistcoat, and he opened his arms to the crowd.

'He's the promoter,' Howard whispered to her.

'Hello, folks! Here we have the undefeated King of the Gypsies, Patrin Romanescu. This afternoon, this champion will take on as many of you men as possible. One at a time, of course. If he knocks you down, then you are to leave the ring. If he fails to knock you down and you knock him down, you win five sovereigns!'

The crowd whistled and cheered. The man glanced around the audience.

'Any takers, please?'

A middle-aged gentleman who looked old enough to be Patrin's father emerged from somewhere in the crowd and the man who had issued their tickets escorted him to the ring.

'Ah, I see we have the first contender!' the promotor shouted.

'That man has no chance,' Howard whispered to her and she nodded at him, for surely he was right. He even struggled to remove his jacket and roll up the sleeves of his shirt. Was he drunk?

Sure enough, the man did not last a minute before Patrin had knocked him to the floor. As the show went on, he knocked man after man to the canvas. Some were young and fit but not one of them could compete with him. It wasn't half as bad as Clara thought it was going to be until the man in the ring shouted, 'I see we have a final contender, folks! A last-minute entrant!'

All heads turned and Clara gasped as a familiar figure began to stride towards the ring with a cocksure expression upon his face.

Josiah Whitman!

People mumbled and Clara shot a sideways glance of suspicion at Howard.

'This just isn't fair,' she hissed.

The lord turned towards her and smiled and then, patting her hand, said, 'What isn't, my sweet?'

'Patrin having to fight Josiah Whitman. Look at the size of him! Not only that, Patrin has already fought with several men, he's exhausted.'

She looked on anxiously as Patrin stood expressionless in the ring. If he was worn out by it all then he was making a good job of hiding it. But the man had been on his feet constantly for the past half-hour or more. One or two of the men who came to challenge him were evidently too old, unfit, or even inebriated, but he had sparred with a couple who had stood their ground for some time. Those ones hadn't made it easy for him.

Clara's mind flashed back to the day when she had lost sight of Meg and Edmund at the fair at Christmas, when Josiah had led them both away to the stall to show off his prowess. The man had angered Patrin so much at the time, especially as he'd offered to take him on in a boxing match the following day that the weather had put paid to. Now it seemed that Josiah was here to go through with what he'd promised back then.

As Josiah stepped into the ring, Clara turned her head in towards Howard's chest, causing him to look at her in an odd fashion as she closed her eyes with fear.

'What's going on here, Clara? You're not frightened? It's only a game, a bit of showmanship!' he chuckled.

'No, it's more than that. These two dislike one another. There was a standoff last Christmas between them because Josiah had led my brother and sister away from safety to show off his strength. I didn't know where they'd got to and became sick with worry. He's a bad man,' she said as she opened her eyes.

The lord's laughter ceased as he straightened up in his seat, causing Clara to remove her head from his chest and sit up herself. 'I'm sorry,' he said, taking her hand in his. 'I didn't realise that. But you mustn't worry. At least everyone can see for themselves what's going on here. There can be no underhand dealings or nasty tricks in front of this audience and the promoter.'

She nodded. She supposed Howard was right about that.

A loud cheer went around the tent as the men began to spar with one another, with a punch landed here and there. Thankfully Patrin was still quite light on his feet as he danced around Josiah, but the man was a powerhouse of strength and his strong right hook was not to be dismissed. The mood of the audience picked up as the match went one round, then two, three and eventually seven rounds. Patrin was now showing signs of tiredness but he wouldn't concede defeat even though Josiah had punched him in the face several times, causing the skin to split beneath his cheekbone. Even the promoter was beginning to look concerned and in between rounds he whispered something in Patrin's ear, to which Patrin shook his head. Clara watched as the promoter shrugged and then dipped a towel in a bucket of water and wiped down Patrin's brow. He was perspiring profusely as a steady stream of blood began to trickle down his face.

'This should be stopped!' Clara said angrily as she made to rise from her chair, feeling she could no longer watch the whole debacle. But it was too late. Josiah brought his right fist up into an uppercut punch just beneath Patrin's jaw, sending him flying through the air so that he landed flat on his back. The referee began to count to ten, but by the time he reached it Patrin still lay there motionless. Reluctantly, the promoter raised Josiah's arm and declared him the winner as most of the crowd cheered loudly.

'But he's not getting up!' Clara shouted and Howard looked on in horror as she pushed past him to rush towards the ring. No one else seemed concerned until the promoter knelt and began to slap Patrin's face. There was no response. The promotor looked at the crowd aghast as the cheering subsided, some of the onlookers now realising something wasn't right.

'Is there a doctor out there?' he shouted in panic as a smartly dressed young man began to rush towards the ring, many in the crowd still unaware of what was going on. Clara lifted her skirts to climb into the ring, not caring whether it was unladylike. She knelt beside Patrin and stroked his head.

The doctor put two fingers to Patrin's neck and looked up at the promoter.

'I'm afraid there's no sign of life here.'

Clara's heart plummeted. Numbly she moved out of the way as the doctor tried to resuscitate the lifeless form before him to no avail.

While all of this was going on, Josiah's voice echoed around the tent. 'Well, where's my money then?' he said cockily as he towered over Clara.

Clara looked at him, bringing herself to her feet and fiercely jabbing him in the chest with her index finger. 'This is your fault! You've killed him! Get out of here right now!' she yelled at him as the crowd began to hum with anger. Josiah gave her a lingering look before turning to flee the ring, the crowd parting.

Everything became a blur as she knelt beside Patrin, tears streaming down both cheeks and dripping onto his extinct form. Looking into his lifeless face, the tent began to blur and she became aware of two strong hands supporting her.

'Patrin,' she whispered, thinking for a moment it was him. But when she looked up at the man's face, it was Howard who was comforting her, hugging her close to him and wiping away her tears.

Chapter Twenty-Four

When Clara came to, she found herself inside his lordship's coach headed for home.

'I'm so sorry,' she groaned, straightening herself up as the coached rattled along the ruts in the road. 'What happened to me?'

Howard smiled at her from the opposite seat, but it did not reach his eyes. 'You fainted for a while back there. I was quite concerned about you.'

'Back where?'

'At the boxing tent. Don't you remember?'

She puzzled about it for a moment. What had she been doing in a boxing tent? Her mind was hazy.

'We were watching Patrin challenging some contenders for his title,' Howard coaxed.

All at once, flashing images ran through her mind like a magic lantern show. Patrin sparring in the ring, Patrin knocking someone over with his fist and Patrin——

'Oh no!' she cried out. 'He's gone, hasn't he? I thought I'd just had a bad dream.'

'There, there,' said Howard as he moved from his seat to sit beside her and take her hand in his. 'I'm afraid he has, and you were right, my dear. That last fight should never have been allowed. The young man was too exhausted and that big brute too powerful for him.'

She began to sob uncontrollably, so much so that by the time they reached the house she had to be put to bed to rest.

***

Hearing hushed voices outside her bedroom door, she sat bolt upright. What were they saying? It was Howard's voice she could hear most clearly and another she thought she recognised. Was that his doctor he was speaking to?

'But I don't want her admitted anywhere, she's in shock. Can't you just give her a pill or some medicine?' she heard Howard saying.

'Yes, we can try that in the first instance,' the man who she thought might be a doctor replied.

Eventually, there was a knock on the door and Howard entered with Doctor Alderman behind him.

'I've brought the doctor to examine you, Clara,' he spoke softly.

'B-but I've only been here for a couple of hours,' she protested.

Howard and the doctor exchanged curious glances with one another. Howard drew close and sat on the bed beside her, taking her hand. 'No, my dear. You've been in your quarters for two whole days.'

Two whole days! She was mortified. *How could that have happened?*

'Grief can do that to people,' the doctor explained. 'Our feelings numb and all sense of time can fly out the window. Don't you remember me examining you the day before yesterday?'

She shook her head.

'I think you are suffering from a form of melancholia at the loss of your friend. I understand your father passed away almost a year ago, and maybe your friend's death has triggered something in you. It might all have been too much for you to handle right now. It would be a good thing if you had a complete change of scenery for a while,' the doctor said, looking at her to gauge her response. 'I can give you some medication to help you if you wish, but my way of thinking is that you need to acknowledge your grief, Clara. Go somewhere peaceful where you won't be disturbed too much.'

'How about I send you on a trip overseas somewhere? At my expense of course,' Howard suggested, causing Doctor Alderman to frown. He looked at the man. 'You don't think it a good idea then, Maxwell?'

Doctor Alderman shook his head. 'No, I do not. Miss Masters needs to go somewhere familiar where she feels safe. What about returning to your family home for a while?'

She smiled at him but realised in the circumstances that would be useless.

'I'm afraid they are living in a small cottage now. I wouldn't get much peace there.'

'Can you think of somewhere else then?' the doctor continued.

She closed her eyes. 'I suppose I might stay with my Auntie Miriam. She's my mother's sister and she lives alone on a lovely property that has plenty of land. It's very secluded and quiet.'

'Perfect!' said the doctor. 'Then that's what you need to do for time being. Maybe for a month or so. I can give you a tonic to take with you if you would like? To help build up your strength.'

She nodded. 'Thank you, Doctor.'

'A month, Maxwell?' Clara heard Howard ask when they had departed from her room.

'Yes.'

'But can't I just visit her now and again?'

'No,' said Doctor Alderman in a firm tone. 'If she is to return to you in mind as well as body, she needs peace and quiet and most important of all, rest.' He lowered his voice as she strained to listen. 'I know from what you told me she had deep feelings for the man who died and he for her, but you won't do yourself any favours by crowding her. She has experienced a great shock, her friend dying like that in such tragic circumstances.'

It sounded as if Howard was now whispering and she could hear no more of what the men spoke. Soon she heard them walk away down the corridor, their voices level and talking of mundane, everyday things.

So, it had been clear to Howard that Patrin had meant so much to her. The very thought of him and their relationship brought her to tears again as her shoulders wracked with sorrow. Burying her head in the pillow, she wept until she drifted off to sleep once more.

When she awoke, she wondered what day it was. It appeared to be morning time as the sun streamed in through the bedroom curtains. She wondered for a moment if the doctor had returned to inject her with something during the night when she'd fallen asleep. As she sat up in her bed, Dilly knocked on her door and entered with a tray of breakfast for her. She asked the girl what day and date it was to discover it was only the following day.

Later, it was arranged for the lord's coach to take her to her Aunt Miriam's home in Stonebridge. On the doctor's advice, Howard said his farewell to her inside the house and did not accompany her on the journey.

'I am not saying goodbye to you, Clara,' he whispered softly in her ear. 'Just farewell for time being.'

She nodded with tears in her eyes. This time he did not passionately kiss her, he merely hugged her to him and dropped his lips to her forehead. He wished her good luck before stepping away and walking down the corridor, leaving her in Mrs Montgomery's capable hands to help her to the coach as the footman loaded up her luggage.

'This is so hard for his lordship,' Mrs Montgomery said as she stood outside the coach to wave Clara off. 'He doesn't want to let you go but knows that he must.'

Clara nodded. As the coach pulled away she waved a gloved hand at the woman. She hoped that time would play a big part in her recovery. She'd even have to miss Patrin's funeral as that would be taken over by his gypsy family anyhow whose culture it was to set fire to the deceased while their body was in the caravan. She couldn't help thinking about poor Flori though, and how she would miss her brother. But for now, Clara reckoned she was the one who missed him most. She knew that she had loved him with a passion she'd not felt for anyone else, and she realised that the lord knew it in his heart too.

***

Clara settled in well at Aunt Miriam's home but although the woman fussed around her and gave her space where necessary, her condition wasn't improving. If anything, it was getting worse. She'd wake at odd hours of the night, sometimes several times, and then when she finally drifted back to sleep it would be time to get up. Her appetite became poor too. When she wasn't crying about Patrin's death, she was sleeping for long periods during the day. Auntie became quite concerned about her niece and sent a message to Mama to visit.

Even Mama's warm embrace couldn't console Clara. Lord Stapleton tried to visit after a month as the doctor advised but Auntie had to explain the situation and send the man away again. Then he began writing letters but she had not the inclination nor the heart to read any of them, that final letter from Patrin still most prominent in her mind. Howard Stapleton was in despair and so were his children – they had lost a mother not so long ago and now to lose Clara as well was all too much for them to bear. Everyone seemed steeped in misery.

Auntie took it upon herself to consult her own doctor, who just smiled and said that the remedy was to allow enough time to pass. That didn't seem to calm Auntie who, in her concern that Clara might take it upon herself to do something foolish, hid all the sharp knives, pills and medicines in the home.

It seemed that nothing would remedy the situation, until news came in the form of an art class that was to take place in the chapel hall in Stonebridge. Auntie tried to persuade Clara to try it, remembering that she'd loved to paint and was forever sketching flowers and trees when she had been a little girl.

'It would do you good to get out and meet people,' Auntie encouraged. 'It's only for an hour or two a week…' her voice trailed off. Every time she had suggested something, Clara had declined as she said she just felt too exhausted and wouldn't be able to concentrate. But today with the midsummer sun shining brightly, something strange occurred. Clara agreed to go.

Not wishing to make too big a deal about it, Auntie smiled to herself. 'That's the spirit!' she said.

Clara's condition did not improve overnight, but the art classes kept her going and lifted her spirits. Auntie purchased some art materials from a little shop in Crownley and even on the days she didn't attend the class, Clara continued to sketch and paint at her aunt's home and around the area. It felt as if she were looking at things anew as she studied them in detail. How delicate the petals of a rose were, how fine were the wings of a butterfly, the light and shade of a room, the colour of the sky at various times of the day and night. She was learning to love life again. She also made one or two friends at the class and looked forward to seeing them to compare their handiwork and chat over a cup of tea at break time. Her purpose in life was being restored.

Chapter Twenty-Five

September, 1886

On Harvest Sunday, Clara began to attend church once again at St. Bartholomew's. It was strange to see a new vicar there in place of her father, the temporary vicar having now departed. Her family were so pleased that she'd taken it upon herself to join them as they'd missed her so much, particularly Meg and Edmund. Mama had explained a little of what had occurred to them: that Patrin had passed away and Clara had been so upset that she needed time away from everyone.

The vicar, Reverend William Matthews, began the service by saying, 'The land has yielded its harvest: God our God has blessed us. Psalm 67:6.'

Clara gazed at the long table to the side of him, laid with all sorts of fayre from the villagers: autumn apples and pears, potatoes, cauliflowers, green leafy cabbages, loaves baked into fancy shapes, a variety of pies and cakes which she guessed were from the Pettigrew bakery. There was an abundance and it was all to be distributed amongst the people most in need within the local community.

The organist struck the chords of the first hymn on the organ as the congregation sang "Come, Ye Thankful People, Come." The song lifted her heart and she smiled as she sang the words. It had always been a favourite of hers from her father's Harvest Sunday services.

After the service, Mama patted Clara's hand. 'Are you ready to return home now, Clara? We've all missed you so! Although it'll still have to be the settee, I'm afraid.'

Through tear-filled eyes, Clara nodded. Unaware of the importance of the gesture, all the congregation could see was a loving family, but she guessed they must have missed her empty place in the family pew on the Sundays since she had been at Stapleton Manor.

Mama had prepared a special meal of roast beef and vegetables and Clara's favourite dessert of Apple Charlotte for them all. Clara appreciated the effort that everyone had gone to for her. 'I don't deserve this,' she said as she seated herself at the table with them all and twisted her napkin in her hands.

'Stuff and nonsense! You've been ill. Now tuck in – you could do with some feeding up, my girl!' Mama urged.

Clara smiled. It was so good to be home. Jake had offered to pick up her belongings from Auntie's house the following morning. After so much peace and quiet, she almost welcomed being back together in their rowdy home, but she hadn't forgotten his lordship. She began to think of him as soon as she woke up in the mornings, and at various times of the day an image of him would flash through her mind. The children were painful to think of as she felt she'd let them down. And Howard too, for they may have been married by now if she hadn't allowed her grief to wrap around her like a blanket. She surmised he'd probably found a new governess for the children by now and was getting on with his life without her. Whenever she could she tried to put them all out of her mind.

***

She soon settled down back at the house and took great pleasure in helping Mama who, due to her arthritic fingers, was no longer making elaborate garments for customers but making easier items like tea cosies, tray cloths and oven mittens which, at Clara's suggestion, she and Emily sold at various market stalls. Oh how she enjoyed it and all, chatting to customers and extolling her mother's virtues as a seamstress.

Autumn soon gave way to winter and Emily announced that Jake had proposed to her. Clara and Mama were delighted by the news and Mama said she'd arrange for someone she knew to make the wedding dress. Seeing how happy Emily and Jake were gladdened Clara's heart, but at the same time made her question what she'd missed out on with his lordship.

It was one week before Christmas and Clara kept hearing Howard's voice whispering to her, repeating what he'd said to her the night they'd first kissed. *'The truth is Clara, I think I began to fall in love with you from the moment you first breezed in to meet me, though I had not realised it at the time…'*

The man had shown nothing but love and kindness towards her since he had asked her to return, and what had she shown him? How hurt he must have been when she'd run to that boxing ring and wept over Patrin's lifeless body. Then she'd buried herself in her grief as she blocked out the world, and him most of all. She now knew what she had to do.

The following day she wore her best cerise dress, donned her navy fur-lined cape and matching bonnet and took a hansom cab to

Stapleton Manor. After the driver had dropped her off, she stood outside the property for a moment, studying the big imposing building with its grand ornate gates and elaborate pillars. She did not feel intimated by the house as she had when she first arrived. Now it was a home.

She pulled on the bell cord to see Mr Snelgrove come limping towards her.

'Well, I didn't think I'd see you ever again, miss!' he said, doffing his cap at her and smiling broadly. What a difference to the first time she'd encountered him. Back then he'd seemed a bit crusty, but now he was genuinely pleased to see her.

He unlocked the gate to allow her entry, offering to escort her up the drive.

'No, thank you, Mr Snelgrove. This is something I need to do for myself.'

He watched in astonishment as she strode up the drive, hardly noticing the first snowflakes that had begun to fall and settle on her bonnet and the shoulders of her cape. She walked with extreme purpose towards the house and with each footfall she took her resolve became stronger.

What if his lordship were out on business? She pushed that thought out of her mind and instead of walking around to the servants' entrance, she walked straight up the main steps and rapped on the door.

It was a minute or two that she waited with bated breath as the door swung open and Mrs Montgomery stood there open-mouthed and blinking profusely. 'Clara!' she said. 'But please come inside, it's perishing cold out there. But what brings you here?'

A deep voice from behind the housekeeper said, 'I think she's here to see me!'

Clara felt a warm feeling inside as she looked in the direction of the voice. 'Yes, I am here to see you, your lordship.'

Mrs Montgomery took her bonnet and cape as Howard led her to the drawing-room with an uncertain smile on his face. He offered her to sit down in front of the fire to warm up a little, but she refused.

'Please hear what I have to say to you, and I'll sit down afterwards,' she said, wishing to get the words she had memorised out as quickly as possible.

He nodded. 'Please go ahead.'

'Dear Howard,' she said, 'I hope I'm not too late, but I've been somewhere else in my mind these last few months—'

'I thought I may have lost you forever,' he interrupted.

She drew beside him and took his hands in hers. Gazing up at him she said, 'No, you did not lose me. I lost myself. I know it may be too late for us as I drew away from you...'

He shook his head and put a finger to her lips. 'None of that matters, now you are here. All I want to ask you is, do you love me?'

He removed his finger from her lips to allow her to reply. She nodded as tears filled her eyes. 'Yes,' she whispered. 'I loved Patrin too, but not in the same way. He was the first man I had seen in that way, but it is you I have deep feelings for and I realised them by how much I've missed you of late.'

He nodded and then she was in his arms.

'I love you too, Clara,' he said. 'Deep in my heart, I knew you'd come back to me someday, but I had to wait for you to make that decision, I couldn't force myself on you – it had to come from you.'

She looked up at him, her eyes glazed with tears. 'And the children?'

'And the children will be delighted you've returned,' he said, wiping away her tears with the pads of his thumbs. 'Come along and we'll tell them the good news. Maybe we can plan a Christmas play for them to put on this year. It's been a long time coming."

'Can we just savour this moment before telling them?' she asked, taking his hand in her own.

He nodded as he drew her towards him and then cupping her face with both of his hands, he kissed her passionately once again.

Printed in Great Britain
by Amazon